Dedication

To my husband John – the wind beneath my wings.
Marrying you was the one exceptional thing I've done in
my life.

Chapter 1

London

A missed period, breast tenderness and nausea. Jenna knew that could mean only one thing; her monster of a husband's baby was growing inside her. The pee sample bottle the nurse handed to her had a bright yellow lid – like a beacon of hope for probable good news . . . not for her, though.

Sitting behind an imposing desk in the smart Harley Street clinic, Dr Furman peered over his half-rimmed spectacles at her, "Yes, Mrs Montgomery, I'm delighted to be able to confirm, you are indeed pregnant."

His smile was congratulatory. And why wouldn't it be? Being her husband's physician, he knew how much Leo Montgomery wanted a family.

"We'll take you through for a scan," he raised an eyebrow enquiringly, "unless you'd prefer your husband to be with you for that? We don't have to do it today."

A scan would mean it was real and she so didn't want it to be real.

"I think I'd better wait," Jenna declined politely, as if she did indeed want Leo to be present.

"That's fine. It will be nice to share the news with your husband and family today and come back later for the scan. I'll get the nurse to book you in."

1

He reached for the phone and her tummy began doing somersaults, which had nothing to do with the news she'd received – it was the overwhelming trepidation of the path she was now on.

Clutching the slick appointment card with a date boldly written in black ink for a scan, she made her way to the waiting Rolls Royce. McNeil, the chauffeur, held the door open for her and she took her seat in the back. Even though he'd switched on the heated seat warmers, she felt bitterly cold. Almost as if ice rather than blood was surging through her veins.

As the car manoeuvred through the busy London traffic, resignation kicked in hard. Her husband was now going to get what he desperately wanted – an heir to the elaborate Montgomery Empire. On the surface, Leo was a dynamic nightclub owner, but hidden behind that façade, he dealt in the dirtier but much richer pickings of drugs and guns. Leo wasn't the brains behind it all though, that accolade belonged to his father, Avery Montgomery. What kind of life is that for any child to be born into? Jenna shivered and hugged herself.

A cheery melody from her mobile phone provided a temporary interruption from her anguished thoughts. She reached in her bag and saw from the caller ID it was her husband. He'd be thrilled to have finally achieved his goal.

She slid her finger across accept. "Hello."

"Peter Furman's just called and told me – about bloody time." Leo didn't do pleasantries, not with her anyway. No how are you, what wonderful news. And Dr

Furman had no business ringing him. What happened to confidentiality? Not that it mattered. There wouldn't have been any excitement telling him herself. It wasn't as if she was deliriously happy and itching to share the news.

Leo carried on. "I've rung Mum and Dad, they're over the moon." The enthusiasm was evident in his voice. "Dad's suggested we organise a party." He must have realised by her silence that was the last thing she'd want, "Nothing too big, just a few close friends to share the news."

What friends? She didn't have any. He'd be meaning the glamorous wives of his business associates she was forced to socialise with. Those that do leisurely lunches and their only topic of conversation is where to buy the latest designer clothes, and who's screwing who.

"Mum's got it all in hand with Bridget who's organising a celebratory dinner tonight for all four of us. Bridget passes on her congratulations, too."

So the evil housekeeper knew before she even had chance to tell her own brother. Bridget, the twisted warden of Oak Ridge with a persona of politeness concealing a deliberate slyness, who reported back anything and everything she knew. Her intrinsic ability to glide around the house and appear out of nowhere never ceased to amaze Jenna. Nothing ever got past her. And the reward for her loyalty to the Montgomerys was a grace and favour cottage on the estate.

"Are you still there?" Leo asked.

"Yes, sorry, the signal isn't very good. It's raining really heavily. Nice your mum and dad are pleased," she responded, purely for something to say. Avery and Susan Montgomery made no secret of the fact they'd longed for a grandchild.

"Are you feeling okay?" Leo asked. The concern in his voice was most unusual for him.

"Not too bad. I just feel a bit sick."

"Only to be expected I would have thought. I guess you'll have to get used to it." She could hear someone in the background, "I'm going to have to go. I'll be home before six so we can celebrate then. Great news, Jen, well done."

He cut the call. Well done, that was it. As if she'd won first prize in a competition. Maybe she had? An heir to the Montgomery Empire was certainly a great achievement especially as Leo hadn't been able to get his late wife pregnant. How many times had she heard her mother-in-law utter the words, *if only?*

The chauffeur raised his gaze to the rear view mirror, "Sorry it's taking so long, Mrs Montgomery, the traffic's really busy today."

"Don't worry," she forced a smile, "there's no rush." And there wasn't. She wasn't in a hurry to return to Oak Ridge, the mansion at Hampstead Heath that had become her prison.

The rain was getting heavier. It was hitting the roof of the car, almost like hail stones. She followed the path of it streaming down the tinted windows. The motion of sitting in the back seat of the car was making her feel

4

even more nauseous. Her tummy being clenched in tightness wasn't helping. And that wasn't a symptom of the pregnancy confirmation. It was the realisation she'd be tied to her husband for the rest of her life. Now that she was carrying his biggest asset of all, she'd never be able to leave. So all the nights over the last three years she'd lain in bed dreaming up ways of escaping, were finally over.

She was never going to be free of him now.

Chapter 2

Oban, Scotland

Lucy Smyth squatted down and buttoned up her four-year-old son Cory's coat. Jordan, his twin, had fastened his own and was playing about with the front door handle.

"There you go, sweetie," she handed him his hat, "put that on and you'll be all nice and warm for nursery."

"Can we go in the van?" Jordan asked all buttoned up with his hat on and rucksack on his back.

"No. It's not far to walk and it will do us all good out in the fresh air. And besides, nursery asked that we don't all come in cars. Come on, quickly," she passed Cory his rucksack.

"Why?" Jordan asked.

"Because the car park gets crowded. Anyway, I like to walk. It's only ten minutes."

Hilda, her dear friend and surrogate grandmother to the boys appeared in the hall, "Don't you look all snugly and warm. I'll see you both tonight," she hugged Cory and then Jordan, "we're going to have your favourite for tea."

"Pizza?" Jordan's eyes widened.

"No, not pizza, another favourite."

"Burger?" Cory asked excitedly. The children didn't get either that often. Lucy didn't like them eating junk food.

"No time for more guesses," she said, "you'll have to wait and see tonight."

She opened the front door and turned to Hilda as the children scampered outside. "You're sure it's okay for Kitty to take you to the shop while I take the van?"

"Of course. I'm grateful you're going to the suppliers for me. It's too far for me to drive nowadays; my eyesight isn't as good as it was."

"Okay, I'll come back for the van and I'll see you at the shop about eleven."

"Okie dokie. Hey, you'd better dash," Hilda nodded towards the children waiting at the gate, "or they'll be at nursery before you."

Lucy walked the couple of blocks to the nursery. Normally in a morning, she'd travel to Hilda's craft shop with her in the van, but her niece Kitty only lived four doors away, so Kitty would take her today while she went to the suppliers and saved Hilda on a hefty delivery charge. And it gave her a chance to browse any new stock, so she never minded going.

Once she'd dropped the children off at nursery, prising Cory from her side and handing him over to the teacher while Jordan barely said goodbye once he spotted his friend, she returned to the house for the van. The drive would give her something different to do in her sedate life which consisted of designing costume jewellery and being the twins' mum. A far cry from her previous life. But she didn't want to think about that – her past had been well and truly archived.

It was a lovely crisp day. She fired up the engine, inserted a Lewis Capaldi CD and set off looking forward to the solitude for a couple of hours.

It was hard to believe it had been five years since she'd arrived in Oban. Somehow it seemed longer. And even though she was forced to live her life constantly on alert, she was settled. Hilda had been the sort of friend that everyone should have. It had been her lucky day when, one dark and dismal Monday morning, she'd set off and visited craft shops in the area trying to get them to engage in her custom-made jewellery. She'd been fortunate to stumble upon Hilda who had been only too pleased to offer her a small area in the shop to sell her designs. And as the designs took off, so had their friendship, and the icing on the cake had been when Hilda invited her and the boys to live with her.

The sun was blinding as Lucy turned onto the dual carriageway and accelerated. She pulled the visor down and reached for her sunglasses from her bag. It was a relief she found them when she did as the traffic ahead appeared to be unexpectedly slowing. She quickly braked, cursing herself for being distracted, but the brake pedal was soft, the firmness she was used to wasn't there. She pressed her foot down again – nothing. The brakes weren't working. The stationary car ahead, zoomed in closer. She frantically pressed her foot down again . . . harder . . . as if that would somehow do the trick.

Panic set in. The driver of the red Mazda ahead flashed his indicators, as if he could see her hurtling towards him and was warning her to stop. There was no doubt she was going to ram right into the back of him unless she did something. With no more than a second to decide, she tightened her grip around the steering wheel and swerved the van off the road and onto the grass verge, coming to a shuddering stop into rutted earth.

The shaking began and she burst into tears. How she'd managed to avoid a head-on collision, she had no idea. An image of her precious boys safely tucked away in nursery made her sob more. If they'd been in the van with her, they could have all been killed.

Once the tears petered out and her breathing became more settled, she took a tissue from her bag and blew her nose. Her hands were still unsteady as she reached for her bottle of water. She stared ahead out of the windscreen with an icy fear snaking through her veins.

What the hell happened?

Had something deliberate been done to the van? What if someone had cut the brakes?

Half a bottle of water later, she reached in the glove compartment for the breakdown card from a local company. The van was five years old so Hilda diligently paid *just in case* she always said. After ringing the number

9

and being told they'd be there within the hour, she called Hilda.

"Hello, love," Hilda's voice felt welcoming after what she'd been through. An overwhelming urge to cry again threatened. Hilda was the nearest thing she had to a mum and she loved her dearly.

"Hi, Hilda," she put as much lightness into her voice as she could, "just to let you know, something's wrong with the van." She quickly realised Hilda might think she'd been in an accident. "Nothing to worry about, it's just the brakes seem to have failed. I've rung the breakdown company and they're on their way."

"Oh no. Where are you? Are you alright?"

"Yes, I'm fine. I'd got onto the dual carriageway, heading out of town."

"Do you want me to get Kitty to come for you?"

"No need. I'll wait here until they come."

"What happened?"

"It sort of cut out," she was intentionally being vague, "I'll see if they'll drop me at the shop. We might have to get Kitty to take us home tonight."

"She'll do that, no problem. I'll wait until you get here, then. So sorry this has happened. Thank goodness it wasn't an accident."

"Yeah, thank goodness." *I could have lost my life.*

"I've just thought," Hilda continued, "I maybe should have mentioned it before. I did notice what looked like a wet patch on the pebbles down the drive yesterday. I didn't think much of it to be honest, but I'm wondering now if it was a leak of some sort?"

The tension eased slightly in Lucy's tummy. That was a better explanation than sabotage.

"Could be. I'll tell the mechanic that when he gets here. See you soon I hope. And don't worry, I'm fine, honestly."

"Alright then love, I'll have the kettle on for when you get here."

Lucy sat in the seat next to the mechanic who'd managed to get the van onto the low loader using a winch. Before taking it to the garage, she'd asked if he would drop her off at the shop.

He started the engine and moved away slowly into the traffic. "It'll only take us a day to sort the problem out. I'm fairly certain it's leaking brake fluid. It'll not take long to fix. It should be ready by this time tomorrow."

"That's good, then," Lucy said, "you're fairly sure that's why the brakes failed?"

"As sure as I can be. I've seen it many times on these older vehicles. And now you've said there was a patch on the drive, it's most probably been leaking slowly for a while."

"And that would definitely prevent the van from braking?"

"Eventually it would, yeah. You've been lucky, though. I don't want to frighten you, but it could have been really serious."

"Yes, I get that. It almost was. I think luck was on my side that I could veer off the road."

11

"Too right. And quick reflexes, you must be pretty skilled at driving to have done that."

She glanced out of her window and kept her voice casual, "You don't think it could be someone . . . I don't know, tampering with the brakes maybe?"

"Nah," he dismissed, "I think those things only happen in Tom Cruise movies, not real life. I'm fairly sure it's as I say. I'll take a proper look when I get it on the ramp though." He glanced at her with a smile, "I can't imagine anyone wanting you in an accident, anyway."

"No, you're right," she smiled back, "it's just been a bit of a shock, that's all."

"Yeah, I bet. You can stop worrying now though. The main thing is you're alright and we'll have the van back and sorted in no time."

"That's great, thank you."

Stop worrying. Easier said than done – worry was her middle name. It had to be. She was on her guard at all times. Even though his explanation seemed plausible, unease still rippled through her veins and it was going to be one hell of a struggle shaking that off.

What if somebody had tampered with the brakes? That would only mean one thing.

Someone knew.

Chapter 3

London

Bridget South, the housekeeper at Oak Ridge closed the door on her employer, Susan Montgomery's bedroom and made her way down the sweeping spiral staircase. She needed to go to the kitchen to check with the chef that everything was in hand for the evening's party. Leo Montgomery, Susan's son, had organised an elite gathering to celebrate the news that his wife Jenna was expecting a baby. The Montgomery's didn't do small. Everything was vast, as if to prove to everyone their considerable wealth and power. And tonight's celebration was important to them all. A much-awaited heir to their empire.

The Montgomery family, Avery and his wife Susan, and their son Leo and his wife Jenna all lived at the Oak Ridge estate. They had respective private suites and offices for their business interests. They'd been Bridget's employers all her adult life. She'd started working for Avery and Susan when she left school and upon the retirement of their housekeeper had taken on the role at twenty-three. If she were sliced open, Montgomery would be written through her body like a stick of Blackpool rock. Loyalty was her ethos, and she knew everything there was to know about the family . . . and more.

As she reached the bottom step, her morning was made much brighter by the dynamic head of the family, Avery Montgomery, striding towards her. He was a tall upright man, who had charm in spades. And unlike many men in their mid-fifties, had a full head of greyish thick wavy hair that she constantly itched to run her fingers through.

"Good morning, Bridget, is my wife up yet?" he asked in a voice all smooth and deep.

"No she isn't." She stood in front of him, getting as near as was respectful while desperately wanting to be much closer. "She's a bit late this morning. I've taken her tea, so once her medication has kicked in, she'll be heading for the shower."

"Ah, right, not to worry, it'll keep. I've got to nip out anyway, can you tell her I'll be back at lunch."

"Yes, of course."

He smiled. The smile that guaranteed her compliance in anything he wanted.

"And everything's all on schedule for tonight?"

"It is." She followed him towards the front door and opened it for him.

"That's great, Bridget, what would I do without you." He winked, "I'll see you later, then."

Oh yes, my darling, you most definitely will.

She nodded courteously as she closed the door behind him.

His warm spicy aftershave lingered causing butterflies to swarm in her belly as she made her way towards the kitchen. Avery Montgomery had captured her heart many years earlier, and one day soon they were going to be together. He would describe often enough how he longed for the days when he could live on an island somewhere away from the rest of the world where he could fish all day and enjoy solitude and relaxation. And when that did happen, she was going to be with him, she'd make sure of it. But until then, she had to make do with hasty lovemaking when his wife Susan wasn't around. Avery insisted that nobody should know about the two of them – his wife would sack her if she got even an inkling.

The aroma of the delicacies being prepared hit her as she approached the kitchen and opened the door. Frank, the family chef, was whisking together some egg whites and looked up as she entered.

"It all smells delicious," Bridget inhaled, "how are things?"

Everything would be under control, she already knew that. Frank wouldn't let the family down. All the staff employed at the house were reliable. Bridget wouldn't have it any other way. There had been a few mistakes with staff along the way, but those that didn't measure up were quickly shown the door. She had no time for shoddy workers. Oak Ridge was too special. It felt to her almost as if it were her house, and there were days when she fantasised about being the mistress. And she hadn't ruled out that could happen one day.

"All good," Frank answered, "just the desserts to finish. The girls are coming early to serve the hors d'oeuvres, aren't they?"

"Yes, both of them will be here at five."

"Good. Are you all set with the drinks?"

"Of course." Was the man bloody stupid? She was *all set* full stop with anything the family required. That was her job. She'd been in the cellar and got the Dom Perignon on ice, the red wines breathing in the house and the white wines refrigerated. Everything would be perfect as usual. There was no room for error while she was in charge.

"Excuse me?"

Bridget turned to see Leah the youngest girl who worked at the house. She was only seventeen and Bridget had taken her on as she'd impressed her at the interview about wanting earn some money so she could eventually go to university.

"Audrey said you wanted to see me."

"That's right. The flowers have been delivered for tonight's party. I've had them put in the outhouse. Can you weave your magic again like you did last time and arrange them in the vases I've left out? I seem to remember you did a fine job when it was Mrs Montgomery's birthday."

The girl coloured, "Thank you," but didn't move to do as she'd been asked.

"What is it?" Bridget asked.

"I was wondering if Mr Montgomery senior was in today?"

"Why?"

"Erm . . . I've brought a photo," she reached in her pocket, "Mr Montgomery said I reminded him of someone he used to know years ago. I mentioned my mother used to work in Scotties Bar in Soho when she was in her twenties. When I got my job here she told me how her and Mr Montgomery senior used to be friends. She gave me the photo of the two of them to show him."

Bridget snatched the photo from her. "He's a busy man and hasn't got time to be chatting to staff. Now you go and make a start on the flowers, please. And when you're done, leave them where they are and I'll bring them into the house. Be careful with the vases whatever you do. They're expensive crystal."

Leah hesitated, "What about the photo?"

"I'll show it to Mr Montgomery and see you get it back." No way was she showing Avery photos of some sort of old flame. The last thing she wanted was him hooking up with another woman. "Now come on, let's get moving."

Leah made a hasty retreat towards the kitchen exit and Bridget headed for the door to the main house, "I'll just go check with the cleaners before they go to make sure everything's as I want it," she said to Frank, "there's nothing you need?"

"Nope."

"Fine. I'll be back shortly."

She made her way to the entertaining lounge the family used for large gatherings. The cleaners had better

17

have done everything properly or there'd be hell to pay. The family relied on her totally and she ran a tight ship. Neither Avery's sickly wife Susan or Leo's dumb wife Jenna were interested in domesticity. Oak Ridge was her province. And tonight's party was going to be an astounding success. A fitting way the family could finally celebrate a much-wanted baby.

Avery had told her that grandchildren were his greatest desire so the family line could continue. He couldn't understand why Leo failed to get either of his wives pregnant. Most recently she'd been tasked with covertly searching Jenna's room to see if she could find any forms of contraception, but she never located any, although she couldn't somehow see Jenna doing anything against Leo such as taking illicit contraception. She was a real scaredy cat hiding behind that brother of hers who ran a newspaper and slagged the Montgomery family off big time. Avery and Leo hated him. Bridget was surprised he was still around knowing how the Montgomery's disposed of anybody and anything that got in their way.

She closed the lounge window she'd left slightly ajar to keep the room fresh. Once Leah had sorted the flower arrangements, she'd place them strategically throughout the house as the aroma would be better than any diffuser.

She ran her hand along the mantelpiece to check the cleaners had actually done the job they'd been tasked with and smiled. Nobody was better at facilitating a party than she was. Her tummy flipped at the thought that sometime during the festivities, Avery would find a way to slip away from all the activity for them to be together. It would be a frantic coupling in one of the downstairs cloakrooms, but they were used to that. They couldn't afford for anyone to know their secret, even though the time was coming when they soon would. Thanks to the dim-wit Jenna, there'd be a Montgomery heir which meant the time her and Avery could be together, was getting closer. And if that didn't work, she had a plan that would make it happen. Sickly Susan, Avery's wife, took an eclectic mix of medication – it wouldn't take much to assist her along the way.

Bridget smiled inwardly, more a sideways twitch of her lip. She had plans – big plans . . . but they were her secrets and she confided in nobody.

Chapter 4

Oban

Lucy rested the crystal stone and nylon jaw pliers on the workbench, switched off the huge magnifying glass and stretched out her arms. She'd been sitting in the same position for two hours and her shoulders ached. But the shop doorbell chiming ruled out a break. She didn't usually serve customers, her preference was working out of sight in the back where nobody could see her, but Hilda had gone to a GP appointment so she was forced to hold the fort.

It wasn't a customer waiting in the shop, though. Stood at the other side of the counter was Alex Vincent, landlord of the local pub, the Golden Lion. Alex was a good-looking man, mid-thirties with all the right attributes to entice a female. He was fit, confident, and had a charm about him that made him easy to like.

"Hi Alex." She painted on her best how-can-I-help-you face, knowing it was highly unlikely he was there to purchase anything. "What can I do for you?" she asked, dreading another request for a date.

"You won this on the raffle Saturday night," he handed her a small wicker basket containing a bottle of wine, shortbread biscuits and chocolate delicacies, all covered in cellophane.

"But I didn't buy a ticket," she said, taking it from him. She rarely went in his pub, so was hardly likely to be taking part in the raffle.

"Someone must have bought one on your behalf then. It had your name on." He shrugged, "Maybe Kitty?"

Kitty worked as a barmaid at the pub, so she'd be the likeliest person.

"That's kind of her," she placed the basket on the counter, "but she should have it, if she bought the ticket. You could have given her first refusal to save you coming here."

"I know I could, but I wanted to see you," he smiled his charming smile, "I thought I'd have another go at changing your mind about coming out with me."

"I'm afraid the answer's still no," she made an apologetic face, "like I keep telling you, it's nothing personal. I don't want a date with anyone, I haven't got the time."

"Can't you make some time?"

"That's the point, I don't want to."

He tried a different approach. "My mate's a guitarist in a group and I've got tickets to see them at a gig. What if you just came with me and see how it goes? We could get some supper first, or just go straight there, it's up to you."

Relief flooded through her as the shop door opened and Hilda bustled in.

"Sorry I've been so long," she spotted Alex, "Morning, Alex, and to what do we owe this pleasure?"

"I've brought Lucy the prize she won in the raffle."

Hilda spotted the hamper on the counter, "Oh, how lovely."

"Yes, it is," Lucy widened her eyes, "considering I didn't even buy a raffle ticket"

"Maybe Kitty bought it for you?"

"Yes, that's what Alex said. I better see if she wants it."

"That's kind." Hilda raised her shopping bag, "I'd better put this milk in the fridge. Nice to see you, Alex."

"You too," he said as she disappeared into the back.

Alone with him again, Lucy felt awkward. "Right, if there's nothing else, I'd better be getting back to it." She picked up the basket, "If Kitty doesn't want it, I know two boys that will. They'll soon be fighting over the chocolates and biscuits."

"Yeah, I'm sure." He raised his eyebrows, "I take it the gig's not a goer then?"

She shook her head.

He moved towards the shop door and reached for the handle. "Well, if you change your mind, you know where I am. Or just call in for a drink sometime, I'm always there."

She wouldn't, but smiled anyway, "Okay, see you," she nodded towards the basket, "and thank you again."

The bell chimed as he opened the door to let himself out. The times she said no to him were mounting up. Rejection would barely dent his pride though, with his looks and charm, he'd soon find someone who was interested in him.

Hilda placed a coffee on her workbench and sat down on the stool next to her. Her eyes focused on the basket of goodies, "Why don't you take the wine out first before you offer that to Kitty, she doesn't need any more encouragement to drink."

Lucy chuckled, "Yeah, you could be right."

"I am right. I bet you Alex has to keep an eye on her when she's working behind the bar. She'll be helping herself every time his back's turned."

"God, I hope not. I'd hate him to sack her."

"I've warned her often enough, but you know Kitty, she doesn't take a blind bit of notice. Just like her mother. I loved my sister to bits but she was weak with an addictive personality. It was only a question of time until she got in with the wrong people and drank herself to death."

"That's so sad."

A wave of sorrow passed across Hilda's face. "Yes, it was. But she'd been on a path of self-destruction from an early age. I know she doesn't like to hear it, but Kitty's a chip off the old block. Anyway, enough about that," she took a gulp of her coffee, "I take it Alex was sniffing for a date again?"

She sighed. "Yes, he was."

"He's a tryer, you have to give him that."

"I know. I wish he'd stop asking, I hate having to keep saying no."

"Then don't. Why not go out with him one night and see how you get on. He's nice enough."

23

Lucy sighed. "I think he is nice, but like I've said many times, I don't want to be dating."

Hilda nodded as if she understood but without knowing her background, she couldn't ever understand. And Lucy would never be able to share it. That could compromise her dear friend and she loved her too much for that.

"It is unfortunate," Hilda carried on, "he favours you and you don't want him, yet Kitty would snap his hand off. She's mad for him."

"That's what makes it worse. Please don't mention he's asked me out. I know that would upset her."

"Oh, I would never say a thing. She's a jealous little monkey at the best of times and has had her heart set on Alex for a while. The punters from the pub she goes out with are not really for her, and don't get me started on that lech, Tricky Monroe she pretends to like. It's all to get Alex to notice her."

"Yes, I know. I wish he'd stop trying with me and ask her instead."

"He's not going to do that though, is he, or he would have done it by now. It seems to me, you're a challenge to him. And men will always chase after you," she widened her eyes, "it's no good looking at me like that. Those large glasses of yours don't hide as much as you'd like them to. Nor do the clothes you wear two sizes too big to detract from your perfect figure. I know you don't want to hear it, but you're a beautiful young woman. Men are always going to be interested in you however many times you turn them away."

Hilda was too near the truth for comfort. Lucy didn't want to think about how attractive she might or might not be. And she certainly didn't want to be desirable. All she wanted was to bring up her boys, design jewellery and be safe. And she could only do that by leading a quiet life. There was no room for anything else. Getting close to anyone would be too dangerous. She was still reeling from the brake issue with the van, even though the mechanic had confirmed it was a leaking pipe that had caused the loss of brake fluid. She'd willed herself to accept the explanation, as anything else was too scary to think about.

The shop doorbell chiming interrupted them and Kitty shouted, "It's only me."

Hilda placed her cup down. "Peace is shattered. What will it be today, I wonder? The car needs new tyres or she hasn't paid her council tax."

Lucy quickly threw a sheet over the basket Alex had brought. She didn't want Kitty to know he'd been to the shop.

"She could just be here to say hello."

Hilda rolled her eyes, "That'd be a first."

Petite size ten Kitty, with her double D surgically enhanced breasts and mop of unruly blonde hair, poked her head around the workshop door. "Morning," she said brightly as she came in thrusting her hands in front of them. "Ta-da! What do you think?" She was waving purple acrylic nails, almost the same colour as a Cadbury's chocolate box, and they were filed like talons. Hilda's face smacked of disapproval.

"They're lovely," Lucy said taking Kitty's hand and examining them more closely, as if she liked painted finger nails, when in fact her preference was for neatly manicured un-varnished nails.

"You should have yours done," Kitty said pulling her hand away, "only twenty quid at Beauty Bazaar," she wiggled her fingers, "I think they're gorgeous."

No way would she go in for any adornments or anything that might draw attention. Nail varnish was reminiscent of her past life and she didn't want to be reminded of that.

"Do you want a coffee?" Hilda asked Kitty.

"No thanks, I'm not stopping. I've just called to give you a date for your diaries. I've decided to have a bit of a birthday shin-dig."

Hilda scowled, "Aren't you a bit old for that sort of thing?"

"No, you're never too old for a party. Anyway," she crinkled her nose, "it's more a few close friends really. I've asked Alex if I can have it at the pub."

Lucy glanced at Hilda, a gentle reminder not to mention Alex had just been in the shop.

"Oh, right, that's a good idea. Won't it be a bit of a busman's holiday for you though at the pub?"

"Course not, I'm not serving behind the bar on my birthday. Alex will have staff on. And the catering is mates-rates so it's not expensive. He says to pay the kitchen staff seventy quid in cash."

"Seventy quid," Hilda's voice went up, "for a few sausage rolls and sandwiches."

"It's fine," Kitty shrugged, "what can seventy quid get you nowadays . . . nothing. Anyway, I've not only come to tell you both about the party, I've come to ask my favourite aunty," she grinned at Hilda, "if you'll make a cake for me."

"Yes, of course, what sort do you want . . . Barbie or My Little Pony?"

"Ha-ha, very funny. Something chocolaty and gooey should do it." She smiled at Lucy, "You'll come, won't you, Luce?"

Lucy had no intention of going. She didn't want to be anywhere near Alex. He'd be sidling up to her all night. "I don't think I'll be able to, with the boys."

"I can find you a babysitter. There are a couple of waitresses at the pub who I bet could do with extra money. I'll ask around if you like?"

"No need," Hilda said, "I'll take care of the boys. I'm not bothered about a party. But you must go, Lucy, it'll do you good to get out with young people."

A wave of sadness passed across Kitty's face at Hilda's rejection of the party.

"No, honestly, you need to be there, Hilda," Lucy insisted. "Kitty's your niece, it's only right you go."

"I'd like you both to be there," Kitty said with a hint of petulance in her voice. But a second later, her face brightened, "I know. I could ask Alex if you could have the boys upstairs, where he lives."

"No, don't do that," Lucy said sharply. Kitty glared at her as if to say why not, so she softened her tone. "We'll sort something out nearer the time, don't worry."

"Great." Kitty was back to her bubbly self, "Right," she checked her watch and moved towards the door, "Got to dash, I'm due at the hairdresser. I'll see you both later."

Once the shop doorbell had chimed and the door had closed behind Kitty, Hilda reached for the coffee cups, "That girl's like a tornado, God help the poor man that ends up with her. He'll need plenty of money, that's for sure." She stood up, "I'll just go and wash these."

Lucy switched the magnifying glass back on to continue working on the piece she'd started earlier. It always appeared to her that Hilda seemed to be a little harsh on Kitty. She might be a bit of an air-head but she was her blood relative, yet Hilda almost treated her as if she was family and Kitty the outsider. But she never voiced her opinion out loud, even though it didn't sit comfortably with her.

Chapter 5

London

The impromptu baby announcement party was in full swing at Oak Ridge. Jenna circulated around the luxurious lounge area smiling and chatting to the invited guests. As per usual, everything inside the house was presented beautifully. You couldn't fault Bridget for organisation. The exquisite flower arrangements were giving off a divine flora, the crystal glasses filled to the brim with the finest wines and were polished and gleamed spectacularly, and their regular pianist was busy tinkering with familiar melodies on the baby grand. It was the kind of evening the Montgomerys loved. A gathering to show off their affluence to attendees who weren't real friends – they were just scared to be their enemy.

Jenna tried hard to circumvent Avery and Susan. More Avery really; he frightened the life out of her. But as she expected, portraying themselves as supportive in-laws, they sought her out.

"How are you doing, dear?" Susan asked with a genuine look of concern. Jenna always imagined that Susan Montgomery was once a nice lady. Sadly though, she'd been brainwashed over the years by Avery and she lived her life under his guise and instruction. What Avery said was gospel. So any personality or character she might once have had, was now long-gone. Jenna did feel sorry for her though, she was crippled with rheumatoid arthritis and while she still was a beautiful woman and lived a full life, the disease had taken its toll and deformed her body. Her wrists and hands were particularly unsightly. And as if that wasn't enough, she was a diabetic also. Jenna couldn't quite make out if her spells of illness, when she spent days in her room, were genuine, or like her, she just wanted to get away from an overpowering husband.

"I'm fine, thank you," Jenna gave a weak smile, "a bit tired that's all."

"You're bound to be," Susan sympathised, "I was just the same in the early days with Leo, wasn't I, Avery, can you remember?"

"You were, yes," he smiled lovingly at his wife, "but you pushed yourself through it," he turned to her, "like you are going to have to do, Jenna. It'll be a long nine months if you don't."

As if she needed obstetric advice from him. Thuggish strategies were more his bag.

"Yes, I'll try my best."

Two waitresses approached under the watchful eye of Bridget, who was wearing a black crushed velour dress that finished just above the knee and showed off rather nice legs. It always amused Jenna to see Bridget dressed up whenever they had functions. As if she was a guest and not the housekeeper.

"Excuse me for interrupting," Bridget said, looking at Susan and Avery, "would you like any hors d'oeuvres?"

Susan shook her head, "No, not for me, thank you."

"Me neither," Avery said, taking a gulp of the whisky he was clutching.

"Can I get you anything light to eat?" Bridget asked her, "you look deathly pale."

Typical Bridget. With an innate ability to state the obvious in a critical way. Nobody else would be so direct. But Jenna had always felt she was above herself. She was cunning with it, though. It was never so much that you could complain, it was a more a subtle slyness.

"Maybe some crackers might settle your stomach?"

"No, I'm fine, thank you," Jenna said, knowing she hadn't fooled the astute housekeeper, who was spot on. The urge to vomit was overwhelming and it wasn't only systematic. Anguish came in waves and she had to keep taking deep breaths to control it. And the fixed smile making her face muscles ache wasn't helping. Any thoughts of slipping away were dashed as Leo approached her.

"I think it's time I said a few words." He put his arm around her and nodded to Bridget who tapped a spoon on a glass to get everyone's attention. The pianist stopped playing and the room fell silent.

Leo made a show of clearing his throat. "Thank you all for coming at short notice to share our special news this evening. He turned his head towards her and gave a totally believable smile, giving the impression of being a devoted husband. "I'd like to take this opportunity to

31

thank my beautiful wife for making me a happy man by giving me the wonderful news she's having our baby in . . ." he paused, looking to her to fill in the gap.

"Almost seven months," she said passively, "November 11th."

He widened his eyes at everyone, "And what a special date that is. Armistice Day. I can't think of a better day to be born on." The outlaws were beaming away as he fixed his eyes on them both. "I know Mum and Dad are absolutely thrilled about becoming grandparents too, so . . . you should have all had your glasses topped up by now," he scanned the room until he saw the jailor, "thank you, Bridget." She gave him her grateful smile, which hid a multitude of deviousness, as he continued, "Would you all raise your glasses to my wife, and our soon to be son or daughter. Here's to you, darling Jenna."

They all muttered her name and she joined them with a sip of her mineral water before the pianist began playing again. It was just the cue she needed. She extracted herself from Leo, "Sorry, you'll have to excuse me," and hastily made her way to the bathroom. One minute more and the contents of her stomach would have been evident for all to see.

She managed to reach a bathroom in time, threw herself on her knees and stuck her head down the toilet. Once she'd finished retching, she eased herself onto her bottom and remained on the floor, leant against the wall. She reached for one of the decorative folded flannels to dry her nose and mouth. They'd all be waiting downstairs for her to return with her happy mum-to-be face which nobody would suspect wasn't genuine. Her brother, Jack would know she was faking it though, if he was there. Jack hated her husband, and Leo hated him. So it was no surprise Jack wasn't at the party to celebrate the good news – Leo would never invite him, nor would Jack have come.

Someone tapped on the door, "Are you alright, Jenna? Leo sent me up to see how you are."

It was docile Susan, the wife who never questioned anything – she wouldn't dare. She just did whatever overbearing thug Avery told her to do, and his son was a chip off the old block. They were as dangerous as each other.

Jenna got to her feet and opened the bathroom door, "I'm fine, just terribly sick."

"Oh dear," her mother-in-law looked concerned, "you do look delicate. I never had it myself with Leo. I sailed through my pregnancy, all text book really."

Yes, she would sail through her pregnancy. She wouldn't dare be sick. A Montgomery had to be stoic.

Susan took her hand and rubbed it encouragingly, "You'll have to try and somehow get on top of this."

"Hopefully, it'll just be for the first part of the pregnancy. Dr Furman did say it's common in some women for the first twelve weeks."

"Let's hope so. Do you feel able to come downstairs and join the others? Leo has organised tonight's celebration especially for you both."

No way was she going back down to join everyone. She knew what Susan's inference was. She was a Montgomery – she needed to get on with it. But Jenna didn't want to go back to the party. All she wanted was to go to bed.

"I think I'll go lie down and hope the sickness passes . . ."

Leo was at the top of the stairs and striding towards her, "There you are, darling, are you alright?" His concern was fake, he'd only be irritated.

Her mother-in-law didn't give her a chance to reply, "I'm trying to encourage her to come down and join the others, but she wants to go and lie down. I was just saying this sickness could go on for a while so she's going to have to try and live with it. Maybe a tonic water might settle it, or something light to eat?"

"Mum's right," Leo agreed, "you'll be better in company. It'll take your mind off things and people want to congratulate us. Come down for another hour or so, then you can make your excuses."

He reached for her arm, "Alright?" he wasn't asking, he was telling. His fingers dug into her as he led her towards the stairs. It wasn't the kind arm of support – more the forceful grip from a man expecting compliance.

By the time she reached the bottom step, Bridget was lurking. "Can I get you anything?"

"Yes," Leo answered for her, "a mineral water with plenty of ice."

"Of course."

Leo led her towards the lounge and, as she entered, it took all her strength to paint on her *I'm so lucky* smile despite an overwhelming urge to open the front door and run. And to keep on running as far as she could to get away from the chains that bound her. Leo's first wife had died, which was sad, but at least she'd got away. Right now that was preferable to spending the rest of her life tied to the insufferable Leo Montgomery and his wretched father, Avery. The days she considered death as an option were becoming more and more frequent. But the thought of her dear twin and how much she loved him spurred her on. He swore he would bring the Montgomerys down. And Jack rarely failed at anything he put his mind to, so if anyone could do it, he could.

It was the only thing preventing her from putting a noose around her neck and ending it all.

Chapter 6

London

Jack smiled encouragingly across the table at Jenna. Seeing her brother each Wednesday for lunch was the highlight of her week. They were dining at a favourite bistro of theirs; Jack's newspaper offices were close by so the venue suited him.

She sipped her mineral water while they perused the menus. It was unlikely she'd be able to eat much but she wouldn't miss her weekly catch up with her brother, even though looking at herself in the mirror that morning, she looked ghastly. The pregnancy was certainly taking its toll. Despite makeup, she looked deathly pale.

"Are you alright?" Jack asked sipping his gin and tonic, "you don't look well."

Jack would be concerned. He knew her better than anyone and loved her dearly, as she did him. And normally she could cope, she was used to putting on a brave face, but today she felt jittery. Jack wouldn't be happy about the pregnancy. He'd never got over her hasty marriage in the Caribbean to Leo. He said it was contrived and, as always, he'd been right.

She took a deep breath in, "You're not going to like it."

"What?" he frowned, concern evident in his brown eyes which replicated hers.

"I'm pregnant."

"Jesus, surely not?"

"I'm afraid so."

His face looked pained, "How?"

"How do you think?"

"I don't mean that. I meant, don't you take contraception?"

"I did, but Leo wanted to start a family."

He leaned back in his chair. "Bloody hell. Fancy bringing another bastard like him into the world."

"I know," she sighed in complete agreement. "I'm praying to God it's a girl. That'll throw the lot of them. Avery keeps saying he wants a boy, to *follow on in the business.*"

"Yeah, I bet he does, another Montgomery thug. I daren't ask if you're keeping it?"

"Err . . . this is Leo Montgomery's child. Do you honestly think termination's an option? Leo knew I was pregnant before I'd even got home. Dr Furman rang him to congratulate him."

"What the hell happened to doctor patient confidentiality?"

"Doesn't exist in the Montgomery world. Everyone's on Leo's payroll."

"Except me."

She smiled lovingly at him, glad he was the only person that wasn't. "No, and you're never likely to be. You're blacklisted."

"Just the way I like it." He widened his eyes, "I can't say I'm pleased you're having his baby, but I do know you're going to be a fabulous mum."

Tears threatened at his gentleness. Nobody had said anything like that to her. She hadn't dared to even consider there'd soon be a little human being that she'd be responsible for.

"I wish I had your confidence. I feel awful at the moment for even wishing I wasn't pregnant." She stifled the urge to cry but couldn't stop her eyes filling up, "How selfish am I?"

"Hey," he reached in his pocket and handed her a clean handkerchief, "you don't have a selfish bone in your body. You are a lovely person and your baby is going to have so much love, from you and me. We'll see it's brought up properly. Just rotten luck who its father is."

She blew her nose, "The controlling has started already about what I'm supposed to be doing and not doing. Right now, I can't even think any further than coping with the sickness."

He took her hand. "Well stop worrying for starters. It's going to be ages yet until you have the baby. It'll all fall into place, you'll see. You've got to get used to things, that's all. Don't be so hard on yourself. Anyway," he took a sip of his drink, "I have some news, too."

"You do? That's good then, I could do with some." She widened her eyes enquiringly but the appearance of the waiter stopped him from answering.

"Can you eat anything?" Jack asked.

"Maybe some tomato soup."

He turned to the waiter, "Tomato soup for the lady and a Spanish omelette for me. We'll go light today."

"Fine, sir. Any wine?"

"I don't think so, not today."

The waiter collected the menus and left.

"Go on," she asked eagerly, "what news have you got?"

"Ah, right, yes, my news," he took a sip of his drink, "you know I've always said to you I want to write, more a fiction based novel rather than journalism?"

"No," she frowned, "I've never heard you say anything of the sort."

"Rubbish. I've always wanted to do it but work got in the way."

She shook her head, "I'm telling you, this is all news to me, but go on."

"Well, I'm sure I've told you before, maybe not recently. Anyway, I've finally decided I'm taking a sabbatical from the paper for a month or so, so I can begin work on a novel."

She sat back in her chair, "I can't believe I'm hearing this. Work's your life – wasn't that why you and Lyndsey split up? She couldn't stand your dedication to work and all the hours . . . and," she widened her eyes, "your fixation on Leo?"

"Yeah, it was a bit more than that, but in essence that was it. I'm putting all that to one side now, though. I'm going to concentrate on my novel. I really want to do this. I've thought about it for a couple of years and now the time seems right."

"But you won't be able to leave the paper, it's your life."

"I will. It's all sorted. Alan Credland is going to take the helm. It'll be great experience for him. And I'm only a phone call away."

"You've really thought this through, then."

"Yep, it's happening, definitely."

"So, are you battening down the hatches and I'll need an appointment to see you?" She grinned, "I wouldn't want to disturb your daily creativity."

"Ah, well, here's the thing. You won't be able to disturb me, not physically anyway, as I won't be here. I've rented a cottage by the sea and I'm going to become a recluse for a month."

"You are joking, you in a cottage? I hope it's got Alexa, remote controlled blinds and an electronic coffee maker."

He grinned, "I'm taking the coffee maker with me."

"Where is it?"

"Cornwall."

"Cornwall?" her voice went up an octave, "why on earth are you going all that way?"

"'Cause I need to get out of London. I want to try something different. I'm still getting used to being single again since Lyndsey left – so I'm looking for a bit of a fresh start really and trying something different while I can, before it's too late."

The waiter appeared, placed their food down and ground some black pepper over Jack's omelette. It would do him good to have a break. He worked far too hard on the newspaper.

She smiled encouragingly as Jack began tucking into his food, "Do you know, honestly, I think it's great. Good for you. I almost envy you. I wish I could up-sticks and join you. A month away in a cottage sounds like absolute bliss."

"That's exactly what I was hoping you'd say. You can come and visit. It'll be like when we were kids, you and me on holiday together."

"Sounds idyllic, but I don't think Leo will allow that."

"Why not? He never objects to you seeing me."

"Yeah, that's 'cause he knows you'll crucify him with your pen if he does and he'll be the feature of the day. You're one of the few people that have any power over him, you and that newspaper of yours."

"Long may that continue, then. So, maybe the pregnancy will help you get away?"

"In what way?"

"Well, I'm no expert, but I reckon you need to develop some symptoms of being unwell, and tell him the doctor recommends a period of rest."

As great as that sounded, she had to pour water on his suggestion. "That would never happen, I'd be more of a prisoner than I am now. He'd have me on bed rest and hire a nurse to make sure I complied."

"Bloody hell, Jen, it makes me so angry you have to live like this."

41

"I know, but we've been over this countless times. It is what it is. There's no way out." She tried a bit of dried bread, the soup was too much.

He put down his fork. "If there was, would you take it?"

"There isn't, Jack, so forget it. Just go away and write your book. I'm pleased for you, really I am. The only downside is, there won't be any negative articles about him for a while. I love your journalism as it riles him so much."

"He's still facing a murder trial. That isn't going to just go away."

"Yes, I know, but they don't have enough evidence to substantiate it and get a conviction. Leo reckons the charges will be dropped before it even gets to court. He has an eminent barrister working on getting the case thrown out anyway. Him and Avery are too clever to be brought down by the justice system. They'll have all angles covered."

"I wouldn't be too sure, my contact in the police reckons there's a good chance they'll nail him. Chauffeurs don't just disappear. And while I'm sure he's clever enough not to have physically killed him, he'll have instigated it. Sadly though, the case is based on circumstantial evidence so it is hard to get a conviction."

"Yeah," she nibbled on some more bread, "but like I've told you, I don't know anything. I keep well away from him and any business dealings."

"You do right. But I am going to expose him and get you away, so you can lead a normal life."

"I wish you could," she shook her head dismissively, "but no-one can. This is my life. Nobody is ever going to testify against him. The cops might have something on him, but they'll never prove it. I bet half of them are on his payroll and the jury will be on the payroll too. It's all been done before."

Jack took her hand and looked directly into her eyes. "You mustn't think I'm abandoning you right now. Nothing's further from my mind. I'll be away one month and if you aren't able to visit me, then we can still speak on the phone and Facetime. And when I'm back, I don't want to raise your hopes, and I can't say anything right now, but there's a plan and we're getting pretty close to executing it."

"Who's we?"

"I can't say. You have to trust me. And you need to promise me you'll sit tight until this plan of mine comes off. I'm not saying anymore. I don't want you having more information than is absolutely necessary in case that arsehole of a husband of yours questions you. So, just give me one month."

"Why a month? Has going away got something to do with the trial?"

"I can't say, Jen. Sit tight for four more weeks and then things will change. I've never let you down before, have I?"

"No," she smiled lovingly, he hadn't. Fortunately, he didn't know the half of how she had to live. She couldn't burden him with it all. He'd be horrified and drag her out of Oak Ridge and then his life would be in danger. She couldn't contemplate anything happening to him.

"You do trust me, don't you?"

She wanted to believe him. But nobody took the Montgomerys on and won. She smiled through watery eyes, "Of course I trust you. But promise me you'll take care. You don't need me to remind you who you're dealing with."

"I will, don't worry. I'll have my sabbatical and then I'll be back. And by then, things will really hit the fan. You need to be prepared for that."

She didn't want to dampen her brother's enthusiasm. Right now it was great he was doing something for himself, much as she'd miss him. "I'm glad you're taking some time off. You're sure everything is okay? You aren't running away because of Lyndsey, are you?"

"Nah. Our relationship had run its course. She was right to move on, there wasn't a future for us." He shrugged, "Maybe I'm destined to be on my own, who knows."

"Don't be daft. You just haven't met the right one. She's out there, I know she is. Maybe you'll find her in Cornwall?"

"I doubt it," he rolled his eyes, "anyway," he looked at his watch, "I'm going to have to run. Do you want to text your driver and I'll see you to the door?"

"Yes, I will do." She reached into her bag for her phone and sent a text to McNeil while Jack settled the bill.

"Will I see you before you go?" she asked as they walked out of the restaurant towards the front entrance.

"Unlikely. I'm hoping to leave on Tuesday."

"As early as that?"

"Yep. I want to be back in time for the trial so we can report on it."

"That's what worries me. Leo will be scrutinising the newspaper each day to see what you write."

"Good," he smiled mischievously, "rest assured, it'll be as bad as I can make it."

Chapter 7

London

It was eight a.m. when Bridget tapped on Susan Montgomery's door and made her way in. Susan had her Earl Grey tea ritual in bed early each morning but not before Bridget made sure Avery had left the room. The thought of Avery and Susan having sex made her sick with jealousy, and it was for that reason she made herself available regularly to Avery. And he certainly took advantage of the opportunity. Whenever he was up for it, he'd twiddle around with his wedding ring, taking it on and off his finger. She knew then to make herself available. And she loved it. Sex with Avery made her feel powerful.

She stared at her employer laid in the bed, her eyes covered with a blackout mask, fast asleep on her back with her mouth wide open. Bridget placed the tea tray on the bedside table next to her and, as was usual each morning, she moved to open the drapes at both windows of the spacious bedroom.

The movement woke Susan and she reached for her eye mask and pulled it off. Confusion was evident in her eyes as she stared at Bridget. "What is it?" she asked as if she shouldn't be there.

"It's eight," Bridget said picking up the tray from the night before that had held some warm milk to *help her settle*. Sickly Susan was constantly bleating on about not sleeping well.

Susan looked towards the window, as if assessing it was daylight. She appeared perplexed. "Eight in the morning?" She scratched her mop of unruly hair, "I must have actually slept through the whole night." She turned towards the ruffled sheets next to her, which her husband had been under only an hour earlier. "I can't believe I didn't hear Avery come to bed. That's a first. Are you sure it's eight a.m?"

Bridget smiled at the stupid woman who looked completely unkempt and dishevelled. If she slept in Avery's bed every night, she'd be up an hour earlier, making sure she looked perfect for him.

"Yes, of course. It's a lovely morning."

"Well I never. I've not slept like that for years. I have changed my medication, so I'm wondering if that's made a difference." She eased herself into a sitting position, picked up the teapot and poured some tea into the fine china cup.

"That's got to be good, then," Bridget said, taking Susan's housecoat off the chair where she'd discarded it the previous evening, and placed it on the bed, "I know you've often said sleeping is a problem for you."

"Yes, it is. And Avery always wakes me coming in when he does. I know it can't be helped with the nightclubs, but I long for the day when he takes things easy and doesn't go out at night. Not that I can't see that happening anytime soon."

Bridget didn't answer. It was more a statement than anything and didn't require a response. When the day came that Avery didn't work, he'd be with her on a tropical island somewhere. And if her newest plan came to fruition, Susan Montgomery might not be around that long anyway.

"Have the boys left for golf?" Susan asked.

It always irritated Bridget how she referred to them as boys.

"Yes they have."

"Great. I do love them to have their time together, and it's good for their health, especially Avery. He is at that age when things can suddenly happen if you're not careful." She took a sip of her tea, "He does love to spend time with Leo. I wish we could have had more children really, Avery would have liked a large family."

Bridget wasn't remotely interested in listening to her ramblings about Avery and their life together. "I'll leave you to enjoy your tea."

"Thank you. I must say I'm still in shock. I just don't know where the night went to. I'm not complaining though. I feel so much better for a full night's sleep."

"I'm glad you feel better," Bridget gave a single nod and made her way towards the door. As she closed it behind her, she looked down at the tray with the empty cup from the night before and smiled with a sideways twitch of her lip.

Gently does it.

48

Chapter 8

London

Jenna was sitting at the dining table with her in-laws and Leo. She'd rather not eat but as always, what she wanted didn't count. She'd managed to sip some orange juice for the first course while they ate their starters, but there wasn't a chance to escape so easily with the main course. Bridget placed a decorative plate in front of her with a totally bland offering.

"It's a plain omelette," she said as if Jenna couldn't see that.

"Thank you." She kept her eyes averted while the others were served their much more substantial roast. Breathing through her mouth was becoming the norm. Anything to avoid strong odours that would make her have to flee.

"Eat what you can, dear," Susan cajoled, as if she were six.

She picked up her fork. Although she hated the effect the hormones were having on her, there was one advantage. Once they'd got through the dinner ritual, she had a legitimate excuse to go to her room and be alone. And Leo would be free to disappear and see his latest. Surely his parent's knew? If not his mother, Avery certainly would. He'd no doubt got a mistress in tow himself. He was a fit looking man for his age. He actually was much more attractive and charismatic than Leo, who favoured his mother's side.

"Have you thought about names, or is it too soon?" Susan asked as she began eating her meal.

She was about to say yes, it was too soon. What she'd like to say was the truth, that their precious son spent hardly any time with her so there was no chance to discuss anything, least of all names. But Leo answered, "I want it to have Leo as its middle name," he said proudly, and looked at his father, "and yours too, Dad."

Avery looked all fluffed up. Mr Important would be thrilled. That was Leo, everything he did was to gain Avery's approval.

Leo continued, "I thought something distinguished like Charles Leo Avery, or George Leo Avery," he turned towards her, "what do you think, Jen?"

She couldn't resist. "I think it could be a girl."

"I doubt that," Susan quickly dismissed with a glare of disapproval, "the last three generations of the Montgomerys have all been boys. We haven't any girls in the family."

Stupid woman. As if that was a guarantee of anything.

Susan turned to Leo, "I think Charles and George are both nice names, they're rather regal and either would sit nicely with Montgomery.

"I think that too," Leo said, looking pleased at her approval, "it's up to Jenna of course, but I think they're good names."

Jenna put her fork down. The omelette was choking her – rather like the family. "Would you mind excusing me," she stood up.

Bridget was there, hovering like a praying mantis. "I'll bring some tea and arrowroot biscuits to your room, shall I?"

She didn't acknowledge her as she fled. Let them think she was going to throw her guts up – it was a legitimate excuse to get away.

Once settled in bed, she called her brother to make sure he'd arrived safely in Cornwall. She'd feel better hearing his voice. Jack was the one constant in her life.

"Hi. Have you got there?" she asked as he picked up.

"Yep. I'm unpacked and all set up in my quaint little cottage. It's beautiful."

"How long did it take to get there?"

"Not that long. The traffic was pretty good."

"Are you near the seafront?"

"Not far."

"Send me some pictures when you go down there. I can't wait to see them. I want to reminisce about the holidays with Mum and Dad."

"Will do, although I'm not sure when I'll be heading down the seafront. Remember I'm here to write."

"Yes, I know, but you're going to have some time off, surely?"

"We'll see."

"Why are you being so vague about it all? It is Cornwall you've gone to isn't it and not somewhere secret you're not telling me?"

"Don't be daft. Why would I do that?"

"I don't know. It seems odd that's all, you taking off to write this so-called book that I've never heard you mention before."

"I guess it does seem a bit out of the blue, but if I don't do it now, I never will. And it's great to try something different. I love journalism but like everything, when you've done it for years, you yearn for a bit of change. So it's great to be able to take off."

"You're sure it's nothing to do with Lyndsey?" She really liked his ex and had high hopes for them going all the way together.

"No, I can assure you it isn't." He yawned, "Sorry, I'm whacked. I'm ready for some shuteye."

"Have you eaten?"

"Yeah, I brought some basic stuff with me but I stopped off at a pub on the way and had a meal."

"That's nice."

"What about you. How are you doing?"

"I'm okay. Wishing I was there with you. I can't imagine anything better than a trip to St Ives right now."

"And I'd love to have you."

"Even though I might spoil your creativity?"

"I'd have a couple of days off if you came. Think about it, won't you?"

"I will, but like I said, it's not going to happen. That's why I want to see some photos."

"Okay, I'll see what I can do. I'll text you tomorrow when I'm less tired."

"You do that. Speak tomorrow. All my love."

"You too, look after yourself."

She cut the call. Every time Jack left the capital, she hated it. It caused her to feel much more exposed. The swift haste of his current trip puzzled her, she wasn't totally convinced he was away on a writing trip. It all seemed too sudden. She knew Jack better than anyone – any vagueness usually meant he was up to something. It would be great to join him for a few days to satisfy herself he was actually doing what he said he was. But that was impossible now, it wouldn't be allowed. Thinking of a way she could escape to Cornwall and relive some of their happy childhood memories was pointless. But the touch of nostalgia was comforting as she rested her head down on the pillow to reminisce about the time when her parents were alive, she was happy and carefree and the evil Montgomerys were a family you read about in crime novels.

Chapter 9

Oban

Lucy polished the oval cabochon gemstone she'd just finished mounting. It was a beautiful deep green colour and she'd used tiny moissanite diamonds around it, which sparkled when exposed to light. It was perfect.

Hilda poked her head around the door, "Ready for a cuppa?" she asked as Lucy held the piece of jewellery up to the light.

"Oh, isn't that stunning," Hilda said moving closer to get a better look, "you've excelled yourself." Warmth flooded through her as she handed the piece to Hilda. As a designer, she loved praise, even though she knew herself it was a lovely piece of jewellery. All the pieces she designed were, but she knew this particular one would be popular. She tended to get a feel for what would sell.

"Right," she stood up, "while you're admiring that, I'll go and put the kettle on. Mine's the easy bit sat on my bottom all day creating stuff, you have to stand on your feet selling it. It's time you had a bit of a rest."

Hilda smiled, "Oh go on then, you've persuaded me, I could do with a sit down. I've put some chocolate digestives in the cupboard, shall we push the boat out and treat ourselves to one?"

"Why not?" As she moved towards the kitchenette at the back of the building, the shop doorbell chimed.

Hilda sighed, "No rest for the wicked. Let's hope they only want to browse."

Lucy filled the kettle and, while she waited for it to boil, she looked out of the tiny kitchenette window to the small play-park where mums chatted and children played. She thought of her own boys, happily ensconced in nursery. Jordan had kicked off big time that morning as he hadn't wanted to go to nursery. A promise of his favourite pizza for tea had eventually cajoled him into complying. Cory never showed any dissent. You couldn't tell them apart visually, both had identical dark hair and dark brown eyes, and were almost the same in height and weight, but their temperament is where they differed. In that, they were total opposites.

She warmed the teapot with some boiling water – no teabag in a cup for her. Most of her previous life she'd managed to erase, but there was the odd thing she couldn't. And proper tea was one of them.

Her phone pinged and she took it out of her pocket. It was Kitty.

Are we still on for you straightening my hair tonight? X

She smiled. Kitty, who spent most of her time searching for Mr Right and kissing plenty of frogs along the way, had the most unruly, thick wavy hair which she felt looked much better straightened. Tonight, much to Lucy's relief, she finally had a date with Alex, the landlord of the pub. She'd been chasing him for a while and it sounded like he'd finally succumbed.

She texted back,

Have I ever let you down? See you at 6 X

As she made her way back carrying the teas, it sounded like a male customer in the shop was looking for a piece of jewellery for his sister's birthday. Hilda was beefing up the *Lucy Smyth* label they'd created. Nobody had been more surprised than she had been when her jewellery had taken off. She'd initially dabbled to see if she could use her creative design degree and began small, but it had soon grown into a full-time occupation. They did a fabulous online trade too, which made her proud of what she'd achieved. Hilda dealt with the marketing and selling, she just concentrated on designing and producing. Her initial reluctance to sell online had been unfounded. Hilda had commissioned an online company to produce a website which focussed on the designs as opposed to giving information about her. Any photographs or details of where she studied for her degree were omitted. Personal information getting into the wrong hands was too frightening to contemplate.

"What about this one?" Lucy listened from the workshop to Hilda's engaging sales patter, "it's so elegant, and we do a range of chain lengths. Your sister could wear it like a long pendant, or as choker around her neck. I always think the shorter ones look nice with open blouses when there are a couple of buttons undone."

"Yes, I'm sure," he replied. His voice had a rich smoothness. One of those voices that made you curious about who was on the end of it. "I think she might like a

56

shorter type. I'm wondering if it's wise to ask her, I'm not an expert on women's jewellery," he joked, "and the stones are so lovely I'd hate to purchase one she wouldn't wear."

"I guess you could always ask, if she prefers a choker type or a pendent although that would give the game away if it's a gift."

"You're right, it would. And I'd like it to be a surprise. I'm tempted to go through some photos and see what she seems to favour. I'm pretty hopeless at this sort of thing."

"I think whichever you decide on she'd be pleased with. We ladies can never have too much jewellery."

"No, I'm sure you're right. I tell you what, I'm going to have a think and come back tomorrow if that's alright?"

"That's fine. Though we close at one, so make it before. Are you staying locally?"

"Yes. I've got a beach house a stone's throw from here, along the front."

"Not Craven's Bay?"

"That's it. I've rented it for a month."

"Mrs Steer's old place?"

"I'm not sure. It's number twelve, I've rented it through an agent."

"That's the one. It's on the same block as mine. She died bless her. I used to keep an eye on her as her son lives in Manchester. He had the whole place decorated and modernised to rent out."

"Well, thankfully, he's not modernised too much. He's done a terrific job trying to keep some of the features but bring it into the twenty-first century. Have you lived here long?"

"Oh, yes, most of my life. It's a lovely part of the world."

"You're telling me. I'll drop in again in the morning, the jewellery's too good not to buy. Do you design it all?"

"Oh no, I have a friend that does all that."

Lucy held her breath – *please no*.

"Lucy," Hilda called, "have you got a minute? There's a gentleman here admiring your jewellery."

She rested her teacup down and reluctantly made her way through to the shop. Hilda was beaming, "He's staying at Mrs Steer's cottage."

"Oh lovely," she forced a smile. The last thing she wanted was making friends with a random holiday maker.

"Good morning," she said to the seriously attractive man across the counter. No wonder Hilda was fawning over him. Tall, dark and handsome didn't come close. He had wavy short hair which looked to have a will of its own but it suited him. He had a sharp high-bridged nose and a well defined face with distinct cheekbones and a sharp jaw. He was wearing a smart jacket and slacks which seemed to afford him presence. She was no expert on men and certainly didn't want to be, but his appeal was evident.

"Hi," he gave her the most charming smile with warm brown eyes that had a kindness about them. "I've been admiring your beautiful jewellery. You're very talented."

"Thank you."

"I'm going to buy a piece for my sister, I'm just not sure about the chain length. I was just saying to," he looked at Hilda, "sorry I didn't get your name?"

"It's Hilda," she replied, clearly smitten.

"I was just saying to Hilda, I'm not good with choice," he shook his head playfully, "I'm better with a couple of pieces to make a selection from. Hilda's sales pitch has been excellent by the way."

"Oh, I'm sure," she smiled. Charm radiated from him. She couldn't remember the last time she'd noticed a man.

"Why don't you show him the piece you've just finished?" Hilda encouraged, "I'll get it, you stay here with Mr . . . sorry, I didn't get your name either."

"It's Jack."

Hilda disappeared into the workshop forcing Lucy to continue making conversation. "I hope the weather holds while you're here, you'll find plenty of places to explore."

"Yes, I'm sure, but I'm not strictly here for a holiday, I'm hoping to start to write a book."

"Oh really, how interesting." She wasn't one bit interested and willed Hilda to get a move on.

"It's something I've always promised myself I'll do but never quite got round to it. But I decided the time was right to do it now. So here I am."

"Why this particular place?" She had to ask — constantly being on guard necessitated it, he could be anyone giving her any old bull. "Sorry, I didn't mean to be nosy."

"Not at all. My father was always suggesting Oban for our family holidays when we were kids, but the poorer weather deterred us from coming. So I thought it might be nice to take a look at what I've missed out on all of these years."

Hilda returned clutching the finished cabochon pendant which she'd slipped into an ornate gift box. "Here it is. I think Lucy has excelled herself with this."

He took the box from her and examined it closely. "This is stunning and just the sort of thing she'd like." He looked up at them both, "I'm going to take it. And I'll pay you now, but is it still okay to come back tomorrow to collect it to make sure I get the right length of chain?"

"Yes, of course you can," Hilda cooed, sounding almost like she'd give it to him for free if he asked.

He reached in his jacket pocket for his wallet but Hilda stopped him. "You can pay tomorrow when you come back. I'll save it for you."

"You're sure?"

"Absolutely. We can package it nicely then, all together as a gift."

"That's very kind of you, thank you."

Even though Lucy was thrilled he'd purchased her latest creation, she didn't want to spend any more time than she had to talking to a stranger. Attractive as he was, he could be anyone.

"I hope your sister likes it," she said moving towards the door to the workshop.

"I'm sure she'll love it. I'll see you both tomorrow then." As he turned towards the exit door a bucket catching drops of water from a leak caught his attention. He raised his head to the ceiling, "Oh dear."

Hilda pulled a face, "It's only just started, which reminds me, I must try the chap again to come and fix it. I did leave a message but he's not rung back."

"It's probably a tile that's come lose," he said, "it won't take five minutes to fix, I'm sure. Right," he opened the shop door, "I'll see you tomorrow then, bye."

Hilda's face was full of devilish excitement as he closed the door, "Oh my goodness, how attractive is he?"

"He did seem nice," she agreed.

"Nice? He's more than nice. You thought so too, I could tell."

"Err . . . I can assure you I didn't."

"Rubbish," Hilda dismissed playfully and picked up the pendant, "I'd better put this in the back for Mr Jack Charming. I'm looking forward to him coming back tomorrow already – there must be a god up there somewhere."

Lucy couldn't help but laugh. She was spot on. He was seriously attractive, that's why she'd dragged her into the shop. Hilda never understood why she wasn't interested in men but she'd never pried into her past. That's what she loved about her. She'd taken her in, given her and the boys a home and never asked questions. She was the best. Over the last few years she'd repaid her tenfold by designing the jewellery and only took a small percentage to ensure she paid her way. Hilda was always saying she could open up her own shop. But she couldn't. There was no way she could ever move anywhere and expose herself.

That was far too risky, and she didn't do risk.

Chapter 11

Dr Furman moved the ultrasound over Jenna's abdomen while Leo looked on.

"There we are, Mrs Montgomery," he turned the monitor towards her, "for want of a better word, the yolk sac is visible and I can just pick out the foetus." He pointed to what looked like a tiny bean.

Leo must have left his gangster persona at the door as his hand reached for hers. He stared at the monitor with an intensity which was most unlike his permanently distracted look.

"It's early days, so I can appreciate it doesn't look much more than a hollow sac right now, but you'll be able to see more in a couple of weeks and then we can take measurements and print some images off for you. What I can tell you is, the baby is implanted properly in the womb."

Leo shook his head at the screen, "You can tell it's all normal then."

"Yes, absolutely." It didn't look anything like normal to her either, but she'd no idea what to expect, "Now, listen carefully."

They did. And the tiny tympanic heartbeat from the ultrasound wand was the outward sign they needed that a new life had begun.

She wasn't an expert on obstetrics but she knew it was early for a scan. However, money talked in Harley Street.

They left the clinic together and walked towards Leo's car. He preferred driving himself around the city. What better way to show off his latest toys that smacked of prosperity, even though the Montgomerys wealth was at the cost of someone else's misery.

They climbed in the exclusive customised Range Rover and set off for Oak Ridge.

"It wasn't what I was expecting," he said.

"No, me neither. I couldn't make anything out. But he did say it was early for a scan. I guess he just wanted us to see it as it makes it more real somehow."

"Yeah, I suppose so."

"It still doesn't feel real, though. It's hard to imagine in just over seven months I'll be responsible for everything that little thing will need. I can't even imagine breast feeding."

"Breast feeding?" he turned his nose up. His eyes were cold and piercing under his black groomed eyebrows, "You don't need to worry about that. Mum bottle fed me. She said it was much better and less restrictive. Have a chat with her if you're worried. She'll reassure you bottle milk is fine."

"I'm not worried," she tried to keep her voice calm so as not to antagonise him, "not at all. But I do want to breast feed. I want him or her to have the best start in life."

"And I've said no, so don't argue."

Leo was exuberant at dinner, which was most unlike him. He didn't do excitement – not with her anyway. But seeing Dr Furman that afternoon for the first scan had thrilled him. It was unusual to see any vulnerability in him, but as he'd looked closely at the monitor, she'd seen he was quite overcome, which made her mourn the passing of the Leo she fell in love with.

They were dining with Avery alone as Susan was out at a charity fundraising event. Jenna had suspected for a while that Susan preferred not to include her husband in her charity work.

Bridget's disdain was evident on her face when she returned for their plates as she'd barely touched hers. Her beady eyes would notice straight away that she'd just moved the vegetable tartlet around the plate, eating only a tiny amount of pastry.

Leo took a sip of wine with the reserved label he'd boasted about opening as it was such a special day. "Cheers, Jen," he raised his glass to her then turned to his father, "It is good wine, isn't it?"

"Excellent." Avery took another sip and licked his lips, "Exactly what we need to celebrate such a momentous day. Shame your mother isn't here, she'll be dying to know how it all went."

"I'll tell her tomorrow. Honestly, Dad, it was amazing, only a tiny bean really, but it made it more real seeing it."

"I bet," Avery smiled, "they didn't have sophisticated scans in our day. You got one only if they suspected something was wrong with the baby."

The conversation stalled as Bridget served them their main course. "Bon appetite," she smiled and left them to it.

Leo took a mouthful of the cod Mornay and looked directly at her. "I wish they'd been able to tell us the sex, don't you?"

He wouldn't be quite as enthusiastic about the sex if he found out it was a girl. That's why she prayed it would be. She didn't want a son who might turn out like Leo and Avery.

She shook her head, "To be honest, I don't really want to know. I'd rather keep it a surprise until it's born. I think there's something exciting about the gender being revealed when it comes into the world."

"I don't agree," Leo said emphatically. "We'll find out at your next scan, that way we can plan. You want the nursery to be the right colour. Which reminds me, we need to consider which room to use as a nursery. Whichever one we choose, we'll need a room next to it for the nanny."

"Erm . . ." she said hesitantly, "I'm not sure about a nanny. To be honest, I'd like to care for the baby myself." His disapproving expression spoke volumes so she quickly added, "It's not as if I've got loads to do."

"Nonsense," Avery interjected, "you'll need some help. You'll still have to support Leo. As his wife, it's expected."

"Yes, I know that." As if she needed reminding that she had to attend certain functions on his arm and mix with other thugs disguised as business men and their cosmetically enhanced wives.

"Look," Leo was irritated if challenged, especially in front of his dad, "I'll speak to Sienna. She'll have some design ideas so don't start stressing over that. Just go with her recommendations."

Her tummy muscles tightened from the way she was being bulldozed along. "Don't you think it's a bit early to be thinking of sorting the nursery out? I don't want to jinx things."

"You won't, everything will be fine, you'll see."

She wished she shared his optimism – she didn't feel it was going to be fine at all. Far from it. And God help her, there was part of her that willed something to happen and she hated herself for even thinking that way, having only just witnessed the tiny spec of life.

Leo's phone rang and he reached in his pocket for it. Good job his mother wasn't at the table. She had a rule that the men didn't answer phones while they were eating.

"Sorry, it's work, I better take it."

He left the room, leaving her with Avery, which made her tummy tighten even more. He had the ability to make her nervous when she was alone with him.

Thankfully, Bridget was fluttering around removing their plates and stacking them onto the server.

"Any desserts?" Bridget asked, crumb sweeping the table cloth, "Frank has made a lemon cheesecake," she looked at Avery, "or maybe you'd like a cheese plateau?"

"Nothing for me, I'm full," he smiled, fiddling with his wedding ring, pulling it on and off. He always seemed to be doing that.

"What about you, Jenna?" he asked, as if he was concerned about her needs, "you're eating for two now, are you having something?"

"No," she shook her head at Bridget, "I'm fine thank you."

She smiled nervously at Avery. "I'm told this nausea will pass in a few weeks. If you'll excuse me, I think I'll go and rest and see if the meal will settle." She made a move to stand up.

"Before you go," her tummy plummeted, "I wanted to have a word with you on your own."

Every nerve in her body was on end. Any words Avery had to say would have a hidden depth.

He paused while Bridget placed a coffee in front of her and then him. "Thank you," he nodded.

She watched him slowly pour cream in his coffee and add a sugar cube. He was waiting for Bridget to leave while she for once, wished she'd stay. The seconds seemed endless. She felt like a rabbit in the headlights not daring to move in case she was flattened.

Bridget left the dining room with a loaded trolley and closed the door behind her.

He stirred his coffee while facing her. Nerves prevented her even touching hers.

"Susan and I are both concerned about how unwell you're looking. I'm sure it isn't easy at the moment for you, so I wanted to check in about the court case. You must be anxious about that."

She nodded. Anxious yes, but not about Leo being found guilty and put in jail. The anxiety was that he wouldn't.

"I don't want you worrying. As I've reassured Susan, nothing will come of it. We've got it covered. Leo is no more a murderer than I am."

That was supposed to give her reassurance, was it?

"The barristers have assured us the court will throw the whole thing out. That's why we're confident. And the fact they granted him bail means they don't see him as a threat of any kind. So nothing is going to happen."

"How can you be so sure?" she asked conveying fake concern.

"We just are. You have to trust us. What you need to do now is concentrate on the baby."

"I'll try," she said, desperately wanting to escape. But he had more.

"Oh, there's just one other thing," he took another sip of his coffee, purposely dragging it out. "Normally it's water off a duck's back what your brother writes in his poxy newspaper. Many before him have tried to bring this family down. They never do. But right now it's a delicate time, and we don't want to give the courts any ammunition to see the Montgomerys in a negative light."

He raised an eyebrow, "You understand what I'm saying?"

She swallowed. "Yes."

"Good." He eased back into his chair. "You wouldn't know this, but when I was a boy, I went to a public school. If you can indulge me for a minute, I want to share something about that time with you."

As if she had a choice.

Bridget tapped and put her head round the door, "Excuse me interrupting, Leo asked me to tell you he's had to go into London."

"Thank you," Avery nodded waiting for her to close the door.

"Where was I? Oh yes, I remember."

With her bottom firmly fixed to the chair, her heart was beating so fast, she could almost hear it. And the hairs on the back of her neck were standing on end.

"I wasn't one of the popular boys," he said, twisting his teaspoon for something to do with his hands, "and I wasn't the most academic either, but I was particularly good at sport. Not as good as Stewart Dalton, now he was something special. Football was his passion and he was good at it. So good that talent scouts from Chelsea spotted him and he was offered a place in their junior academy when he finished his schooling." He put on a pensive expression, "I still remember now that feeling of complete jealousy and envy how anyone could be so lucky."

He appeared as if he was reminiscing but it was phony and all for effect. There was a purpose to all of this and it wasn't going to be a pleasant chat, she was certain of that.

"Anyway, for some reason Stewart Dalton didn't like me," he shrugged, "I never understood why. He started to bully me. And do you know what the worst thing about a bully is," he stared directly at her, upping the intimidation, "they play with your emotions. Some days, he would draw me into his group, and other days, I was ostracised. Things frequently happened to me, my PE kit would go missing, while another day money was taken. I think it's fair to say, over a couple of years at school, he made my life pretty miserable. I got beaten up more than once, never by him, of course, but he instigated it." He widened his eyes at her, "Now I don't know if you believe in karma?"

Fear surged through her veins. Whatever was coming next?

A darkness passed over his face, "Well, I believe in it, and Stewart Dalton certainly must have done because do you know what happened to him?"

The question didn't require a response.

"Unfortunately, on a dark evening walking home from football practice, he was hit by a car. Oh, don't look so worried, it wasn't fatal. But both his femurs were shattered and required endless surgical procedures to put them right. It took months of physiotherapy to actually be able to walk properly. Sadly though, that was the end of his football career. He never did get to play for the Chelsea first team."

The silence in the room seemed almost loud.

Avery took an exaggerated deep breath. "So that's why I believe in karma. It's always out there waiting and you can't get away from it. It's a force to be reckoned with." He wiped his mouth, "Memories eh, they come up when you least expect them to." He tossed the napkin on the table. "I'm glad we've had this little chat," he pushed his chair away and stood, "now, if you'll excuse me I've got some work to do while Susan's out. You get your rest and let's hope you're soon feeling better."

She watched him stride out of the room. If hate could kill, he'd be a dead man. With legs like jelly, she made a hasty retreat out of the dining room to their suite of rooms and didn't breathe again until she was safely inside her bedroom. Her hands were shaking uncontrollably as she undressed – he'd scared her exactly as he'd intended.

She rushed to get into bed, wrapping the duvet around herself as if it would somehow keep her safe. Although the house was warm, she felt bitterly cold and alone. Relief flooded through her that Jack was currently in Cornwall and out of the way. As soon as he was back, she needed to warn him about Avery's threat. And as terrified as she was for his safety, an even greater fear was Jack's response. He'd never back off – not when his driving force was to bring the whole lot of the Montgomerys down.

Chapter 11

London

Bridget got out of bed and wrapped her house coat around herself as Avery dressed. They'd had a frantic sex session as Susan was out for the evening, so he'd been able to come to her cottage. She knew as soon as Avery declined dessert and fiddled with his wedding ring he'd be paying her a visit. And what a visit it had been. He was a stallion for a man his age.

As she watched him put his trousers on, a yearning flooded through her for Avery to spend more time with her after lovemaking. While she knew their coupling couldn't be leisurely, she longed for him to hold her afterwards and talk to her. Like lovers do. He rarely did that. Occasionally he would, but not tonight. It had just been frantic sex.

He fastened his trousers and belt. "You don't know how much I needed that tonight."

Her tummy did the usual flip when he spoke nicely to her. "You do seem tense. What is it?"

"Susan's on my back about the court case. She's terrified Leo is going to be sent to prison."

"You said that's unlikely though?"

"I know what I said, and the brief says that too, but it's still a concern. Especially now Jenna's pregnant. This

73

baby means the world to us all. We can't afford the upset of her losing the baby with any stress."

She moved round the bed towards him and stroked his arm, "I'm sure that won't happen. I don't know how they've even put a case forward against him. Of course it's sad about Isaac disappearing, and I'm not daft, Avery, I do realise in business you have to be ruthless, but murder? I don't know how anyone could think Leo would be capable of that."

"Let's hope the jury see it that way, too."

"I'm sure they will. And once the case is over, Jenna will have the baby and you'll all have a new future to look forward to."

He took her in his arms. "You are such a good woman, Bridget, I'm bloody lucky to have you."

"And I'm lucky to have you. You mean the world to me, you know that, don't you?"

"I do and that's what keeps me going." He put his jacket on for the short walk back to the house. She knew he'd only come to her tonight as his wife was out. It saddened her that Susan got to spend the night with him, while she slept alone. But it wouldn't always be like that. One day Avery would truly be hers, totally. And if her little plan came into fruition, she was going to make it happen. Nothing was more certain. They were going to spend the rest of their lives together on that Caribbean island and nothing was going to get in their way.

"Right," he kissed her one final time, "I'd better get back to the house. Susan should be back soon."

"I'll get dressed and come across."

"No need to do that."

"But Susan will want her warm milk when she gets in. She finds it helps her sleep."

"Yes, so she said. But she can miss one night, I'm sure. If not, I can quite easily warm some milk up for her."

"No, honestly, it's fine." She didn't want him doing anything for Susan. "I'll come across. I've nothing else to do."

"You have such a heart," he smiled tenderly at her, "it was this family's lucky day when you came into it."

She kissed him gently. "That's such a lovely thing to say, thank you. I do try."

"I know you do. You're more like family to us than an employee."

"I hope so. I'd do anything for you, you know that don't you?"

"Of course I do. We both do. Susan knows your worth and trusts you implicitly."

"That's nice," she smiled with a sideways twitch of her lip.

Susan shouldn't trust her . . . not one bit.

Chapter 12

Oban

After Lucy dropped the children off at nursery, she doubled back to Kitty's house. As she opened the gate, the front door opened at the same time. Mortified didn't come close as she saw Kitty letting Tricky Monroe, *her boyfriend with benefits* out. Lucy's face coloured as he walked down the path.

"Morning," he smiled smugly, displaying his uneven yellow teeth. To her, he always had an expression which smacked of arrogance. His nickname of Tricky spoke volumes about the calibre of the man he was.

She nodded to be pleasant despite disliking him and moved aside to let him pass. He'd unnerved her ever since she'd met him. Nothing to do with her past, he just had the ability to make her feel uncomfortable whenever she came into contact with him, which fortunately for her, wasn't often. The left side of his neck was heavily tattooed with stars which looked unsightly enough, but it was his shaved head that smacked of aggression. What Kitty even saw in him, she never understood.

She pulled a pained face walking towards Kitty. "Sorry."

"It's fine," she held the door open, "come in, it's bloody freezing. I'm in desperate need of coffee and lots of it."

She followed Kitty into the kitchen area at the back of the house. Judging by her appearance, it had been a heavy night. It looked like she'd just thrown on a tee-shirt, which barely reached her knees, and her morning-after-the-night-before face was still smeared with last night's make-up.

"I was on my way to town but I thought I'd call in to see how it went last night. I feel awful now though, how embarrassing."

"Don't be daft. We're all over eighteen. Why should you be embarrassed? I'm not."

"Well I am. Anyway, you look a bit delicate," she screwed up her face and hoisted herself onto a bar stool.

"Cheers," Kitty groaned making her way to the coffee maker at the side of the sink. "I've just made a pot, have you got time?"

"That'd be nice. Are you going to have anything with it? You look like you could do with some food."

"I might in a bit," Kitty grimaced, sitting down opposite and placing a mug in front of her and taking a huge gulp of hers. "Thank the Lord for coffee. My saviour."

"So why was Tricky here? What happened to Alex?"

"He bailed on me."

"Bailed?"

"Yeah, said something had come up, maybe another time."

"That's a shame, you were looking forward to it."

"Yeah, I was. But Tricky's a good laugh. And," she raised her eyebrows, "he's got plenty of stamina, if you know what I mean."

Lucy held up a hand, "Er . . . spare me the details, would you."

Kitty laughed, then winced as if it hurt her head, "Unlike you, I don't want to live a celibate life."

"I can see that, but you could do so much better than him."

"Says who?" Irritation was written all over Kitty's face, which wasn't unusual. She was fickle and her moods fluctuated – jolly one minute and morose the next.

"I'm just saying you're lovely and deserve someone nice," she said, trying not to antagonise her further, "but it's entirely up to you who you see. I'm not here to fall out."

"Well don't say anything then 'cause I'll see whoever I want."

"Don't be like that. He just always looks to me like he's looking for trouble. Does he even have a job?"

"Yeah, he does labouring. But what does that matter? Not all blokes fit into a nine to five office job. It doesn't make them any less of a person if they don't."

"I'm not saying it does. Look, I didn't mean anything by it."

Kitty sighed, "I know you didn't. But lay off judging me, would you. I've enough of that with Hilda. Just because she sees you as the perfect friend and me the poor relative, doesn't make it right."

"That's not true and you know it. Hilda loves you dearly and helps you out all the time. She's as good as any aunty could be."

Kitty's face looked pained because she knew it was true, Hilda was really good to her. "Forget I said anything, it's this bloody hangover making me twitchy."

Lucy nodded, "Look, I better go," she picked up her cup and took it to the sink to rinse. "What are your plans today . . . after you've sobered up. Are you working at lunch?"

"No, I'm off today. So, a shower first, maybe a bit of a fry-up and then I'll have a shopping day. There's a licensee ball a week on Saturday. You never know, Alex might invite me to that, so I'll need a decent dress."

"Right." She daren't suggest waiting to see if she gets an invite first. "Oh, before I forget, Alex dropped a hamper off at the shop and said I'd won it in a raffle at the pub. I didn't buy a ticket so I thought you must have, which makes it your prize really. I can nip home and get it?"

"I didn't buy you a raffle ticket," Kitty frowned, "not that I recall."

"God knows then." She'd been right, it wasn't a legitimate prize. "Maybe it was a name card or something? Do you want it anyway? It looks to have some nice biscuits and chocolates."

"Nah, you keep it. Share them with the boys."

"Are you sure?"

79

"Course I'm sure. I need to keep the kilos off at least until after the ball. I want to get something slinky and figure-hugging," she grinned.

It was a relief to see Kitty back to her bubbly self as they made her way to the front door. "I'll call in the shop later and show you my dress if I get one."

Lucy gave Kitty a hug and squeezed her extra tightly. She didn't have anyone else in her life only Hilda and Kitty and she couldn't afford to alienate either of them.

"Okay, see you later."

"Yeah, see you soon."

Lucy closed the gate behind her and checked her watch. It was still early and she didn't want to return to the shop as she might bump into the chap returning for the necklace for his sister. It bothered her that she found him attractive. There wasn't room for anything in her life like that, ever. To delay things a little longer, she decided rather than catch a bus, she'd make her way on foot to the High street, but she was still relatively early once she'd reached the shops, so decided to pop into a café to kill another half an hour.

It was crowded with holidaymakers but she managed to find a vacant table. She caught sight of herself in the mirror on the wall and as always when it unexpectedly happened, her appearance caught her by surprise. Her natural blonde hair was now brunette courtesy of a bottle of hair colour every six weeks, and the tinted clear glasses which detracted from her eyes, while a necessary permanent fixture, still took some getting used to even after five years. Her pierced ears had closed up as she never wore ear-rings or any jewellery that might draw attention. She was as far removed from how she used to look as was possible without plastic surgery. Her objective when she'd arrived in Oban was to fit in with the crowds. Even her name was carefully thought out. Nobody would be interested in plain Lucy Smyth.

As she leisurely sipped her coffee, she glanced out of the window at the busy High Street and spotted Tricky across the road talking to another dodgy looking individual. He somehow had the ability to make her flesh creep, even from a distance, so seeing him twice in one day was two times too many.

Lucy returned to the craft shop clutching a small bag of cakes for her and Hilda to legitimise her shopping trip. As she walked through the door, it was evident her avoidance strategy had been in vain. Handsome Jack was pulling on his jacket and talking to Hilda.

"Ah, you're back," Hilda said, "Can you believe Jack has fixed the leak for us?"

"How kind," she said, wishing to God he'd been long gone – she didn't like the way her heart seemed to quicken around him, "Thank you."

"Not a problem," his smile lit up his warm brown eyes and she hadn't noticed his long, sooty black lashes before. "It was a couple of loose tiles that had moved. I nipped to the hardware store and bought a bit of felt, borrowed the ladder from the shop on the corner, replaced the felt and tapped the tiles into place. It didn't take long at all."

"Well, we are grateful."

"No problem, you're more than welcome." His charming smile showed off his perfectly even white teeth. If anything, he was more attractive seeing him the second time. "And I went for the long chain, by the way."

"Long chain?"

"For my sister's pendant . . . the one I chose yesterday."

"Oh, yes, of course," she flushed, "that'll be nice. I'm sure she'll like that."

"Me too." If he was staring at her expecting her to carry on a conversation, he was mistaken. She smiled at Hilda, "I'll just put this in the back," she held up a small bag and moved towards the workshop, "Bye then, and thank you again," she nodded to Jack.

As she hung up her jacket in the workshop, she considered why he unsettled her. The fluttering in her tummy was alien to her. Where men were concerned, especially new arrivals, she was always wary, assessing if they were possible predators, and even though he seemed like one of the good guys, it could all be subterfuge, so she couldn't afford to let her guard down. It was a relief when the doorbell chimed and she heard Hilda say goodbye. That was the end of him now, she wouldn't see him again.

Hilda came into the workshop gushing, "Wasn't that nice of him to fix the roof? I wanted to pay him but he was having none of it, so I've invited him round for dinner tomorrow night. I thought it was the least I could do."

"Dinner?" Lucy's voice went up an octave, "What, at home?"

"Yes, of course at home, where do you think?"

"And he's said he'll come?"

"Yes," Hilda frowned, "why wouldn't he?"

"But you don't know him. He could be anybody."

"It's just a bit of dinner. I hardly think there'll be a problem."

"But what about the children?"

"I don't think he'd mind them being there."

"I don't mean that at all Hilda and you know it," she snapped, "I mean a man in the house. I don't want the children exposed to that."

"It'll be their bedtime," Hilda dismissed, "anyway, have you ever stopped to think a man might be good for them to be around? They're only ever exposed to us two."

"And that's all I want them to be *exposed to*. I wish you'd asked me before you invited him."

"Why, so you could take the children somewhere out of the way? Lucy, love, I don't know what has gone on in your life, nor do you need to tell me, but you're a young, beautiful, woman and you can't keep hiding away like this. Whatever trauma you've been through in the past, won't shape your future if you don't let it. Now might be a good time to move on a little."

"What, by having a fling with a man that's here for a month?"

"Why not? What's wrong with that? You don't have to fall in love with every man you meet. You can just enjoy the moment, no strings attached, and then one day, you'll meet someone you want to be with. You might even have more children, you're only young."

"Oh, please." She found herself struggling to find the right words. Hilda was a huge part of her and the children's lives, she didn't want to upset her, but she had to put a halt to her match-making. "I love you very much, you know that. And the children do. I can't ever repay you for the kindness you've shown me. But I'm begging you, please don't encourage this man with regard to me. Even if he was interested and it doesn't strike me he is, but even if he was, I really don't want to get involved. The only life I want is one for me and the boys. That's it. Nothing else."

"But you should have more, that's what I'm saying. You can't hide away for ever. You'll have to one day face your demons. Only then will you ever be free."

She had to fight back the lump in her throat and the overwhelming need to let the threatening tears flow. "Trust me, Hilda, there's not a single person that can ever free me. I only wish there was."

Chapter 13

Oban

Lucy sat on a chair in between the children's beds and exaggerated the animal noises of the characters in the book. The children adored story time and each night she'd make it special, adlibbing to make them more exciting. It was her favourite time of day, when the children were settled in bed in their pyjamas and the fragrance of the bubble bath still lingered, and their little cheeks, still pink from the bath were protruding out of their quilts. She loved their precious time together.

"Right," she closed the book with a big thump, "that's it for now, we'll read the last bit tomorrow."

Jordan started to get up from his lying position, "Aww, we need to know what happened to Mr Policeman Badger. Please, Mummy, just 'till the end."

She stood and gently eased him down again smiling. She loved their enthusiasm for a story, just as she had as a child.

"No, you're tired, you need to go to sleep now, it's getting late." She tucked the quilt around him, "And it's something to look forward to tomorrow night." She kissed his head and turned towards Cory who was almost asleep. Dear compliant Cory, he'd never protest like his brother. She kissed him too.

"Night, night, sleep tight," she waved as she made her way towards the door, smiling as the boys said in unison, "and make sure the bed bugs don't bite." She dimmed the lights. "Love you to the moon and back. See you in the morning."

She made her way downstairs and approached the dining room which Hilda had gone to town on for her dinner guest. It looked beautiful with the ornate lace tablecloth, matching napkins, and with tea-light candles floating in an oval dish of water in the middle of the table. Hilda shone at creating a warm welcome.

"Can I help at all?" Lucy asked knowing it was all in hand.

"No, it's all done. You need to get a move on though, to get ready."

"Get ready?" she frowned, "I am ready, well, as ready as I'm going to be."

"What, that's it?" Hilda said exaggerating her eye movement from Lucy's head down to her toes, "you aren't getting changed?"

"Er, no." Lucy shook her head, "he's your guest, not mine."

"I know, but it would be nice to make an effort. It's just one night."

"And why would I be doing that? I've told you, I'm not interested."

"Yes, I know what you said, but how are you going to feel if he turns up in smart clothes and you're in jeans and a jumper. It's a bit rude. People do dress for dinner you know."

Lucy took a deep breath in. "Okay, okay, I'll go and change, but I'm not getting glammed up, that's for sure."

The door bell rang, "Go on then, off you go, that sounds like him now, he's early. You better hurry up."

Lucy made her way upstairs smiling inwardly. Hilda had got it completely wrong if she thought she was going to be entertaining him all evening. She intended to be polite, but that was all. And dressing up wasn't a priority for her – dressing down was. She reached in the wardrobe for a plain grey dress which would suffice with black tights and shoes. It was the one she'd had in mind until a brighter red print caught her eye, which she'd bought the year previously but never actually worn. She held it against herself in the full-length mirror and decided on it purely because it was less drab than the grey one. That was the only reason – *wasn't it?*

Much as she wanted to be indifferent towards Jack, Lucy couldn't. His appeal and considerable charm was almost magnetic, which made her wonder how he could possibly be single. She could only conclude that maybe all wasn't as it seemed and he had a darker side. He was witty and amusing, reciting anecdotes about his childhood spent with military parents. His eyes had clouded over when he'd explained about their death in a car accident in Malta. For some bizarre reason, she had an urge to reach out to him when she saw the sadness in his usually vibrant eyes. But he quickly moved on, telling them about his sister who was a twin. That led to Hilda interjecting about Lucy's boys.

"Oh, you have children," Jack said, "I know I'm a bit biased but twins are rather special."

"Yes, they are, but at four they can be little minxes."

"Is there a dominant one?"

"Oh yes. That would be Jordan. Cory is a little sweetie that does whatever I say, whereas Jordan challenges every time. What about you and your sister . . . who was the dominant one growing up?"

"Ah, me of course, but Jenna was a bit bossy," he looked over his shoulder playfully, "but I wouldn't dare say that if she were here."

They laughed. He was easy to like and wasn't at all inquisitive. That's what she feared most of all, that he might start asking about her past. Hilda assumed she was hiding from an abusive husband, which seemed the likely explanation so she never corrected her.

"I'm trying to get my sister to come for a weekend while I'm here," Jack said, "I hope she will, then you both can get to meet her."

"That'll be nice," Hilda said, "we'd love to, wouldn't we, Lucy?"

"Yes," she smiled encouragingly, even though that was the last thing she wanted. There was little point in building friendships that couldn't go anywhere. Being close to someone meant explaining things. Questions always came up, 'do you have siblings' 'did you go to university' 'what job did you do before you had children'. She found it easier to steer clear of making friends. The twins were her life, and she hoped one day she'd have saved enough money to buy herself a small property for her and the boys. That was the dream, even though she had a long way to go.

Jack wiped his mouth on his napkin, "That was a truly lovely meal, Hilda, I'm so grateful to you. I must say, it's a long time since I've tasted good old-fashioned home cooking like that. I love lamb."

Hilda beamed, "I hope you've left room for some apple pie and custard?"

"Oh, go on then, if you insist."

Lucy stood to clear the plates. "Sit still, Lucy, I'll do them," Hilda said, "you keep Jack company, I'll only be a minute." She piled the plates up and headed for the kitchen.

She inwardly cursed Hilda for leaving her alone with him, it felt awkward. And she couldn't control the nervousness swirling round her tummy.

It's just tension, she told herself, with always having to be on guard.

"How's the book coming on?" she said quickly to deflect from him asking her a question.

"Good. I've managed to make a start. I can't imagine I'll get much done while I'm here but I'm enjoying doing the research, that's interesting."

"What's it about?"

"It's a love story stroke thriller."

She widened her eyes. "Really? Isn't it unusual for a man to write a love story?"

"Not really, there are many that do. Mine focuses on the thriller aspect more, but I do like a happy ending. Do you?"

"I'm not a great reader I have to say." Her stare seemed intense so she carried on, "Too busy most of the time."

"What about while on holiday, do you like to read then?"

How could she tell him she'd hadn't had a holiday in five years? She daren't go anywhere outside of Oban. *Where the hell was Hilda?* "Yeah, maybe then. Just excuse me a second, would you?" She stood up, "I'll see how Hilda's getting on."

She fled the room. Hot and sticky didn't come close to how she was feeling. He had the ability to knock her equilibrium off its axis with those warm eyes of his that were becoming so addictive. Hopefully after tonight she wouldn't see him anymore. Maybe just a nod if she saw him around. He wasn't likely to come to the shop anymore as he'd bought the necklace, he'd fixed the leak, and Hilda had repaid him by inviting him for dinner. That should be the end of it.

She accompanied Hilda back into the dining room feeling better having her there. Being alone with Jack was too much. But she was amused to see the delight on his face as he tucked into his dessert.

"Oh my God," he put his spoon down, "if you ever get tired of the craft shop, Hilda, you could set up a tea room. That was something else."

Hilda's face was a picture, but the front door opening stopped her replying.

"It's only me," Kitty called. She'd been invited for dinner but she'd been working at the pub. She must have got away early.

"In here," Hilda called. Kitty stepped into the dining room looking as loudly dressed as usual in a figure-hugging red top which showed off her ample cleavage, and an equally tight mini skirt.

"This is my niece, Kitty," Hilda said, "Kitty, this is Jack I was telling you about."

Lucy knew exactly what Kitty's reaction would be to Jack. He had trousers and a pulse so was a dead cert.

"Hi," Kitty smiled, her eyes quickly drawn straight to him as he stood up and towered over her.

Hilda carried on, "Kitty lives four doors away from us to the left, so we're all neighbours."

Jack held out his hand and Kitty shook it. Lucy knew she'd find Jack appealing, any woman would. Her tummy twisted at the thought he might find Kitty attractive too, which was silly. It wasn't as if she wanted him for herself.

"How nice to meet you," Kitty said pulling out the chair next to him and sitting down. "Hilda tells me you're going to write a book."

"Yes, that's right, but I'm only at the research stage. There'll be a long way to go before it actually seems anything like a book."

"How exciting though. You've picked a great place to do the research, I hope we get some nice weather while you're here."

"That'd be good, although I am here to work really."

"Yes, but you must have some time off. Isn't there a saying about too much work makes Jack a dull boy?"

He grinned at her clever words, "I think you might be right. But I'm afraid dull is what I'll have to be for the few weeks I'm here."

Hilda interrupted, "Kitty works at the Golden Lion if you do get fed up, it's a lovely local pub and they do a tasty venison pie."

"Sounds nice, I must remember that."

"Oh yes," Kitty flirted outrageously with her doe eyes, "call in anytime and let me buy you a drink. And I can easily show you round here if you get bored. It can get a bit lonely when you don't know anyone."

Lucy cringed at her brazenness.

"Thank you," he said politely, "I'll bear that in mind." He turned to Hilda, "I can't tell you how much I've enjoyed tonight and your lovely food," his eyes met hers, "you've both been so kind. I think it's about time I made a move."

"Are you sure?" Hilda asked, "won't you stay for coffee, or something a little stronger?"

"No, honestly I'm fine. You've spoilt me enough, thank you so much for your hospitality."

"Oh, you're welcome anytime. We love company, don't we, Lucy?"

She smiled as if the answer was yes, when nothing was further from the truth. Jack moved his chair and stood up.

"I can see you out," Kitty jumped to her feet.

"Thank you," he smiled with those warm rich brown eyes. No wonder Kitty had taken a liking to him. "I'll say goodnight then, and hope you'll let me repay you sometime."

Hilda smiled, "There's honestly no need."

Lucy and Hilda were clearing up and loading the dishwasher when Kitty came back into the kitchen drooling, "He's rather nice, isn't he? And single too."

"Well you're not." Lucy hadn't meant to snap, "What about Tricky, I thought you were with him?"

"I keep telling you, we're just friends. I'm not bothered about him that way, and certainly not when drop-dead gorgeous Jack's around."

Hilda pressed start on the dishwasher. "Shame he's dashed off and didn't want a night cap. I'm going to have a whisky," she winked, "to help me sleep. Anyone else?"

"Go on then," Kitty said, "I'll have a Bailey's for the road."

"I'll get the ice," Lucy smiled, amused at one for the road for Kitty when she only lived four doors away. They carried their drinks into the lounge and made themselves comfy on the sofas.

"Do you know if he has anyone at home, like a girlfriend or anything?" Kitty asked, looking directly at her.

"Don't ask me," she dismissed, "I have no idea. It's Hilda that knows him."

Hilda shook her head, "I don't think there's anyone. I can't imagine a wife or girlfriend would let him come here on his own for a month. And when he bought one of Lucy's necklaces, it was for his sister. So no, he doesn't strike me as a man with a girlfriend."

"Don't you like him, Luce?" Kitty asked taking a sip of her drink.

Kitty would want her to say no so she could make a move. More of a move than she already had – she couldn't have made it any more obvious she liked him.

"Not like that, I don't."

"In that case, I'm going to invite him out. He can't sit at his computer all the time he's here. Where's the fun in that?"

Hilda scowled, "Why don't you, for once in your life, leave things alone. All this chasing men does you no good. You'd do much better if you took a more laid back approach. Then, if it's meant to be, he'll ask you out."

"Hilda, you're living in the Dark Ages. Women these days go after what they want. And now I know I'm not stepping on anyone's toes, there's no harm in asking him out. It's just a date, that's all."

"Yes, but we know it won't end there. You'll be rushing into something like you always do. And then you'll get hurt when he leaves for home. He's made it clear he's only here to do some research on his book. He's not stopping."

"All the more reason to have a bit of fun while he's here, then. Stop worrying, Hilda. I always manage my own love life don't I?"

"Yes and that's what worries me. None of them stick around."

Kitty's expression was one of irritation. Lucy could tell she didn't like Hilda's tone. It was too near the truth.

Kitty downed the last of her drink. "Right, on that supportive note," she said sarcastically and stood up, "I'll make a move. Don't get up, I'll see myself out. Thanks Hilda as always for the vote of confidence in me."

Hilda waved her hand, "Go on with you. I only give advice, what you do is entirely up to you. But I wouldn't push that one, he's nothing like the men round here."

Kitty rolled her eyes as she left the room.

Hilda yawned. "I don't know about you, but I'm whacked and going up. Were you just saying it for Kitty's benefit, or don't you really like Jack?"

"Course I like him. Just not how you want me to."

"Well, I'm telling you now, Jack is not, nor would be interested in Kitty while you're around. It's you he likes and, if you were truthful, you like him too. You might think you can hide attraction, but trust me, you can't. It's there." She stood up, "Okay then, I'll say goodnight. I'll lock the front door on my way up. Put the lights out, love would you?"

"Course I will. Goodnight." Lucy got out of the chair, picked up the empty glasses and put the lounge lights off before heading for the kitchen.

Hilda was talking rubbish, as if she was interested in Jack. She'd been reading too many of the Mills and Boon novels she favoured. And even if there was a smidgeon of truth that she did found him attractive, she could never go there. Letting her guard down could never happen.

Chapter 14

London

Bridget was sitting in the kitchen with the chef planning the menus for the family. They worked on a month at a time.

"Does Leo's wife actually eat anything anymore?" Frank asked, "Everything we give her comes back hardly touched."

"Yes, I know, she barely eats anything."

"That can't be good for her with a baby on the way. Have you asked if there's anything she fancies I can do specially for her?"

"Of course I have," Bridget said curtly, "she doesn't want anything. We have done our best. We can only hope she's getting sufficient nutrients from the fruit juices she has and the bread and yoghurts. If not she'll end up in hospital on a drip."

The internal phone on the wall interrupted them. Bridget got up to answer it.

"Hello."

"Ah, Bridget," her heart raced upon hearing Avery's voice. They'd not been intimate for five long days so her anticipation was high he was going to suggest meeting up.

"Susan's not out of bed yet," he said, "can you bring her some coffee, she has a luncheon appointment and doesn't want to miss that."

"Of course." She hoped he didn't think she'd been slacking, "I did go in at eight with her Earl Grey."

"Yes, so she said, but she had that and went straight back to sleep apparently."

"I see. I'll bring a cafetiere up. Do you require a cup?"

"No. I have to go out."

Her excitement faded at his focus on sickly Susan. She hated that their unions were always instigated by him when he was ready with no consideration for her needs.

"Okay," she replied cordially, "leave it with me. I'll help Susan get ready."

"Thank you."

Bridget tapped on the bedroom door and opened it. Susan was sitting by the window with the sun directly on her face, fast asleep. She put the coffee down on the console table and gently gave her a shake.

Confusion was written over Susan's face as she opened her eyes. "Oh dear, not again. Honestly, what am I like? All I seem to do these days is sleep."

"You must need it," Bridget said encouragingly, pouring her coffee into the cup from the cafetiere. "Would you like me to run you a bath?"

"Oh, would you? Thank you, that'll be such a help." Bridget made a move towards the bathroom.

"Before you do that, please don't mention anything to the boys about this sleeping all the time. Avery is already pussy-footing around and treating me with kid gloves. I keep telling him I'm fine but I can see he's concerned. They have enough on with Leo's case without worrying about me."

Bridget's tummy clenched with jealousy at Avery's concern for her. Susan Montgomery was her boss and for that reason she showed her respect, but she'd never really liked her, and more recently not liking her had turned into something much more sinister. She wanted her gone so that Avery would be free and with her. But she needed to be careful. At any time she could go and see a doc and then it would all be over. So she needed to tread carefully. *Softly, softly catches the monkey.*

"I won't say a word. I think maybe your tiredness is all to do with the months you've been worrying about Leo. One minute he was going to be charged, the next he wasn't. It must have placed a terrible strain on you and Avery. You've probably missed more sleep in the past months than you realise and it's finally catching up with you."

Susan gave her a relieved smile. "Do you know, I think you could be right, dear. I must say, I am worried sick about it all despite Avery and Leo reassuring me everything will be fine. And on top of that, now I'm worrying myself to death about Jenna and the baby as well."

"It's all bound to have an effect on you," Bridget said.

"Yes, quite. And Jenna's been so unwell and virtually living in bed. She's not keeping anything down as far as I can see. Do you see her eating anything? All I see is her doing a good job of pushing food around her plate. Does she eat any of the snacks you take her?"

"Sometimes. But you mustn't worry. I have a friend who was just the same. She was fine though after the first three months and I'm sure Jenna will be too. She's a fit young woman."

"I do hope you're right. But do let's keep my worries between you and I. I think the boys have enough on their plates right now."

"Of course."

"Good. Well, if you don't mind running me that bath, I'll have my coffee and then get ready. My friend Celia is taking me out for lunch and a bit of retail therapy. It might be the last chance for a while with the trial looming closer by the minute."

"That'll be nice then. You'll enjoy doing something different other than sat about worrying."

"Yes, you're right, I will." Susan smiled kindly at her, "Thank you, Bridget, you always say the right things and manage to cheer me up. I really appreciate you, we all do. We're so lucky to have you."

"That's a nice thing to say. Thank you. I'll just go and run that bath." She made her way into the luxurious ensuite, turned the bath taps on and reached in the cupboard for the decadent La Mer bath foam Susan favoured. She unscrewed the top and poured a generous amount in and, as she watched the bath water thicken with the luxurious rich bubbles, she smiled to herself. Susan's statement, *'we're so lucky to have you'* had a certain irony attached to it. Lucky? Little did Susan Montgomery know, – her luck was about to run out.

Chapter 15

London

Jenna woke to find she was alone in the bed. Leo rarely slept more than five hours – too busy planning who he was going to screw next. He'd either be playing golf or downstairs in the annex of the house. He and Avery had adjacent offices they used for business. She never ventured there, she was too frightened of what she might find.

Laid on her back contemplating the day ahead, she relished the fact that for the first time since she'd found out she was pregnant, she didn't feel the usual morning sickness. She glanced at the time on her phone. The boring day ahead held no excitement for her. She was meeting a friend for lunch which she could barely face as she hated having to paint on the happy wife mask. She wished Jack was around, she'd much prefer lunch with him. She missed him since he'd gone on his latest jaunt. Jack being away meant less about Leo in the newspaper so it kept Avery off her back. She was still nervous about her brother returning to London after Avery's veiled threat to harm him.

Her full bladder made it impossible to lie any longer so she headed for the ensuite. It soon became apparent something was wrong. She was bleeding a significant amount, which could only mean one thing – she was losing the baby. She showered and quickly dressed. The tension in her tummy was palpable. Leo was going to be absolutely devastated. That's why he'd hastily married her – just to get the child. He needed an heir, but more important than that was his need to prove his masculinity. He wanted his father's approval too. That was most important to Leo Montgomery.

Dr Furman was running a scanner over her abdomen. The silence was palpable. She could tell by his face there was no baby.

"I'm terribly sorry, Mrs Montgomery, you've miscarried your baby."

She felt Leo stiffen beside her.

"I'm afraid it's not uncommon early on in the pregnancy. One in ten pregnancies end in miscarriage and, as sad as this news is," he looked at Leo to include him, "there is absolutely no reason why you can't go on and have further healthy pregnancies."

Leo wouldn't be interested in anything he had to say. Yes, he'd want more sex to make sure she conceived again, but right now he'd be furious. He hated failing at anything and he'd very much see this as failure. There'd be no comfort for her, that was for sure, it'd be straight on the baby-making wagon as soon as they were able. That caused her greater angst than losing the baby. And God forgive her, but it was almost a relief not to be bringing his child into the world.

They remained silent in the car on the journey home. They had a driver so it was difficult to speak, which she was relieved about. Even when they got home there'd be no comforting words, or a calm arm of reassurance around her. No, there'd be none of that. Leo would just disappear into the secret criminal world he thrived on.

"Do you want to tell Mum and Dad?" he asked, "or shall I?"

She shrugged, "You can."

"They're going to be upset."

"Yes, I'm sure."

As she stared out of the window at the busy London traffic she considered if she'd somehow caused the miscarriage. Tears threatened at the thought she might have contributed, but she held them back. If she cried, Leo wouldn't console her, he'd just be irritated.

The car pulled up outside the house. "I'm going to lie down," she said moving to exit the car before McNeil even had chance to open the door, "and don't send Bridget. I'm fine."

He nodded and she quickly made her way into the house and towards their rooms. For once, Bridget wasn't lurking. Right now she couldn't face speaking to anyone.

She got into bed and cried desperately for the little bean that hadn't made it. Was it karma? She hadn't wanted the baby, not with Leo. Nevertheless, she would have loved it and tried to be the best mother she could. She'd had the perfect role models. Her and Jack's parents were the best. The thought of her mum and dad made her sob even more. If only they were still alive.

When she woke up, she had a desperate need to speak to her brother and reached for her phone to call him.

"Hello, you," he sounded out of breath. Hearing his cheery voice stopped her from saying she'd lost the baby. It didn't seem fair to burden him with that. Not right now. He was only away for a few weeks so she'd tell him when he got back. There was nothing to be gained by him worrying about her. He needed to enjoy his time in Cornwall.

"Hello to you too. You sound breathless."

"I've just come back from a run and about to jump in the shower."

"Do you want me to ring you back?"

"No, I can sit and get my breath back first. How's things?"

"Fine, I'm just a bit fed up. How about you? I still haven't received those photos you promised."

"Ah, well, there's a reason for that."

"And what's that?"

"I want you to come and visit me and see it for yourself."

"How long are you likely to be, do you know yet?"

"Not sure. Alan's doing a good job at the paper, so there's no rush. But I've got to come back to London to sign a couple of documents at some stage. You could always come back with me. A break might be nice for you."

She'd love a break with him, especially right now when she was feeling more vulnerable than usual.

"I'll speak to Leo. Maybe I could fly down."

"No, don't do that. It'll be fun driving. It'll be like old times. We could stop off in Plymouth."

Her heart constricted. Plymouth was where their mother had been born.

"That would be so nice," she stifled the threatening tears, "I'd love that."

"Yeah, so driving would be better. And it's perfect with me having to come back to London."

"Are you sure? You're not away that long, won't it wait until you're back?"

"Not really. And if you're coming back with me, you'd be doing me a huge favour as it's lonely on my own. I like solitude and it's great for writing, but I do yearn for some company."

"So there aren't any women in Cornwall then?" She knew her brother was a good catch and there'd been plenty of women who had tried to snare him, but they never did.

"Not that I can find. So what do you say? I can come up on Thursday and bring you back, on Monday."

"Can I have a think about it?" She'd have to run it by Leo first of all. There might be a smidgeon of a chance now with her losing the baby. "It does sound tempting."

"You do that, then. I'd love to have you here with me."

"Me too. I'll see what I can do. Speak later."

"Okay. All my love."

"You too. Bye."

Would Leo let her go? He might, but only because he was distracted right now with the lawyers and the court case. Leo was an overbearing bully and used threats to get his own way. He rarely used physical violence towards her, he didn't need to as his threats made sure of her compliance. He'd made it clear she could never leave the marriage, and he was more than capable of killing her if she attempted it. She prayed daily there'd be enough evidence to lock him up, even though that seemed unlikely. Who would possibly go up against Leo Montgomery and his father, Avery?

Nobody would dare.

Chapter 16

London

Bridget tapped on the door and went into the sitting room after the family dinner to see if they wanted any liqueurs. Susan wasn't there, only Avery and Leo, sitting together on the leather Chesterfields, both looking intense.

"Can I get you anything else?" she asked, aching to know what was going on. Something was. During dinner, Avery, Susan and Leo were making polite forced conversation every time she entered the room, which was purely for her ears. She wasn't stupid. And why wasn't Jenna eating with them?

Avery turned to Leo, "Are you working tonight?"

"Yeah, but I'll get McNeil to drive me."

"Make it two large brandies then would you, Bridget?"

She nodded, "What about Susan?"

"She's gone up as she has some phone calls to make. Can you give her a knock to see if she wants anything?"

"Yes, I will do."

She made her way across to the drinks cabinet containing an array of premium alcoholic beverages and selected two elegant brandy schooners. The atmosphere was tense as she poured them a generous measure each of Rémy Martin. As she left the room, she pulled the door to, but slightly ajar. She didn't move away – she stood quietly and listened to their conversation.

"I thought something was odd with all of her sickness," Avery said, "makes you wonder if it's her temperament that's half the problem."

"Yeah, I know, I'm gutted. I was so looking forward to finally having a son. I reckon that's why Mum's taken off to her room. She seemed upset over dinner."

"She was. But she'll get over it, there'll be other babies, you'll see. At least Jenna can get pregnant, so you'll just have to keep trying. The thing that's pissing me off is the brief saying her being pregnant could well sway the jury."

"Yeah, exactly."

Bridget had heard enough. She made her way up the stairs to Susan's room. So, dim Jenna had miscarried – it wasn't a surprise. She hadn't been taking care of herself, spending far too much time in her room, wallowing in self-pity. It irritated her to death that all she had to do was carry a baby for nine months and she couldn't even do that. It just confirmed how useless she was. But his first late wife had been no different. That was the trouble with Leo, his type was beautiful looking women with no brains. And both times he'd ended up with bimbo's.

She returned to the sitting room thirty minutes later to clear the glasses away and was surprised to see Avery sitting on his own.

"Oh, I am sorry, I would have knocked. I thought the room was empty."

"It's okay," he gave her his, oh so sexy smile, "come in. Leo's gone out, Susan's upstairs, so I'm a bit of a Billy-no-mates tonight. I'm contemplating going to my office for an hour or so to do some work."

"I see." She desperately wanted to say he didn't need to be alone but she held back. They were in the family sitting room and it was important they maintained the employer, employee relationship. Anyone could walk in.

She moved towards the console tables and collected the brandy schooners, placing them on the small silver tray she was holding.

"We've had a bit of unfortunate news this evening," Avery said, "it's not public yet, but it will be in the next day or two."

Bridget stood silently, waiting.

"I'm afraid Jenna's lost the baby."

"Oh dear. How is she?"

"I haven't seen her, but Leo's upset, more than he's letting on. And Susan too, that's why she dashed off after dinner. We were so looking forward to having a grandchild."

"I'm sure," she muttered sympathetically.

"And please don't think me cold-hearted, but Jenna being pregnant might have helped with the trial. You know, a happily married family man with a baby on the way."

"Yes," she agreed, hating seeing him so sad. "I can see how that might help to sway a jury."

"It wasn't me saying it either, it was the brief. He was the one that suggested the party, to make the announcement, so it was well known she was pregnant."

"Such a shame. But does it need to be made public?" she raised her eyebrows, "nobody would know if she didn't say anything. Her medical history is confidential, so things could carry on as if she was still having a baby. Then after the trial it wouldn't matter."

"I see what you mean. But it was more about the pregnancy being visible. You know, a baby bump getting Leo sympathy from the jury. Who doesn't love the miracle of babies?" He looked genuinely upset and she wished she could throw her arms around him and tell him not to worry, she'd be there for him and always would be.

"Anyway," he sighed, "I'd better be making a move. Thank you, Bridget." His voice became no more than a whisper, "You always have the ability to lift my spirits."

She'd like to do so more than lift his spirits, but he wasn't indicating any intimacy was going to happen that evening, even though she desperately wanted to offer him some comfort and relief. He stood up and she hated the thought of him being alone in his office.

"Just a thought," she said, stalling for more time with him. She screwed up her face, "Oh, no, it doesn't matter. It's probably a bit far-fetched anyway."

He frowned, "What, tell me?"

"Well, there are fake bellies you can buy online that imitate a pregnancy. They're used mainly for advertising or stage performances. They come in various sizes depending what stage of a pregnancy is to be replicated. So," she shrugged, "if Jenna was willing, she could wear one of those, showing she's in the early stages. Nobody would know any different and, if it helps Leo . . ."

"Bloody hell, Bridget," Avery's face became animated, "you're not just a pretty face . . . you're an absolute genius. And you might just have saved Leo's bacon."

She smiled coyly and gazed at him longingly. If he was so pleased, he should be thanking her properly.

Merriment flashed in his rich brown eyes turning him from handsome to godly. "I'll give Leo a call and put that idea to him. But before I do, I'll nip up and let Susan know I'll be working for the next couple of hours in my office. Could you bring me another brandy in about thirty minutes," he winked. "Oh, and if you could keep the news between us for now."

"Of course," she nodded, her body now flushed with warmth, "see you shortly."

Chapter 17

Oban

Lucy was enjoying the afternoon sunshine as she wandered along the beach with the boys after nursery. It was a bright, pleasant afternoon and she always liked them to get plenty of fresh air. She'd given them a bag each and they were collecting shells. The teacher had encouraged them to bring some so they could create a collage.

"Mummy, look at this," Cory held up a large shell.

"I think that might be a bit too big, darling, Mrs Scott said just small shells."

"I like it. Can I keep it?"

"Erm . . . if you want to. I know, I'll polish it up a bit and maybe we can put it in the bathroom, or better still, you could give it to Hilda for her birthday."

His little face was a picture. "Is it soon?"

"It's not for a little while, but you can give it to her before then if you like. She'd love a present from you."

Jordan picked up a huge shell. He'd not want Cory to upstage him. "I've got one."

"That's a bit big, sweetie."

"But I want to give a present to Hilda too."

"Okay then. I'll give you each a tag and you can write your names and a funny face. Right, come on, my

113

tummy's rumbling. Let's put what we have in your backpacks and walk to town for your McDonalds."

The High Street was busy by the time they'd walked to it from the seafront, which wasn't unusual. Residents living in Oban were on their way home and it was the main street for tourists arriving or leaving. She held onto the boys' hands tightly as they approached the crossing.

"Can I press the button?" Jordan asked eagerly.

"No, sweetheart, someone already has. The cars will stop in a minute."

She felt her phone vibrating in her bag and let go of the boys' hands to open the zip. In a split second, Jordan made a move towards the button. She attempted to grab him, and as she did so, someone barged into her from behind with enough force to send her flying into the road. As she plunged towards the ground, almost in slow motion, out of her peripheral vision, two men ran onto the road to stop the oncoming traffic. An almighty screech reverberated in her ears as the oncoming cars braked and juddered to a stop.

"Stupid cow!" someone called as she scrambled on her knees. Strong arms wrapped themselves around her, "You're alright, love. Come on, let's get you off the road." The man gently helped her up and moved her towards the safety of the pavement.

Relief flooded through her to see an older lady was clutching the children's hands. Cory had started crying and Jordan was staring at her in complete shock.

"It's okay," she said and grabbed the boys, wrapping her arms around them. "Mummy's fine, I'm not hurt," she reassured while at the same time frantically glancing around to see who'd pushed her.

"You're bleeding," Cory sobbed, pointing to her knees.

"Oh dear," her tights were ripped, revealing scuffed knees, and her wrists were grazed where she'd stretched out her arms to save herself, "I'll put a plaster on to make it better. I'm alright."

She turned to the man that had helped, "Did you see who pushed me?"

"No, love. I just saw you going headfirst into the road and rushed out with that other chap to stop the traffic." He looked around, "He's disappeared though, and whoever it was that barged into you seems to have vanished too. You'd think he'd have hung around to at least see if you were alright and say sorry."

"It was one of those joggers, coming up too fast," the woman said, "they're all the same, they never look where they're going. Think they own the pavements, they do."

Lucy scanned everywhere for any sign of a jogger. Pedestrians had moved on and more were arriving so it seemed hopeless and unlikely she'd find out who it was.

The man continued, "He must have hit you with some force to send you flying like that."

"Here, dear," the woman handed her some tissues, "press those on our knees. You've had a lucky escape, it could have been really nasty."

It was like déjà vu. The mechanic had used similar words when the brakes failed.

"Yes, thank you." She pressed the tissues into her knees to stop the bleeding. The boys were clinging to her as if they'd never let her go.

"Would you like a taxi to take you home? There's a taxi office just there," the woman pointed, "they might even have a first-aid kit."

Lucy nodded, "I think I will. We were on our way for a burger, but that can wait for now. Thank you so much for your kindness."

"Not at all." The woman bent down to the boys' level and took out her purse, "I think it's best Mummy goes home to wash her knees, and you can go for a burger another time." She gave both of them a pound coin each, "When you do go, ask Mummy to get you some sweeties for being such good boys."

Tears welled up as the little mites eagerly took the pound offered and said thank you in unison.

"You're welcome." The lady stood upright and grasped her arm in a comforting way, "I'm glad you're alright, love, that's the main thing. But take it easy today. Accidents can really shake you up."

"I will. And thank you again," she looked at the man, "both of you."

They smiled kindly and walked away. She limped towards the taxi office with an overwhelming urge flooding through her to get home, pack their suitcases and flee from Oban. First the van brakes, and now a push into the road – two accidents in the space of weeks

116

had her fear antenna on full alert. Had someone found her?

The journey home was short in the taxi. She paid the driver and opened the front door to let the boys into the house. They ran ahead to find Hilda and she followed them to the kitchen, only then remembering her phone had vibrated before she was pushed. She took out her phone. The missed call was from an unknown number.

"Mummy's hurt," Cory squealed and Hilda quickly turned to look at her standing in the doorway. She eased her skirt up and showed Hilda her torn tights and bloodied knees.

"Oh my goodness, sit down." Hilda pulled out a chair from the kitchen table, "What on earth has happened?"

"Nothing too dramatic," Lucy reassured as Hilda reached up to one of the higher cupboards for the first-aid kit. "A jogger ran into me and I fell over and grazed my knees."

"We got some money for sweets," Jordan showed Hilda his pound coin and Cory reached in his pocket for his to show his as well. "I'm hungry," he said, "we didn't have McDonald's."

"Aw, didn't you?" Hilda sympathised, "Right, you go upstairs and put your pounds in your piggy banks while I clean Mummy's knees up, and then we'll have something nice to eat."

The boys ran towards the stairs and Hilda smiled tenderly, "You poor love, you're sure you're okay?" She gently wrapped her arms around her.

117

"I'm fine." Lucy hugged her tightly, desperately trying to hold back the tears. Her knees throbbed, her wrists ached, but it was the thought of having to leave Oban that was causing her the most anguish. What if she was wrong and it had just been an accident? Moving the boys from the only home they'd ever known, their happy and secure little nursery around the corner, and Hilda who they all loved so much, would be devastating and traumatic for them all. She swallowed down the lump in her throat. Maybe the two incidents weren't connected? The garage had confirmed the brake was erosion, and the couple who'd helped both said it was a jogger running too fast and he probably ran off because he felt guilty. That was the most likely explanation and the one she desperately wanted to believe more than anything. Because deep-down in her heart she knew that if her actual identity had truly been discovered, she wouldn't be sat in Hilda's homely kitchen right now having her grazed knees attended to.

Chapter 18

London

Dr Furman had called into Oak Ridge to see Jenna, no doubt wanting to justify his large fee. At least Leo had the grace to join them, even though he wouldn't be interested in miscarriage after-care for his wife. He'd be more interested in moving forward which she dreaded — she couldn't face sex with him again.

"How are you feeling, Mrs Montgomery?" the doctor asked from over the top of his designer framed glasses.

She gave him a pained expression. "A bit down to be honest." She wanted to say it was a relief, she didn't want to bring another Montgomery into the world. But she had a part to play to get what she wanted.

"Yes, you're bound to be, that's only to be expected."

"I've read about why early miscarriages happen, and I've come to the conclusion, it could well be there might have been something wrong with the baby. Sort of God's way . . ."

"That is a good way to look at things, my dear, but don't be afraid of grieving. It was a much-wanted baby, so it's perfectly natural to be feeling down." He looked at her husband. "Maybe you could think of having a break away somewhere nice together?"

Bingo!

"Yeah, that's something we can think about," Leo replied, which was code for get lost. She knew that if the doctor didn't.

"My brother said exactly that," Jenna said, "he's currently on a sabbatical from work and staying in Cornwall. He suggested a break there with him," she was on a roll. She could see the doctor was taking it all in. "We used to go there for holidays as children and it has such fond memories for us both. Sadly, my parents are both deceased so it's just my brother and I now," she glanced at her husband, "and Leo, of course. So a trip away is certainly something to think about."

"I think that would be good for you both. Cornwall is lovely."

Leo shuffled. She had the urge to laugh out loud. As if he'd be interested in a break in Cornwall. He'd opt for San Tropez or someplace like that. He wouldn't be seen amongst the minions in Cornwall.

Dr Furman must have sensed Leo's disinterest and moved on to what he knew her husband would be keen to know. To the Montgomery family, an heir was important.

He cleared his throat. "There's no reason why you can't start trying for another baby," he looked sympathetically at her, "as soon as you feel ready, of course."

She faked a sad expression. "I'm still bleeding at the moment."

"Yes, quite. That's completely natural. It could go on for a few days, if not weeks. Give it some time for the bleeding to stop and then your cycle will return to normal. If not, do get in touch."

She was glad the doctor was spelling it out. Sex could mean another pregnancy. She'd have to fake the bleeding for longer, Leo wouldn't touch her then.

Dr Furman smiled, "Right, I'll bid you both a good day. If there's anything you need, you have my number, Mrs Montgomery."

"Yes, thank you."

He looked at them both, "And do try to have some time together. Losing a child, however new the concept was, can be difficult. Some women do need a bit of time to come to terms with it." He stared directly at her husband and she loved him for it. He would know exactly what type of man Leo was. He wouldn't have time for a miscarriage. He'd see that as a failure and would be desperate trying to get her pregnant again.

"I appreciate you visiting, Dr Furman, I'll show you out."

Jenna returned to the lounge expecting Leo to have gone, but he was still there flicking through his phone. She took a seat on the sofa opposite him.

"Nice of him to call, I thought."

"He should be doing house calls the amount he gets paid."

"He was kind, though, and understanding. It's hard getting my head around losing the baby," she ramped up the sorrow, "I feel a bit numb, to be honest." Even though Leo didn't do sympathy, she piled on the regret,

121

"It's hard to believe that a little life that was growing inside me has now gone."

He continued scrolling through his phone. They'd lost a baby and he was flicking through emails.

"We need to start trying again," he said without looking up.

How she loathed him. "Yes, but like I said, I'm bleeding."

He looked up from his phone, "You might as well go and spend some time with that imbecile brother of yours in Cornwall. You're no good here. But only for the weekend. I want you back after that."

The urge to shout halleluiah was overwhelming, but she kept her tone calm. "That'd be nice. I'm sure a rest and a change of scenery might help."

"I'll arrange the helicopter."

"No need, Jack's home this week so I can go back with him."

"What, he's coming all the way back to London and then going back to Cornwall?" he scowled.

"So he says, reckons he's got some papers to sign."

"Long as he's not back slagging me off. The last thing I need right now is any of his negative crap. He should be showing me some respect being your husband. Instead he takes every opportunity to write crap in that tin-pot rag of his."

She ignored him, there was no point in antagonising him. He could snatch the offer away as quickly as he'd given it. She'd got what she wanted, so it was best to appear grateful. It was still a mystery as to why he'd agreed.

"At least going by car, we can make it a bit of a road trip. I'd like to go back to Plymouth to where my mother was born."

"Whatever. He's prepared for you being travel sick, is he?" He looked almost gleeful that she might be ill on the way.

"Yes, there is that I suppose. I'll have to take some pills."

"Fine, then I'll allow you to go."

He was bored. He'd moved on she could tell.

The fact he'd said he was allowing her to go irritated her beyond words. What gave him the right? But it was better not to antagonise him. Not when she'd got exactly as she wanted. The trial had to be troubling him despite his bravado that it would be thrown out of court – normally she'd have had a real battle getting to spend some time away from home, yet he'd given in easily. And not a mention of any of his gorillas chaperoning her.

"Anyway, I've got a bit of headache," she was keen to get away before he changed his mind, "I'm going to lie down. Will you be here for dinner later?"

"Doubt it." He put his phone in his jacket pocket and stood up. Typical. He was happy to leave her to have dinner with his insufferable parents while he'd no doubt be shagging his latest mistress.

"Okay then," she gave a half smile as she stood as well, "see you when you come to bed."

"Yeah, and tell that prick of a brother of yours when you see him, he owes me. I could have easily said no."

He made his way towards the door but there was more. "And don't be saying a thing to him or anybody else about losing the baby."

"What do you mean?" she glared, of course she was going to tell Jack.

"I mean," he was gritting his teeth with irritation at her, "it'll be better for the trial if the jury think you're still having a baby."

"But they'll see I'm not."

In two strides he was in front of her and he grabbed her arm. His breath was on her face and his fingers dug in. His eyes darkened as he scowled, "Don't say anything to anybody. Just carry on as if you're still pregnant. That's all I'm saying. It's not that difficult, even for you to understand. And if you can't do that, you're not going anywhere."

She nodded in compliance and he released his grip. "Don't let me down. And remember, you owe me."

Her whole body began shaking as she watched him leave the room. The elation she'd felt minutes earlier was now replaced with deep anxiety. Now she was going to have to continue the lie of being pregnant when she wanted Jack's support for losing the baby. She still blamed herself for not wanting it.

How long could she go on living like she did?

The option of death reared its ugly head again.

Chapter 19

London

Jenna exited the Rolls Royce outside of her brother's town house and McNeil closed the car door behind her. Jack was coming out of the elegant Georgian front door and down the steps to meet her. McNeil took her luggage from the boot.

"Cheers," Jack said taking it from him.

"Have a good trip, Mrs Montgomery," McNeil nodded and made his way into the Roller and gently pulled away.

Jack wheeled her case towards his car and put it in the boot. "You good to go, or do you need the bathroom?"

"No, I'm fine."

"Okay, I'll just lock up, you get in."

She sat in the passenger seat marvelling at the way she'd got away from Leo and the confines of Oak Ridge. For three nights she could forget about the life she loathed. Quite how she was going to return to it, she didn't want to think about, nor the sex-on-demand to try for another baby.

Jack got into the car. "You okay?"

"I'll let you know when I get there," she joked. "I've taken a couple of my travel sickness tablets though, so I'm likely to nod off on you."

"That's okay. Are you alright taking them while you're pregnant?"

"Yeah, it's fine," she lied. Leo's threat was still ringing in her ears so she daren't tell him the truth.

"Sleep when you want to, it's quite a way, so it's best you do." He glanced at her, "I'm so pleased you're here, Jen."

"Me too, I still can't believe Leo agreed, but he is distracted now preparing for the trial."

"I bet. Let's hope they convict him and he gets life."

"Not a chance. He's got the best lawyers on the case and nothing sticks to him, as you well know."

"Maybe this time we'll get lucky?"

"I wish. Remember though, if they do get him, there's still Avery, they can't lock them both up."

"You could be right," he sighed, "although my contacts reckon they will get Leo this time."

"Well, he's certainly nervy, that's for sure."

"That's good to hear. I like the thought he's crapping himself."

She relaxed into the heated leather seat of Jack's Range Rover enjoying the warmth. "Are you still in touch with Lyndsey?" she asked, still secretly hoping they might reunite.

"Yeah, just friendly though, so don't be buying a hat."

"As if," she rolled her eyes, "I'll be buying a walking stick by the time you tie the knot."

He grinned as he changed gear, "How you feeling anyway?"

"Fine," she said, her eyes becoming heavy. The tablets were doing their job, she was going to have to give in.

"There's a blackout mask in the glove compartment if you want it. Lyndsey got travel sick on long journeys and she swore by blocking the light out."

She'd give it a try. The last thing she remembered was reaching for it before sleep took over.

The car came to a halt, jolting her awake. She lifted the eye mask.

"I need the bathroom, do you?" Jack asked.

"Yes, good idea." She unclipped her seatbelt and followed him out of the car towards the service station. "Where are we anyway?"

"A good way. You've been asleep over two hours. I thought we'd crack on for another hour or so then grab some lunch. How does that sound?"

"Perfect. We're still stopping at Plymouth, aren't we?"

"Erm . . . we'll see."

They returned to the car clutching take-away coffees and continued on the journey. She took a sip of hers, "I'll give this a go, I'm not sure if it'll settle my tummy or make it worse. Maybe we should have flown up?"

"Nah, Leo would have known where we were going and I didn't want that."

"What do you mean? He knows where we're going, I told him."

"Yeah, you told him what I told you."

"You've lost me, you're talking in riddles."

"That's me. Do you trust me?"

"I did, but I'm not sure now," she scowled as he rejoined the motorway. A sign caught her eye and even with her limited knowledge of motorways she knew they weren't on their way to Cornwall. She felt uneasy. "Jack, where are we going? Leo will go ballistic, he thinks I'm going to St Ives."

"Blame me then. Tell him I changed things."

"But why? I was looking forward to going."

"Yeah, but you'll like it where I'm taking you."

"Where? I don't get it. Why lie?"

"I just changed the plan that's all."

"But he'll ask me. He'll ring. I'll have to tell him."

"Tell him you're in Cornwall. He won't know unless he's got a tracking device on you."

"He probably will have."

"If he asks, just tell him. But if he doesn't, no need to offer the information."

"Yeah, but why all the secrecy?"

"No secrecy," he shrugged, "I just don't want him knowing what I'm up to. It's none of his business. If he gets stroppy, tell him it was my idea."

She sighed. "He won't be happy."

"Who cares? Let's just enjoy some time away from him."

"Okay. But where are we going? You might as well tell me now."

"Oban."

The pitch of her voice went higher, "Oban? What, in Scotland?"

"Yep."

"Why on earth are we going there? What's the attraction with Oban for goodness' sake? We're travelling the full length of the UK."

"I like it there."

"What's going on, Jack? Something is and I really need to know."

"There's nothing going on. I'm there to write my book and I want you to have a break. Simple as that, nothing else."

"Funny how I don't believe you."

"Yeah, funny that." He took a gulp of his drink, "Great coffee I must say."

Chapter 21

Oban

Lucy was sitting with her sketchpad in the workshop when she heard the shop door open. Each day since the level crossing accident, her antenna had been high alert. At night, the demons urging her to pack up and move on had her tossing and turning into the early hours, but the thought of uprooting the boys from the only life they'd ever known, held her back. She loved Oban. In the winter, its population was small, but in the summer it was vibrant. She'd chosen it as a suitable place to hide as far away from her previous life as she could get. She still felt that way, constantly reassuring herself that if she had truly been discovered, it would be something far more sinister than opportunistic accidents letting her know.

"Good morning, Jack," she heard Hilda say, the delight evident in her voice.

"Good morning, Hilda."

Her tummy did the usual flip when she heard him. His voice was warm and silky; he could do a voiceover for a hot chocolate advert. She gave herself a shake.

"This is my sister I was telling you about." Even though she couldn't see him, she could hear the affection in his voice. "Jen, this is Hilda, my friendly neighbour who's keeping me supplied with delicious baking. I'll be ten kilos heavier when I leave."

"As if," the female playfully dismissed, "pleased to meet you. You'll win my brother's heart if you feed him, that's for sure. But don't be fooled by his woe-is-me face, he can actually cook pretty well."

"Hey, don't you be spoiling it," Jack playfully chastised.

"You look alike," Hilda said, "you can tell you're related."

"Yes, seemingly we do. So we're always told."

"How long are you staying for?" Hilda asked.

"Just the weekend I'm afraid."

"Ah, not long then. If you get the chance, there's an exhibition on at the Memorial Hall about the history of Oban. We went last year and it was really good. I'm sure you'd both enjoy it."

"Thanks, Hilda," Jack said, "we may call in and see that. Is Lucy about?"

Tightness clenched her tummy. She didn't want to see him let alone meet his sister. He unsettled her and was getting too close for comfort. But her heart gave an extra thump because he'd asked for her.

"Lucy," Hilda called, "have you got a minute?"

A curse escaped her lips as she tossed her sketchpad down. No way did she want to be involved in playing happy families. But Hilda had given her no choice, so she'd have to say hello. As she made her way into the shop, she hoped the warm flush of her cheeks wouldn't

131

be too noticeable, especially if she put on a bright welcoming face.

"Good morning."

Jack looked as masculine as ever in his wax jacket and walking boots. "Morning, Lucy, this is my sister, Jenna." It was the first time she'd noticed how his eyes crinkled at the edges when he spoke. His voice did strange things to her tummy as he smiled affectionately at the striking lady at the side of him. "This is Lucy who lives with Hilda along with her boys."

Lucy shook Jenna's outstretched hand, "Pleased to meet you. Welcome to Oban." She went on to ask the same question Hilda already had so it didn't appear she'd been listening, "How long are you here for?"

"Only the weekend I'm afraid, then I need to get back."

"I hope the weather stays nice. It's a lovely place but like anywhere, much better with sunshine."

Jack was watching her, almost scrutinising, as if he knew her inner most secrets, which unnerved her. In the depths of the night when she lay awake wondering if someone knew who she really was, she'd considered Jack might be something to do with the van brakes and the push at the crossing. But her instincts which she'd had to rely on so heavily over the last five years, told her that Jack was one of the good guys.

"I hope it stays nice too. But if not," Jenna glanced at her brother, "Jack's promised to take me exploring so a bit of rain isn't going to put me off."

Hilda laughed, "You may end up eating your words. I hope you don't see the rain we can get, but if you do, you'll not be doing any exploring, that's for sure."

"Oh, right, fingers crossed then."

Lucy was about to make her excuses when Jenna said, "Jack says you have twin boys, how old are they?" Although she smiled when she spoke, it wasn't a smile that reached her eyes. There seemed to be almost a sadness about her. She looked pale too, as if she wasn't entirely well.

"Four."

"Are they identical?"

"Yes, they are."

"How lovely." Lucy didn't miss the fleeting wave of sorrow pass across her face. She seemed fragile, nothing like her robust brother.

"I'd better get on," Lucy said. "Enjoy exploring, both of you. It was nice to meet you," she nodded at Jenna.

Hilda chipped in. "I've just had a thought," she looked directly at Jack, "I don't want to spoil your plans while you're here, but could you manage afternoon tea, maybe on Sunday, if you're around that is? We'd love to have you, wouldn't we, Lucy?"

Hilda would know categorically she wouldn't *love to have them* – nothing was further from the truth. She had to call a halt to the friends-round-for-tea idea, "I'm sure you'll be having full days out and not want to be tied?"

"No, that sounds great," Jack answered enthusiastically, "we'll definitely make it, won't we, Jen? But only if we get some of your fabulous cakes, Hilda," he turned to his sister, "you need to sample Hilda's cakes, they're to die for."

"Sounds lovely," Jenna smiled politely, "thank you. Now," she turned to her brother, "we better start doing some of this exploring and let these people get on."

Lucy's tummy churned. She could throttle Hilda. She was going to have to take the boys somewhere. Jack unsettled her and it wasn't just fear about her past. For the first time in years it hit her, she was attracted to him. And she couldn't afford to be attracted to anyone – that would be a step too far.

Chapter 20

London

"Typical of Julia, late again," Susan Montgomery sighed. She was standing at the bedroom window that overlooked the huge sweeping drive leading up to the front door of Oak Ridge.

Bridget folded the king sized duvet and eased it off bed, "It's probably the commuter traffic holding her up."

"I'm sure you're right," Susan glanced at her watch, "I do wish she'd get a move on though. If she's not here soon, I might not even bother going."

"It'd be a shame to miss your day out."

Susan sat down on the small window chair, "Sometimes it's easier not to go."

"But it's a lovely day and it might do you good?"

She peered out of the window again. "I know," she sighed, "take no notice of me, I'm having another off day."

"Are you still not feeling well?"

"Nothing I can put my finger on, that's half the trouble. It's more a constant feeling of weakness, grogginess and forgetting things. And this sleeping all the time isn't helping. I'm in two minds about making an appointment with the doctor even though I hate going. Test, tests, tests, that's all they seem to do and then mess around changing tablets which take for ever to get used to."

Bridget painted on a sympathetic expression, "I guess the court case getting closer is having an impact too?"

"It is. I'm worried sick despite Avery and Leo assuring me it'll be thrown out."

"I'm sure if they're confident, then it will."

"I know I should trust what they say," she pulled a face, "but it's difficult. The thought of what could happen is sending my blood pressure through the roof."

"I bet once the trial's over, you'll start to feel better. If not, maybe see the doctor then rather than rushing to see him now. I'm sure he'll say it's anxiety. That can play havoc on your physical health."

"Yes, you're probably right. Perhaps it's best to leave things for now and let those that are genuinely poorly get the help they need."

"That sounds sensible."

"Ah, halleluiah, here's Julia coming down the drive now."

Bridget moved towards the bedroom door and opened it, "I'll come down and see you out."

She offered Susan her arm to walk her down the huge spiral staircase. "Let's hope the weather stays nice for you," Bridget smiled, "and you have a lovely day out."

"Yes, let's. Now, I haven't forgotten anything have I?"

"No, we checked earlier. You've got your glasses, your phone and I've put your gloves by the front door so you don't forget them this time."

"Oh good, my hands seem to be getting so much colder lately. Thank you, dear. You really are such a jewel."

Bridget nodded appreciatively. She never forgot her place as an employee – not noticeably anyway.

They walked towards the huge oak front door and Bridget picked up the leather gloves.

"You're cleaning our room today, aren't you?" Susan asked putting on the gloves that matched her leather patent boots which would cost more than a month of Bridget's salary.

"Yes, I'm going to do that now while you're out," Bridget replied, irritated as she hated the term *our* when Susan referred to Avery . . . hopefully she wouldn't be saying that for much longer.

"It's well ready for it, I must say. I've spent too much time in it this week, it's starting to feel stuffy. Do be careful though won't you, with the other cleaners," she gave her a knowing look.

"Always."

"Good. I'll be back around four. Please don't mention anything to the boys about me not feeling well. They've got enough on right now."

"Of course not," Bridget held the door, "do enjoy your day." Susan nodded and made her way across the pebble chippings forming the drive-way to the house. It was evident by her unsteady gait that her mobility was becoming erratic. She waved as the Mercedes moved away. Stupid woman, as if she needed reminding when to clean the bedroom when she did it religiously every week.

Bridget made her way back up the stairs to the enormous master bedroom. The lounge in her cottage was about the same size as the ensuite. She locked the door behind her as she always did when Avery and Susan were both out of the house. Her first task was to strip the bed, but before she did, she reached for Avery's pillow. His smell was exhilarating and she fantasised that it should be her lying in sickly Susan's place next to him. Her heart raced at the thought Susan might not be sleeping there much longer, and her fantasy was that she'd be the one getting into bed with crisp fresh linen and Avery making love to her.

She removed the sheets, carefully scrutinising them for any obvious stains. The thought of the two of them making love horrified her. It was one of the reasons she always made herself readily available to Avery. Not that she could imagine Susan would be up for anything regular – she looked far too sickly for any sex Olympics.

Once she was satisfied there wasn't any evidence of intimacy, she re-made the bed, perfectly smoothing out the creases and tightening the envelope corners. The finishing touches were with the pretty bedding accessories. She stood back admiring her work. Susan was lucky to have her.

Next, she moved towards the decorative marquetry table with a single drawer which had one purpose – it housed a small handgun. She opened the drawer to check the pocket-pistol was still there wrapped in its pouch. Avery had explained it was loaded and there for Susan's protection, but she never believed that. It was more for giving him peace of mind that he had a weapon should he need it. That's why it was next to the side of bed he slept in.

He'd explained he didn't want any of the cleaners inadvertently coming across the gun especially with it being loaded, so he'd asked her alone to clean the bedroom each week. She diligently took up the task despite being confident the staff wouldn't dare search in any drawers – she'd sack them if they did. Each Wednesday, being in Avery's intimate and personal place became her weekly delight, especially when both he and Susan were out and she could take her time.

A loud knock startled her. Staff knew not to disturb her. She quickly closed the drawer and moved to unlock the door. It was Leah, the young domestic.

"Audrey said to come up to see if you wanted a hand with anything?"

"No," she said curtly, "I don't." The cleaners would be cracking on and not want to be bothered with supervising the young girl who needed direction all the time. "Can you get a bowl of soapy water and go to the main dining room and wash the table legs. Mrs Montgomery spilled her coffee last night so there may be some sticky patches." Her tone remained curt. "And while you're doing that, give all the chair legs a wash."

"Okay. When I'm done, shall I go and find Audrey, or you?" Leah asked.

"You shouldn't be done if you do a thorough job. I'll be down to check when I've finished up here," she said firmly.

Leah's face flushed and she quickly turned and headed for the stairs.

Bridget relocked the door and made her way to Avery's dressing room. Each time she went inside his personal domain, a quickening rushed through her. She ran her fingers along his endless colour-coded jackets all lined up, and imagined she was selecting one for him to wear as a wife might. Next, she located the jumper he'd worn for golf the previous day and removed it from the hanger, rubbing the wool against each side of her face, savouring the intimacy of the man she adored. She reached for one of her favourite aftershaves of his from the few on display and placed a tiny dab of the musky scent on her wrist. Avery's sensuality and masculinity would be there for her to smell all day.

She made her way back into the bedroom towards the ensuite, glancing again at the gun drawer which held a deep fascination for her. As far as she could tell, the chances of anyone getting past the sophisticated security system installed in the house was minimal, but what if they did? And what if somehow the gun got into an intruder's hand and he blasted Susan's brains out. Her skin prickled with excitement – Avery would be all hers then.

Chapter 22

Oban

Jenna had her arm in Jack's as they walked along the beach and stopped at a coffee shop. It had been a busy couple of days exploring the area's beauty, and she'd relished being in the company of her brother, but the following day she had to return to London. Jack had bought her a hot chocolate with cream on top and she felt like a child again as she took a spoonful of the whipped cream. "I think I've died and gone to heaven."

"It's great you've got your appetite back now the sickness has stopped."

"Yeah, it is." The hot chocolate suddenly seemed less appealing. She hated lying to her brother. But she daren't tell the truth that she'd lost the baby as she was scared of what Leo might do.

She smiled at him wanting to detract from baby talk. "This has been the best few days I've had in ages."

"I knew you'd like it. That's why I wanted you to come."

"I've loved it. I wish I could stay here."

"You could. Just say the word and I'll extend the lease on the cottage."

"Don't be daft. Leo would come to get me and take me back."

"How could he, he doesn't know where you are. He thinks you're in Cornwall. Let him try." Jack laughed.

Jenna sat back in her seat. "You devious little monkey. That's not why you changed from St Ives to Oban, is it, so Leo wouldn't know where I was if I stayed?"

He grinned, "No, but it would have been a good plan."

"Yeah, it would, but it'd never work. You know that. He'd find me. There isn't a way you could successfully get away from the Montgomerys. You might escape for a few days, but they'd get you in the end. I wouldn't put it past him to torture you to find out where I was."

"Not right now he wouldn't," he fiddled with the sugar sachet on his saucer, "there's too much hanging over him with the court case. He can't afford to put a foot out of line."

"Yeah, true. But that's another thing. Even though I'm dreading it, I have to be there for it. You know, supportive wife and all that. Apparently it helps to sway the jury."

"What, even though you want him to get locked up?"

She could always rely on Jack's directness.

"I know I do. But nothing would change. I'd just have Avery holding the leash until Leo came out of prison."

"I hate that family and the way you're tied to them. And now with the baby coming, they'll up their ante I guess and keep you locked up even more than you already are."

142

"Don't go over this again, Jack, not now. We're having such a lovely time together, let's not spoil it. You know as well as I what they're capable of. If I left, they'd come and get me and then you'd pay dearly. And I'm not putting you at risk."

His expression was painfully sad as he stared at her. He knew what she said was true. The Montgomerys were ruthless and would stop at nothing to get what they wanted. Even murder she suspected.

"Okay," he said, "enough about them for now. We've got Hilda's afternoon tea to look forward to."

"She's a sweetie, isn't she? But why do I get the feeling it's not the afternoon tea you're interested in?"

He frowned playfully, "And what else might I be interested in?"

"Lucy."

He took a sip of his coffee. Stalling.

She raised her eyebrows, "Am I right?"

"Nope, not interested one bit."

"Yeah, right. You are, I can tell."

"Well even if I was, there's no point in pursuing anything. I'm not here long enough. I'll soon be back in London full-time."

"Ah, obviously you haven't heard of long-distance relationships, you know, where couples visit each other and communicate via social media."

"I can't see Lucy being up for anything like that. She seems to me to be a private person. I think she wants to concentrate on her boys."

"Where's the father of the kids, do you know?"

"No idea. As I say, she's quite private. If I'm ever on my own with her, she asks the questions, almost as if she doesn't want me to ask anything about her."

"Maybe it was a volatile relationship?"

"Yeah, I reckon it possibly is something like that. Who knows? Anyway, there's one thing I do need to tell you before we go to their house."

"What's that?"

"There's this niece of Hilda's called Kitty and she might well be there."

"And . . . ?"

"She's a bit of a maneater."

"Oh right. And you daren't tell her it's Lucy you fancy?"

"I don't *fancy* anyone. And I don't flatter myself I'm Kitty's dream man either."

"So what's the problem?"

"There isn't one . . ." he screwed his face up, "I might have stretched the truth a bit that's all."

Jenna smiled, "This just gets better. What have you told her?"

"Well . . . I haven't said I'm from London for a start."

"Really?" she frowned, "where have you said you're from?"

"Birmingham. And I might have mentioned I'm a freelance journalist as opposed to owning a newspaper."

She was highly amused at him behaving uncharacteristically, "Why? I don't get it."

"I don't want her knowing anything about me really. I've temporarily deleted my social media stuff for now."

"All this for someone you say is a maneater but not really interested in you? What are you worried about, she's going to decide she does like you and turn into a stalker?"

"I dunno," he shrugged, "I just don't want them knowing stuff about me. I'm only here for a couple more weeks, to be honest I've not even told them my surname."

"So why are you telling me all this?"

"To make sure you don't inadvertently spill the beans."

"Right. So am I supposed to be from Birmingham too?"

"Yeah, that's along the lines of what I was thinking."

"It seems a lot of trouble you're going to. What if you do get together with Lucy? She won't be impressed at you telling lies."

"They aren't lies. It's more . . . creative license. And as I'm not going to *get together* with Lucy, there's nothing to worry about. So, do you think you can back me up if some odd things come out of my mouth?"

"I guess so. It all seems strange if you ask me. But then again, it's been odd since we left London supposedly heading for Cornwall and ending up here."

"Yeah, but you've enjoyed it, haven't you?"

"Absolutely," she smiled lovingly at him, "being away from London with you has been perfect." She reached across and squeezed his hand, "Thank you."

"You're welcome. We'll be able to do more of this when the baby's growing up, I hope."

"Yeah, you bet," she swallowed the lump forming in her throat, loving him for his thoughtfulness. Even though she was biased when it came to Jack, he truly was a good man. Ruthless, yes, but he had a charm about him that was easy to love. How he still remained single she had no idea, but she desperately hoped one day soon he'd meet someone, settle down and have plenty of his own kids. Only then could she get away from the chains that currently bound her.

A time when death would no longer be just an option.

Jenna and Jack arrived at Hilda's promptly at three. Hilda opened the door.

"Hi, welcome," she greeted, "do come in. So pleased you could come."

"We wouldn't have missed it for the world," Jack smiled warmly, "would we, Jen?"

"Definitely not. It's so lovely of you to invite us."

Jenna knew why they'd been invited. Jack was infectious and a real hit with women whatever their age. There was a charisma about him that seemed to have most women flocking round him. That's why she suspected that Lucy's indifference was really put on. She was going to watch carefully and see if she could spot whether it was genuine disinterest, or if she was working at it. That was her intention anyway until she entered the dining room and saw another woman sitting at the table instead of Lucy.

"This is my niece, Kitty," Hilda introduced.

The small blonde woman stood up and reached out her hand, "So pleased to meet you."

"You too."

"Please take a seat," Hilda nodded at the beautifully set table, "the kettle's just boiled. "Is tea okay for you, Jenna?"

"Lovely thank you. Can I help?"

Lucy came through the door, and gave a bright welcoming smile directed at her, "Hi Jenna," she barely acknowledged Jack, "I've got the kettle on, so you sit and chat and I'll see to it."

Why no welcome for Jack?

*

Lucy looked at Hilda, "You sit down too Hilda and talk to Jenna and Jack, I can make the tea." The boys came running in from the kitchen and stopped in the doorway when they saw people they didn't recognise sitting at the table.

"Come and say hello," Lucy said to them, "then you can go back to your colouring."

She proudly introduced them. "This is Jordan and Cory," she put her arms around them both, "these are Hilda's friends and are here for a little holiday."

Jack pushing his chair back and walking towards them threw Lucy completely. She'd only expected him and Jenna to smile, as people usually did around children and then she could scoot the boys away.

He squatted down to the children's level. "Did your mummy just say you're colouring? I love colouring."

Jordan's face lit up, "Do you want to come and see?" He reached for Jack's hand and led him towards the kitchen. Cory followed, not quite sure who the man was, but not wanting to be left out.

Blast.

"Excuse me, I won't be a minute," Lucy smiled and turned towards the kitchen. Her strategy of keeping out of Jack's way hadn't worked. He'd taken a seat at the kitchen table and made a show for the boys of selecting a special colour from the crayon box.

"I know," he said in a most engaging voice, "How about I draw a picture for you both and you can colour it in. And if you do it really nicely with lots of different colours, I can take them to put up in my house."

"Yeah," they squealed in unison.

She tried to ignore Jack at the table by fiddling around with nothing, but the image of her boys with a man, clenched at her gut. He looked up and his eyes met hers. It was a split second, but an emotion she didn't recognise flooded through her and she had to turn away. Her face felt hot. He was far too close for comfort.

She distracted herself by warming the large tea pot and brewing the tea. She placed the tea and a hot water pot on a tray to take through before making an attempt to extract the boys from Jack. Biscuits usually did the trick. She put a plate of chocolate animal ones in front of them with their squash.

"You'll have to colour on your own for a little while so we can have our tea."

Jack stood and moved a few paces towards her, which caused her heart-rate to accelerate. "Let me," he reached for the tray and, as he lifted it, the sleeve of his jumper rolled up. Her eyes had a will of their own and focussed on his large clean hands and traced the fine hairs tracking to his wrist. It was hard not to appreciate his attractiveness.

The dining table had been ably prepared by Hilda who loved any sort of gathering. She'd washed and starched a beautiful ornate lace tablecloth, dusted down the Royal Doulton china she kept for special occasions, and dug out the antique cake stands bequeathed to her by her late mother.

Hilda beamed as they all tucked into the sandwiches and cakes she'd prepared. She had every reason to be proud, the feast was as good as any restaurant offering. Lucy purposely sat at the end of the table so she could flit in and out, keeping an eye on the boys. Being in the kitchen was her preference, as far away as possible from Jack who had an almost magnetic pull. But she had to admit, it was enjoyable to have Jack and Jenna there, they were nice people. Covertly observing Jenna, it was evident that she had none of Jack's vibrancy. There was a sadness about her which she covered well, as if she was putting on a front, like playing a part. And the reason Lucy was aware of that was – it was like looking in a mirror at herself.

The chat around the table was pleasant. Kitty was overtly in Jack's face, as was the norm in the company of anything wearing trousers. "I've just thought, Jack," she cooed getting as close to him as was possible at a table, "you'll be here for my party. I'd love you to come. It's on Saturday at the Golden Lion."

"Oh right. That'll be something to look forward to." Lucy could tell he wasn't keen, even if Kitty couldn't. And for some unfathomable reason, she didn't want him to go her stupid party."

"Please say you'll come," Kitty pressed, "Hilda and Lucy are coming, aren't you?"

Kitty's stare implied she'd better say yes.

"Erm . . ." she hesitated.

"Sounds like it could be fun," Jack looked encouragingly at her, in contrast Kitty's face was full of fury. She wouldn't be happy about the way Jack was coaxing her. Neither was she.

"It all depends on if I can get a babysitter."

The boys came barging through from the kitchen, "I need a wee," Jordan announced, much to everyone's amusement.

She rolled her eyes, "Excuse me," she said, pleased for the excuse to leave them to it and take the boys to the bathroom, knowing full-well Jordan wouldn't need the toilet, he just wanted attention and knew that was the best way to get it.

When she returned with the boys, having spent as much time away as was politely possible, it appeared Jenna and Jack were getting ready to leave. Kitty had taken Jack to the bay window in the lounge and was pointing out which was her house. Jenna was beginning to clear the table.

"Leave those, love, you're the guest," Hilda said, "we'll do them when you're gone."

"Thank you, you've been very kind. I have enjoyed it today, being here, and the food was so tasty."

"Ah, it's nothing," Hilda dismissed, "just a few cakes, that's all. I've loved having you both. Is it tomorrow you're leaving for home?"

"It is, yes."

"Your husband will be pleased to have you back, I bet."

"Yes, I'm sure he will."

Lucy watched Jenna carefully. There was something about her that wasn't convincing. It seemed almost like she was giving a performance. As if she was pretending to be happy. And why wasn't her husband in Oban with her?

Jack returned, closely followed by Kitty. "Can we say goodbye to the boys?" he winked at her, "I need to collect my pictures."

It was just a wink she told herself, nothing more. But it still had the ability to unnerve her.

"Of course." He really was quite something. What man would be interested in two boisterous boys?

"Boys," she called and they came rushing back clutching their pictures. They were so eager to please and her heart melted at their little faces.

Jack reached for both of their pictures and studied them carefully. "Do you know what, I think they are beautiful and just right for my office. I'm going to pin them up straight away when I get home."

"Can we come and see them?" Jordan asked eagerly.

"We'll have to see," she cut in. Visiting Jack's house would be far too much. She could barely cope with being in the same room with him at Hilda's.

"Anytime," he said looking directly at her.

"Come on," she turned away and took the boy's hands, "Shall we go and get your shoes and we can go outside and wave goodbye?"

The sooner Jack was gone the better – she really couldn't cope with him a minute longer.

Chapter 23

Oban

"I'm really not keen on this party, Hilda. I'd much rather you went, she is your niece."

Hilda picked up her mug from the table, "I'm too old for parties, I'd rather have another cup of tea and stay with the boys. But it'll do you good to get out. And you look so lovely in a dress for a change."

She'd put on a plain grey dress with black shoes and tights. It was hardly party attire, but she didn't own anything that was."

"And if you take the van," Hilda gave a wry smile, "you can be as late as you like."

"I'm not going to be late," Lucy dismissed, "I'm going to walk along the seafront to the pub, have a quick drink and then I'll be coming home." She slipped her jacket on, "Kitty will be sulking for days, you not turning up."

"Well that's nothing new. She'll get over it."

Lucy took a leisurely walk along the promenade determined she wasn't going to stay long at the party. As she approached the Golden Lion, much to her distaste, Tricky was stood outside having a cigarette.

"Evening," he sneered. Somehow he had the ability to make even the most innocuous greeting sound threatening. She nodded to him and went inside, heading straight for the bar.

Alex, the landlord, came to serve her, "Hi," he smiled warmly in complete contrast to Tricky.

"Hi, Alex. I'll have a lime and soda please."

"Lime and soda," he pulled a playful face, "isn't this supposed to be a party?"

"Yeah, but I'm only calling in for a drink. I don't want to leave the boys for long. They're quite a handful for Hilda."

"Okay, lime and soda it is then. How are you keeping?"

"Fine, busy, and you?"

"Yep, all good." He handed her the drink and she opened her purse.

"Put it away, it's only a soft drink."

"Yes, but I'd rather pay."

"Pay me with a dance later," he grinned.

She rolled her eyes and moved away, confident she'd be long gone by the time the music started.

She headed for Kitty and the crowd around her. Socially mixing was alien to her so it was an effort to make small talk with people she barely knew. A memory flashed before her of a time when socialising was a major part of her life, but it was quickly crushed by Kitty's scowl, "I'm so furious with Hilda, I could barely speak earlier when she rang."

"Aww, don't be hard on her. Parties aren't really her scene, she probably just wants to sit and watch a bit of TV."

"No, she doesn't. You know as well as I do, she'll be sorting the online orders for the jewellery. That's what pees me off. She'll do anything for you but not me."

Arguing with Kitty when she was sober was a challenge, but when she'd had a drink she was best left alone.

"Is your dress new?" she asked wondering how Kitty could possibly look in the mirror at herself and not see how cheap she looked in the halter neck dress which showed off so much cleavage, it was almost indecent.

Kitty twirled around giving a glimpse of her bare back. "Yeah, what do you think, do you like it?"

Lucy widened her eyes playfully, "It's . . . unique."

Kitty's eyes were drawn towards a movement at the pub entrance, "All the better to catch someone with."

Lucy followed her gaze and the one person she secretly hoped for, but wouldn't admit even to herself, walked through it. Jack was dressed in a jacket and slacks, which on him looked like he'd stepped out of an outfitter's window. She hadn't seen him since he came for afternoon tea with Jenna, but Hilda kept him supplied with cakes and never missed an opportunity to coo about him. And, watching him walk through the door – it was a good thing. Seeing him did strange things to her.

155

"Bingo, here's the man I've been waiting for," Kitty handed Lucy her empty pint glass, "get rid of that for me would you, while I go and say hello."

Two more drinks and a respectable time spent chatting, Lucy stepped outside the pub to get some fresh air. She'd grabbed her jacket as she was in two minds whether to go home. It was still early, so she felt bad about leaving, but she'd had enough. For some reason, Tricky seemed to be watching her. Each time she caught sight of him, he almost leered, which made her feel uneasy. She was twitchy enough since the brakes and crossing incidents without him adding to her anxiety. And as if that wasn't bad enough, Alex had sidled up to her and asked her to say the word when she was ready for a dance, which she had no intention of doing. There wasn't even a chance of talking to Jack as Kitty was all over him like a rash, which was embarrassing.

As she came out of the pub and closed the door, she was surprised to see Jack leant against the wall smoking a cigar. "Ah," she widened her eyes playfully, "so this is the place to hang out."

He blew out some smoke and reached to crush the cigar, "Don't tell anyone about my guilty pleasure, will you? I can't resist sometimes when I'm out."

She smiled, the man was seriously growing on her. "Rest assured your secret's safe with me."

"What about you, why are you out here? Hiding from your beaus?"

"Beaus?" she frowned.

"Yeah, the two blokes. One I think is the landlord, who can't keep his eyes off you, and a dodgy looking individual in the corner who I reckon has a more creepy agenda."

He'd have no idea how uncomfortable his statement was. "That'd be Tricky, he is a bit odd."

"Tricky? That says everything. You need to be careful, I don't like the look of him at all."

"No me neither and now you've said that, I think I'd better make a move."

"Do you want some company?"

"If you want to." Why did her heart lift to be walking home with him? If it had been Alex asking, she'd have said no.

"Do you think we need to go in and say our goodbyes?" she asked, "it seems a bit rude not to." She really didn't want to. Kitty would be furious that she was leaving with him.

"Nah, I might just lose you to the landlord."

His jokey remark made the heat rise inside of her. He bent his arm for her to hook hers into and playfully smiled. "Ready when you are."

She surprised herself by linking her arm in his. It felt comfortable walking alongside him like a couple would. They headed down to the harbour. It was a clear evening with the sound of the water lapping. Rather romantic if they were both inclined, but of course, she wasn't. She'd be relieved when he left Oban – that's what she kept telling herself.

As they steadily walked a few metres, he paused and stared across at the perfectly sheltered horseshoe inlet with the panoramic view of the mountains. "No wonder this place has captured artists, authors and poets for centuries. I must say I'm going to miss this little piece of heaven when I return to the city. It's been a great few weeks. Hilda's a diamond, isn't she?"

"She is."

It was one of those nights that showed the harbour at its best; the stars were twinkling in the night sky, the waves were rippling gently, and the smell of sea salt was in the air. The moon was playing tricks, making it a perfect evening for lovers – but not for her. She needed to steer clear of anything romantic.

"I'm looking forward to reading your book when it comes out," she said as they continued walking, "have you actually got much writing done while you've been here?"

"Erm . . . well, I might as well confess, I've only got a rough draft and bullet points. But I read somewhere, I think it was Stephen King that said it, the draft is telling you as the author what the story is about, and only then does the hard work begin."

"Ah well, that's good then if you've got a draft. What genre is it, I've forgotten."

"A thriller. My biggest headache though is the ending. I'm really struggling with it."

"Oh, why's that?"

"'Cause it could go one of two ways."

"I see."

"Yeah. I want the bad guy to get his comeuppance and spend the rest of his life in jail. That way justice will be done. That's how I want it to end."

"Can't it end like that? Surely you can tell the story how you want?"

"I only wish I could."

"I'm sure you'll come up with something. The best ideas come when you aren't looking for them. Perhaps when you get home you'll get some inspiration."

"Yeah, you could be right. Maybe you can advise on how you think is should end, if I give you an outline of the story?"

She pulled a face, "Crime isn't really my scene so I'm not sure how much help I'd be."

They approached a bench. "Let's sit down for a minute," he said.

She sat down with him. His eyes scanned her face with such intensity, for a moment, she considered he might try and kiss her. But his face looked pained when he started to talk.

"It starts with a woman's obituary. I've done a prologue to wet the reader's appetite. It's more of a headline grabbing introduction. It starts off, *'The terminally ill wife of billionaire ends her own life in a Swiss clinic'.*"

Her heart missed a beat. She put a hand to her chest as it started to palpitate.

He continued, "There's shock, horror and an outpouring of sympathy for the devoted widower, but few would mourn her passing," he shrugged, "a trophy wife who'd outlived her purpose, which became abundantly clear when she failed to conceive and produce an heir. She'd become a wife who'd expired."

Breathe, you need to keep breathing.

"There's a funeral, a fitting tribute to the wife of the rich tycoon. Many attend out of duty and respect, and the grieving husband struggles to come to terms with how cruel life can be that his beautiful young wife saw no option but to end hers. But here's the twist . . . the character, I've called him Leo Montgomery, his wife really didn't die . . . she's actually alive and hiding away in a remote seaside town . . ."

"That's enough," Lucy snapped and stood up. Flashing lights danced in front of her eyes, blinding her. Her limbs became suddenly weak. Strong arms eased her back onto the bench and into a sitting position, pushing her head downwards encouraging the flow of blood to her brain. A voice in the distance was reassuring her, "You're alright."

Get up. Run. You have to get away from him.

The uneven ground was centimetres away from her face. She could smell the concrete mixed with sand. And as uncomfortable as it felt with her head pushed downwards, she wanted to stay just as she was. She didn't want to sit up and have to face him. Despite all the precautions she'd taken, all the years spent in hiding, she'd been found.

And he knew everything. She had to get back to the boys.

He eased her gently back up into a sitting position. "I'm sorry. I shouldn't have sprung it on you like that."

She got up to her feet . . . far too quickly. Her legs were like jelly and it took every bit of effort. But she had to get away.

"I've nothing more to say to you," she said, "don't contact me again."

She started to run.

"Wait. You haven't heard the rest."

"Leave me alone," she shouted and broke into a faster run which would either get her home, or not. She didn't care. She just ran – the same way she'd been running for five years. Panic propelled her on. For years she'd lived in fear this day would come.

The day her life in Oban would be over.

Chapter 24

Oban

Lucy ran as fast as her legs would carry her and didn't look back. Within minutes the house was in sight and she speeded up so she could get inside and shut him out. As far as she could see, she had only one choice now and that was moving on. Five years she'd escaped them and now she'd been found. And ever since Jack had been in Oban, he'd played her. It was her own fault – she'd let her guard down. She felt physically sick. How far behind were Leo and Avery? Was Jack working for them?

She quietly opened the front door and let herself in the house, locking it behind her and then swiftly moved to the back door making sure it was bolted. Fortunately, Hilda had gone to bed. She grabbed a bag from the closet under the stairs and speedily moved around the house filling it with personal items. First thing in the morning she'd have to get a train out of Oban. She worked her way around the lounge grabbing the children's iPads, her phone charger and their pyjamas which were airing on a radiator. A tap on the front door made her panic levels soar. Frozen with fear, she stood still, hardly daring to breathe. She listened. The tapping continued. Her breathing was shallow, as if that somehow might stop her from being discovered. On and on the tapping went relentlessly, until as she feared, it woke Hilda. As she listened to her footsteps coming down the stairs, Lucy rushed into the hall. "Don't open it," she barked.

"Why not?" Hilda frowned fastening her dressing gown, "whoever it is will wake the boys." The anguish on her face must have been evident as Hilda scowled, "What on earth's the matter? You look like you've seen a ghost."

"I have to leave."

"Leave? Leave where? What are you talking about?" She turned her head towards the knocking, "Who's out there?" Hilda moved towards the door.

"Don't open it, please don't," Lucy begged frantically.

"You're scaring me," Hilda scowled, "what's going on? Do you want me to call the police?"

"No." The tears she'd been holding back flowed freely down her cheeks. "You'll get hurt if you let him in. We all will."

"What do you mean? Why am I going to get hurt? I'm going to see who it is." Hilda bent down, opened the letter box and peered through. She gave a relieved sigh, "It's only Jack."

"Hilda," Jack called back, "please let me in. I need to speak to Lucy. I've frightened her and I didn't mean to. I need to explain something. Tell her I'm not here to harm her."

Hilda remained squatted down to the level of the letter box but turned towards her. "For goodness sake, what's going on? Why is he saying he didn't mean to harm you?" By the change in her expression, it seemed to dawn on Hilda what might have happened. "Tell me what he's done!" she urged.

Lucy shook her head frantically, realising which way Hilda's mind was going. Hilda bent her head down again and lifted the letter box. "You'd better go, Jack. I've never seen Lucy like this. Whatever has gone on between you, leave it for now. There's nothing to be gained by this tonight."

"Tell her Jenna's married to Leo. Tell her that please, Hilda. Then she'll know I mean her no harm. Tell her I don't work for the Montgomerys." There was a pause, "Please, while I'm here and then I'll go."

Hilda turned, "Did you hear him? Who are the Montgomerys?"

Lucy stared at the door. Jenna was married to Leo? Was he lying? It could be a ploy and he'd been sent by them to get to her.

She could barely whisper, "I don't believe him. Come away from the door. He might have a gun."

"A gun!" Hilda's voice went up. "Why would Jack have a gun?"

Hilda peered through the letter box again, "We're calling the police Jack, right now."

"Don't do that . . . please," he pleaded, "Tell Lucy not to. Let me talk to her, Hilda, let me in. I don't have a gun. I'll show you, I don't have any hidden weapons."

Hilda stared through the letter box for a second before pulling her head back. "He's taking his clothes off."

164

"What?"

Hilda peered again. "What the hell are you doing, Jack?"

"Look Hilda, I don't have a gun. I'm not hiding a weapon, I promise. Tell Lucy that. Please. I mean her no harm, I just need to explain. Get the iPad and look me up. I'm Jack Carr and I run a newspaper in London called the Daily Gazette. I'm not going to expose her. Check, and then for Christ's sake let me in."

Hilda moved away from the door, "I'm going to check him out. The man's half naked out there, he'll catch his death."

Lucy was frozen to the spot staring ahead with only a door separating her from Jack. Jenna married to Leo? God help her if she was. But how had they found out she was alive?

Hilda came back into the hall. "It's all here as he says. There's a photo of him. I'm going to let him in."

Lucy wanted to stop her but she had an overwhelming urge to see what Jack knew. She had to know how he'd tracked her down.

Hilda held the door open and he walked in wearing just boxer shorts, shirt and his shoes and socks. He was clutching his other clothes. His deep remorseful eyes stared directly into hers. "I am so sorry, truly I am for the way I told you."

Hilda took a deep breath. "Put your clothes on, Jack and I'll get us a brandy to calm us all. And I'm not going anywhere tonight so anything you have to say to Lucy, you say it to me. And if I suspect you're here to hurt

165

Lucy, then I'm calling the police. I have the phone ready," she lifted her mobile up.

"I'm not here to cause any harm, I promise. Hear me out both of you and then I'll go," he pleaded.

It was almost laughable. The three of them stood in the hallway, Hilda in her dressing gown, her still wearing her outdoor jacket and Jack half naked. But rather than put his clothes on, he carried on speaking, his eyes focussed on her. "Jenna is married to Leo. She's terrified of him. I want to get her away from Oak Ridge but she's frightened for my wellbeing and what they might do to me if she leaves him."

"Will somebody tell me who this Leo is," Hilda interjected, "and what have you got to do with him, Lucy?"

She swallowed the bile in her throat, and in barely a whisper said the words out loud she'd banished from her mind for five years.

"I'm Grace Montgomery, Leo Montgomery's first wife."

Chapter 25

Oban

Hilda came in the lounge with a tray of brandy glasses and tea. Dear sweet Hilda, who had given her the home she loved, which she was now going to have to leave.

Lucy removed her coat and, while Jack put his clothes on, she switched on the monitor with a camera in the boys' room. As she stared at them both fast asleep, Cory sucking his thumb and Jordan laid like a starfish, she had an overwhelming urge to go and scoop them up and run away with them as far as she could from Oban. But it was eleven o'clock at night, they couldn't go anywhere.

"Now, can we please start from the beginning because none of us are leaving here until we sort this out," Hilda said firmly, sitting on the sofa next to her.

Lucy took a mouthful of brandy, grateful for the warmth flowing through her chest. She took another gulp and looked at Hilda who was sipping hers. She cleared her throat. "The Montgomerys are a family of thugs. They run nightclubs in London, amongst other things. They stop at nothing to rule – even murder."

Jack interjected, "And Jenna is married to Leo, who Lucy was married to. He's going on trial shortly for murdering a chauffeur."

"So, I take it you aren't here to write a book, then, Jack? How many more lies have you told because it sounds like you don't live in Birmingham either?"

"You're right," he looked awkward and Lucy knew despite her anxiousness, he wasn't a man used to telling lies. "It's true, I have lied to you both ever since I've been here. I wanted to get closer to Lucy."

"Why?" Lucy glared at him, "Why do you need to get close to me?"

"I want you to give evidence at the trial to convict Leo of murder."

"What?" As if there was any way she was doing that. Why would he even think she would?

"Who sent you?"

"Nobody sent me. I found out about your existence and realised you might be able to help Jenna. I just had to find you."

"Who told you about me?"

"That's the biggest mystery of all, and one I keep asking myself. I don't know. I got an anonymous email saying you were alive. And following that a text. They can't be traced, I've tried. I just did my own searching until I found you."

"What about the accidents I've had?"

"What accidents?" he frowned.

"The brakes failing on the van and someone pushing me into the road at the crossing."

"They were just accidents," Hilda said, "they weren't anybody trying to harm you, I'm sure of it."

Jack's face looked pained. "I swear to you, I know nothing about any accidents. You have to believe that. The only reason I lied about my job and where I came from was so I didn't scare you. I've never physically hurt anyone in my life."

"So who knows you're here, love?" Hilda asked her, "You must have some idea who tipped Jack off."

"I don't." She blew out a breath, "It has to be the Montgomerys."

Jack shook his head. "I don't think so," his vibrant brown eyes looked directly into hers, "And you don't either. We both know if they'd found you, we wouldn't be sitting here drinking brandy."

"Well, who then?" Hilda asked.

"I don't know," Jack said, "I truly don't. I brought my sister here for you to meet, so that when I eventually told you who I was and that she was married to Leo, you'd understand why I have to get her away from that family."

"You can't, Jack," Lucy said emphatically, "nobody can get away."

"You did."

"Yes, love, how did you?" Hilda reached for her hand, "You don't have to go over it if you don't want to, but it might help for us to understand all of this mess."

Her gut clenched at the thought of having to live through it all again. But Hilda was right, she deserved to know what she was able to tell her. But not everything . . . there was one thing she couldn't discuss. Not with anyone. It was her secret that she'd take to her grave.

"Okay," she sighed and lifted up her brandy glass, "we'd better top up our drinks – it's going to be a long night."

With Hilda next to her and Jack sitting opposite, her whole body ached, most probably due to the drop in adrenaline. It was going to be painful to delve into the part of her life she'd buried deep. But she had to. She took a breath in, preparing to turn back the clock five years.

"I hated Leo and hated his father even more. For some unfathomable reason, Avery has a massive hold over Leo. From when we first married, I never understood why we had to live in a suite of rooms at Oak Ridge. I wanted my own home with Leo to bring up our children, not live with his parents and have dinner with them every evening. Leo was quite a charming man, that's why I fell in love with him, but Avery kept him tied down. Leo never saw that, of course, he hero worshipped his father."

She took a sip of her brandy. Hilda and Jack were watching her intensely. Hilda gave her hand a squeeze, "Go on, love."

"I had a cat that meant the world to me. One day, it just disappeared. I was terribly upset. She was all I had to love – there was certainly nothing endearing in that house. On a typical gloomy day at Oak Ridge," she looked at them both and raised an eyebrow, "there weren't any good days, Avery took me to one side and told me he'd got rid of my disgusting cat and he wouldn't hesitate to get rid of me if I didn't conceive a child. I was

170

terrified. He said if I tittle-tattled to Leo, there would be consequences. So I stayed quiet." She shrugged, "Even if I'd told Leo, he wouldn't believe me. He'd always believe his father. He was like God to him.

"But then, a tremendous amount of luck came my way and a glimmer of sunshine came into my life. I went for my usual facial and massage and was taken into one of the private rooms. That was when I was introduced to undercover police officers; they wanted to prosecute Leo. They expected me to answer questions about exactly what I knew about some of his illegal dealings, of which there were plenty, but I wasn't going to tell them anything unless they helped me. I'd fantasised for years about a plan in which I supposedly took my own life to get away from the Montgomerys." A sly smile escaped from her lips, "My thoughts were they wouldn't come looking for me if they believed I was dead. I explained my plan to the police and suggested that, if they helped me to facilitate it, I would help them by giving evidence against Leo. They wanted, Avery, too but I didn't have anything on him other than the gut instinct that he was ten times worse than his son."

Lucy took another sip of her brandy. "I left that beauty salon and sweated for a week. Would they help me? It was a cunning plan and would take weeks and a degree of ingenuity. And even though I didn't honestly think they'd help me, the only thing I had was hope and a resolution if they did somehow agree, I would help them. I received a text from a," she made air quotes,

"Nadine, who told me there had been a cancellation at the salon and they could fit me in that day.

"The police agreed to facilitate my plan, and in return, I'd go to court and provide the evidence to put Leo behind bars."

Hilda cut in. "Faking your death seems a bit extreme, couldn't they have smuggled you out somehow?"

"That's what they would have preferred, but I wanted it to appear as if I was dead. If I'd agreed to just go to a safe house, I wouldn't have been able to sleep at night, knowing Leo was out there looking for me. And he would have come looking, I had no doubt about that. I just couldn't take the risk." She brushed away a stray tear that ran down her cheek. "I just needed some space to be able breathe."

She blew her nose before continuing. "So, that day, the undercover officers changed my life. The subterfuge began. It started slowly, a stumble as the chauffeur held the car door open for me; spilling my food, gently shaking, headaches, taking to my bed. Eventually, I explained to Leo I was worried and needed to see a doctor. I even went through the motions of seeing one in Harley Street who of course gave me a clean bill of health and told me my problems were due to anxiety. But I didn't tell Leo that. I told him I'd been referred for further tests. When we went for the results, it was a fake doctor that the police provided who revealed the terrible news. I was in the early stages of motor-neurone disease and the prognosis wasn't good.

"Leo was actually devastated. I do believe he cared for me in his own way. Oh, I know he had mistresses, men like him and Avery always do, but he was genuinely upset. I started to talk about dying, which was going to be the eventual outcome. Leo wouldn't discuss it, he buried his head. I told him about a specialist in Switzerland I wanted to get a second opinion from and Leo facilitated a jet for me to go. I returned in a more upbeat mood with the so-called advice the doctor had given me. I'd explained the diagnosis was not always as bleak as people imagined and it didn't mean immediate death. I could have up to ten years left to live. Leo was delighted, and in fairness to him, he became more attentive. I managed to steer clear of Avery. He scared me. He'd be pleased I would be leaving the family. It wouldn't bother him it was going to be in a coffin.

"For a while, outwardly my health was stable. I faked another journey to the Swiss clinic. Leo was happy to fly me there. Over those weeks, I meticulously planned my death. It had to be realistic. I had every angle covered. I told the police that Leo would want to see a body. That was the hardest part of the whole process. Not that he would suspect my death was fake, but he may want to see me. I wasn't certain either way really. He was terribly squeamish with hospitals and that sort of thing, which was a joke considering the life he led, that's why he was fine for me to attend medical appointments on my own as they troubled him.

"So," she gave a sigh, the tension was enormous reliving it all and explaining the harrowing experience,

173

"on the day I supposedly died, I flew to Switzerland. Leo thought it was for another appointment so facilitated the private jet again. I remember vividly looking at Oak Ridge as the chauffeur pulled away to take me to the airfield. I even turned at the gates to take one last look as we were driving out. It was a goodbye to the most terrible three years of my life – and goodbye to Grace Montgomery.

"That day, I supposedly ended my life in a Swiss clinic and my new life in witness protection would begin. But first of all, we had to convince Leo I had died, as he, of course, flew over supposedly to accompany my body back to London. And that was the hardest part of the whole operation.

"I had to literally be put to sleep, via anaesthetic, and laid in a coffin. It was of course all supervised with a qualified anaesthetist carrying out the procedure accompanied by the police. I was literally in their hands. And even though death was preferable to going back to Oak Ridge, I was still petrified. Seemingly the drug they gave me, Midazolam, reduces the respiration rate so it wouldn't look as if I was breathing. It was risky as they only had minutes to leave me without oxygen. But fortunately for me, luck was on our side. I was told Leo took one look at me through a screen and cleared straight off. As soon as he'd left the room, they were able to oxygenate me before waking me up.

"Once I recovered from the anaesthetic, I was in the hands of the police. I was taken to Glasgow and put in a safe house. I was still scared, but for the first time in three years, I was happy, or maybe relieved is a better word. I was content to walk, eat, and sleep. Just everyday things that normal people take for granted and I'd forfeited when I married into the Montgomery family. I was in their fold and expected to do whatever I was told.

"Leo was accused by the police of murdering the chauffeur, Isaac Davey . . . but that's a story for another day."

"So how did you end up in Oban, love, you said you were taken to Glasgow?"

"After the police facilitated my escape, it was payback time. I was to testify against Leo as we'd agreed. The police had played their part and got me away from Oak Ridge and the family, now I had to carry out mine. And I would have. I had every intention of doing so. Even though I would be turning up from the grave to help convict the bastard, but by that time it would be too late for him to get to me. But I found out I was pregnant and everything changed. I couldn't go back. As much as I knew about the family, I had to protect the young lives growing inside me. The police were acutely disappointed, we all were. There were promises to keep me safe, they'd move me, but I knew he'd find me. Leo Montgomery's greatest desire is to have children.

"The trial date was fixed and I'd have been seven months pregnant by then, so there was no chance of hiding it. I made a decision. I couldn't give evidence, and as a consequence of that, the charges were dropped against Leo. It was crushing for the police and for me too. I was then left to make my own way. There was no need for police protection because as far as the Montgomery family were concerned, I was a dead woman. They wouldn't come looking for me. I was on my own. I had legitimate documents to say I was Lucy Smyth and a place to live for a period of time. I won't bore you with the things I had to do to live, but I survived though sheer determination and the knowledge I wouldn't have to ever see the Montgomerys again. I gave birth to the boys and then," she smiled at dear Hilda, "God was kind and I got lucky and met you. And you saved me."

Hilda wiped her eyes, "I am so sorry. I cannot believe you've come through all of that, unscathed. You poor, poor girl."

"It's okay, Hilda," she squeezed her hand. "I'm telling you now," she stared at Jack, "so you'll understand why I can't go back. I'm sorry about your sister, truly I am. But I'm not going to London again, ever. So your stay here has been wasted. I have to leave first thing in the morning now."

"You can't leave," Hilda said firmly, "not now we know all of this. You have to stay here where we can look after you."

"Nobody can look after me. Don't you see? Now someone knows I'm here, the boys and I aren't safe. It's only a question of time."

"There is another way," Jack said, "if you'll hear me out."

She willed him to say her secret was safe, that he wasn't going to expose her. Surely her instincts hadn't been so wrong about him?

He cleared his throat. "I am really sorry for lying to you about why I'm here. I'm not a person that lives my life like that. But what you must know is, everything that happened to you, my sister is going through now. I have to get her away. And you're my only hope. If you'll give evidence, we can get Leo put behind bars where he belongs."

"But that wouldn't be the end of it. They have contacts. Someone will come after me, and the children. Why would I risk that?"

"They could come after you now. Clearly someone knows you're alive. They contacted me, so it's just a question of time until the Montgomerys find out and come looking. You have to come back and help put those lowlifes behind bars for good. Maybe it was your intention to spend the rest of your life here hiding, but you can't any longer. You'll never be safe. You'll spend the rest of your life looking over your shoulder."

She did that anyway but now wasn't the time to talk about it.

"You were fortunate and managed to escape from them, unfortunately my sister isn't as lucky. Help her, Lucy, I'm begging you. Come to London with me and I'll protect you. And when it's all over, you can come back."

"Why would I do that and risk my own life?"

"Don't you see, you're at greater risk by not doing so? Listen, if you tell me all you know about the

Montgomerys and their dodgy dealings, we can write it all down. Every single thing. We won't use it, but we'll let them know we have it. And threaten them that if anything in the future was to happen to us, then it will be given to the police."

He turned to Hilda, "You can see what I'm saying makes sense, can't you?"

"I have to agree, love. It sounds better than the option of running and hiding until they do find you."

"What you are asking of me is massive," she scowled, "I've built a life away from them, I can't go back."

The stillness in the room was thick – no wonder. The details she'd shared sounded like a TV drama. Hilda broke the silence. "What I want to know is, what evidence can you possibly bring regarding this chauffeur you say has been killed? What do you know about it? How would you know this Leo chap definitely killed his chauffeur?"

Lucy didn't flinch. It was a nightmare she'd relived over and over again, like a revolving door turning round and around . . .

"Because he forced me to watch while he did it."

Chapter 26

London

Jenna was messaging her brother when Leo opened the lounge door. "You need to come and meet Curtis Grantham; he's in the sitting room."

Jenna didn't want anything to do with meeting his barrister or the court case, not when her greatest desire was that he was found guilty. She wished she could go to sleep, and when she woke up again, it would all be over.

"Why do I have to meet him?"

"Just come, would you, and stop arguing. He wants to explain things to us all as a family."

She followed him through the hall to the sitting room. Bridget was hovering by the door and opened it for them. No doubt she'd have her ear to it once they'd gone inside.

Avery and Susan were already sitting on the leather Chesterfield when they entered. Both Avery and the man sitting in the chair opposite stood up. The man holding out his hand was thin and small and looked to be about sixty. He was clearly eccentric, going by his attire, which included a waist coat with a pocket watch, and a grey moustache that was curled at the ends.

"This is my wife, Jenna," Leo said and she shook his hand.

"Pleased to meet you, Mrs Montgomery, I'm Curtis Grantham."

Avery indicated to the seat he'd vacated. "Would you like to sit here, Jenna, next to Susan?" She took her seat. Anything was preferable than sitting near him.

Bridget cleared her throat. "Can I bring some refreshments?" she asked Susan.

"That would be nice. Would you like tea or coffee, Mr Grantham?"

"Coffee, thank you. Black, no sugar."

Jenna wanted to laugh. Bridget wouldn't be able to listen in if she had to go and fetch coffee.

As Curtis Grantham took his seat again, Jenna glanced at a deathly pale Susan at the side of her. Something wasn't right about her, which could well be the looming trial. Whatever she thought about Susan, she loved Leo and must be desperate thinking about the possibility he could go to jail.

The barrister continued, "I'll come straight to the point as to why I wished to speak to you both together," he addressed her and Susan. "As I've already said to Leo and Avery, I'm confident we can get the case dismissed and the jury discharged if not that first day, then certainly the next. We're going for a complete dismissal due to the lack of any hard evidence."

Susan, in true Drama Queen form, raised a hand to her chest, "But why are they bringing the case to court then. . .?" She seemed to struggle to find her words, ". . . What's the point in even having a trial?"

"The point is, a man has disappeared and is most likely dead. The police have an obligation to search for him, and despite not having a body, they have reached the conclusion he's been murdered. They've built a case which they've take to the Crown Prosecution who have endorsed Leo's arrest and subsequent charges. The fact he's been allowed out on bail, works in our favour. And the evidence they are presenting is purely circumstantial. They don't have any witnesses, and while they may be able to present a compelling case which they feel will secure a conviction, I am equally confident it won't." He paused as if to give them time to digest his explanation so far.

"However, we do need to remember, a man is missing presumed dead and, while we don't have any idea what happened to the chauffeur, Isaac Davey, we must ensure a significant amount of dignity and respect is afforded to the victim and his family. And this is where you both come in," he directed his gaze at her and Susan, "despite the trauma this has brought to you, your family and the Montgomery name, part of our defence has to be to portray Leo as a family man, which will be evident by you all in court supporting him each day. And the fact that you," he smiled kindly at her, "are having a baby, most certainly will help." Jenna desperately wanted to interject and say she wasn't pregnant anymore, but she was terrified to do so. She could almost feel the heat of Leo's glare telling her not to utter a word . . . or else.

Bridget tapped on the door and waited for the command to come in by Avery. With her Miss Important

181

hat on, she fluttered around making sure everyone had their requirements, and while she did, Jenna looked closely at Avery and Susan. A desperate urge surged through her to get up and run. They were monsters, the whole family, and in that she included the old witch of a housekeeper who nodded as she left the room but didn't close the door fully behind her. It amused Jenna as she watched Leo get up and close it firmly.

Curtis Grantham took a drink of his coffee and rested it down. "Where were we? Yes, the trial. That's where you all come in," his odd little moustache twitched as he smiled. "You'll all have a part to play which is crucial. Cases are often won not just on the skills of barristers, but the behaviour of the suspect and their families."

"So what must we do?" Susan asked, "I'm sure we'd do absolutely anything we can if it helps."

"You need to display a united front. As you attend court, you'll be seen together supporting Leo as a family. The press will be there, so remember, no acknowledgement to them at all. Keep your heads down as you make your way to and from the courts. Security will get you safely into the court and back to your car. And, Mrs Montgomery," he looked directly at her, "don't be afraid to wear something that highlights you're pregnant. Anything loose fitting that will accentuate you're having a baby."

How the hell was she going to be able to do that when she wasn't even pregnant? Why hadn't Leo told him?

And what about Susan? She knew categorically that she'd lost the baby. Why wasn't she interjecting? A quick glance to the left made her realise she'd be no help at all. She could barely keep her eyes open.

Curtis Grantham went over a load of other mundane stuff but she wasn't listening. She needed to get out of the room, away from the oppression. As soon as the barrister indicated he'd finished, Jenna politely excused herself and Susan followed. No surprises that Bridget just happened to be in the hallway next to the sitting room. "All finished?" she asked as if it was anything to do with her.

"Yes, for now," Susan replied. "I'm going to have to lie down. This is all far too stressful, my poor head's throbbing. I just don't know how I'm going to get through it all."

"Would you like some of your pain killers? I could bring you up some warm milk."

"Would you, Bridget? That would be helpful."

Susan turned to her, "Are you alright, dear? Can Bridget get you anything?"

"No, I'm fine thank you. I'll go and have a rest myself."

She made her way to her and Leo's suite of rooms. What on earth was wrong with them all? Why didn't someone tell the man she wasn't pregnant?"

She sat in their lounge overlooking the rear gardens. Leo came in and closed the door behind him. Fury made her stand up and challenge him, which she didn't do often, "Why haven't you told the barrister I'm not pregnant? All this talk of me swaying the jury is completely irrelevant. I can't look like I'm having a baby when I'm not."

"Then you'll have to make an effort, to make it look like you are."

"And how on earth do I do that?"

"I've got you a fake thing you can wear. Nobody will see the difference. You'll just look pregnant."

"A fake thing?"

"Yes, a fake pregnancy belly."

She couldn't believe what she was hearing. "Are you mad? I won't do that so don't even ask."

"If it helps me get acquitted, it's the least you can do."

"I am not doing it. Have you any idea how it feels to lose a baby. It's actually painful. Not that you'd understand that. And you expect me to stick a fake belly on to imply I'm still pregnant. You should have told the barrister I lost the baby."

"Listen," his face screwed up with fury, "I allowed you go and spend time with your brother, now you can do something for me." The penny dropped, she thought at the time it was odd he'd said she could go. And he never questioned her about the trip when she came back. For that reason she never let on she wasn't in Cornwall. Now she knew why he wasn't bothered. He obviously been thinking up ridiculous plots that he thought she'd comply with.

184

"Do your mother and father know about this absurd idea?"

"Yeah, they do, and unlike you, they agree if it helps me then it's a damn good idea."

"Then shame on them, and on you for expecting it. I'm not doing it."

"You'll do exactly what I tell you to do."

He moved towards her, pushing his face into hers. "It's for one or two days at the most, then afterwards you can announce you've lost the baby. Is that too much to do? To sit in court and look pregnant? I'm the one on bloody trial and could end up going to jail."

"And whose fault is that?" she glared.

"Shut your fucking mouth," he grabbed her face with one hand and squeezed her cheeks. "All you had to do was carry a baby for nine months and you couldn't even do that, you useless bitch."

"Yeah, well maybe the baby didn't want to be born into this dysfunctional fuck up of a family."

The blow knocked her off her feet. She put out her hands to save herself as she skidded along the floor. Stunned, she put her hand to her face. It was already heating up and throbbing through her fingers. Pain she could cope with, she'd learned to. But looking at his face she knew worse than the physical blow of his hand was to come. Only a man who thrived on violence could be aroused by it. She tried to get up but he forced her back on the floor and pinned her there.

"Please don't," she pleaded.

She shut her eyes tightly. As if by doing so it wouldn't happen.

His disgusting breath was on her face. "You fucking asked for this."

She prayed hard, as she'd done many times before, that he'd put his hands around her neck and strangle her. Anything to release her from what was about to come.

Chapter 27

London

Susan Montgomery's medication supplies had been delivered to Oak Ridge and Bridget had taken the bag to her own cottage and emptied them out by the kitchen sink. She had boiled the kettle and carefully steamed the labels off the bottles that contained tablets. The ones that came in blister packs she couldn't do anything with but that didn't matter – it was the analgesia ones she wanted, especially the paracetamol which she knew could do the most damage. The previous month she'd managed to order an extra supply, claiming that one of the orders had gone astray. She needed the perfect bottles to replace with the ones she'd tampered with when the time came.

Once she was satisfied she'd managed to jumble them up enough to fool the increasingly confused and sickly Susan, she packed them back into the bag and took them over to the main house intending to leave them in Susan's room. But as she came through the back corridor and passed the area the cleaners used to store their equipment and cleaning products, Avery appeared and was heading towards her.

"Have you got a minute?" he asked, his dilated pupils telling her exactly what he was after. Excitement flooded through her, as eager as him to comply as he ushered her into the linen cupboard. She barely had chance to remove any clothes, such was his wildness. There seemed a certain irony that as she bent over and moaned for him as he thrusted into her, she was steadying herself with the linen stand and still clutching his wife's medication she'd tampered with.

Avery was all she wanted. She loved him desperately. And as he panted and roared his release, she vowed he'd soon be all hers and they'd be together. And, due to her tenacity, the time when she'd be with her love on that tropical Island . . . was getting closer by the day.

A short time later, Bridget carefully deposited the medication in Susan's drawer and made her way downstairs. Leo was striding towards her.

"There you are. Jenna isn't feeling brilliant. I'm out this evening and she says she'd rather not have dinner with my parents. Could you get the chef to do something light and take it to her about six."

"Yes, of course."

Bridget had heard some sort of shenanigans coming from their lounge earlier. It sounded like an animal being strangled.

"Thank you," he nodded and moved to walk away but stopped. "Erm . . . there's one other thing. Have you noticed my mother doesn't seem herself lately?"

"In what way?"

"Unsteady, sleepy, anxious."

"Ah, I see what you mean. Yes, I have. And to be honest, I think she's getting worked up about the court case. I'm helping as much as I can."

"I'm sure you are. Dad's worried about her too, and the trial of course, so I think there's a high degree of anxiety all round."

"Yes. But rest assured I'm doing my best to take care of your mother and offering that extra support. She is becoming a little confused with her tablets, I have noticed that. To be honest, I was getting a little worried she was having too many, so I'm keeping a watchful eye on her as best I can."

"Thank you. We do appreciate it."

"You're welcome. I have taken the liberty of suggesting she pays a visit to her doctor and has a thorough assessment. I thought sooner rather than later but she isn't keen right now. Says she wants to wait until after the trial. You'll understand it's not my place to challenge her decisions."

"No, I do understand. And she knows best. It's good you're keeping an eye on her, though. Thank you, Bridget."

"You're most welcome," she nodded and watched as he walked away.

She sighed. He was such a dumb boy. Nothing like his dynamic father.

Chapter 28

Oban

It was five a.m. and Lucy's head was throbbing relentlessly, she'd hardly slept. Two questions kept going round and round in her mind – who could possibly know she was alive and where could she disappear to where she wouldn't be found. The past she'd kept hidden successfully for five years was finally out in the open and it scared her senseless. Now, not only did Hilda and Jack know she wasn't Lucy Smyth, someone else did too. She'd have to leave Oban, there wasn't a choice. She'd got some money saved so could make a fresh start somewhere else. And she could continue making her jewellery, she'd just need to use a courier company to transport it.

She got out of bed, put her dressing gown on and went into the boys' room. They were still snuggled down fast asleep. Her heart was bursting with love for them and their innocence. She couldn't allow Leo and Avery to find them. She had to protect her children.

Downstairs in the kitchen, she filled the kettle and put it on. As she reached into the cupboard for some aspirin, Hilda's voice surprised her, "How are you?"

She turned her head quickly, "Gosh, you made me jump."

Hilda leant against the doorframe, "I couldn't sleep," which was evident by her appearance. Her hair was dishevelled, as if she'd been fighting with her pillow half the night, and she looked pale. It was unusual to see Hilda not showered and ready for the day. She was old school and got up early to make sure she was well-turned out before the children even stirred.

"No, me neither," Lucy tightened her dressing gown belt. The house wasn't cold – she just felt cold.

"I'm worried sick you're going to up-sticks and leave." Hilda's face looked pained, "I understand how you must be feeling, and I'm selfish I know, but the future looks bleak without you and the boys in it. It's nothing to do with the business either. I just can't face the thought of you leaving and never see you again."

Lucy had to be strong and not give in to the tears that were threatening. "I'll make us some tea."

It was still dark outside as they sat at the cosy kitchen table. There had always been warmth to the seaside house she loved and called home. If only she could turn back the clock to her quiet life before Jack gate-crashed it. She took a deep breath in. "I can't stay, I have to go. I don't have a choice."

Hilda rubbed her forehead, "There's always a choice. You could go to London and give evidence at the trial. That's an option. Then you wouldn't have to spend the rest of your life running and hiding."

"You have no idea what this family is capable of. They'll have me killed."

"But surely you'd be in a better position by giving evidence. Then they'll not dare hurt you. Honestly, love, think about it. Yes, you can flee now and build a life somewhere else, but what sort of life? You'll be looking over your shoulder constantly, especially once they find out you're alive. This way, you might actually see justice done. And you'll finally be free. You can build a life on honesty and who you actually are."

"Maybe I don't want a life like that. I was happy with what I've got right now. Jack's spoilt all of it."

"He hasn't. Don't you see, it was always going to come out, it was only a question of time. And Jack's not going to hurt you, he cares about you. Anyone can see that."

"You say that but he's not whiter than white. He used me, and you, for his own ends. He wants to help his sister and I get that. But he's nothing to me, nor is Jenna. I don't have to help them. Why come after me?"

"Because he loves her. You can't blame him for wanting to help her. It sounds like a terrible situation in that house with those monsters. There's no wonder he wants her out of there. You should know that more than anyone."

"Yes, but that doesn't make it a reason for me to go back. There's so much you don't know about, and quite honestly, you don't want to know. The family are poison. They have committed the most heinous of crimes."

"Then expose them," Hilda said forcibly, "it's the right thing to do. And by doing so, you and the boys will be much safer than you are now. And once it's all over, you'll be free to live a normal life with your ex-husband in jail."

"Yes, but his father, Avery won't be. And to be perfectly honest, he's even scarier than Leo. Leo loved me in his own warped way, whereas Avery hated me. Once Avery finds out I'm alive and outsmarted them, he'll be out for revenge." She sipped her tea. The heat of it helped with the numbness.

"Do it, love. Do it for Jack and his sister condemned to a life you escaped from. You have two beautiful children and a future, if you let yourself have one. Don't throw it all away by packing up in the middle of the night and heading off. I love you and the boys – I don't want you to go anywhere." Hilda's eyes welled up, which was unusual for her. "If you stay, I'll help anyway I can. I'll even come to London with you."

She'd never seen her so emotional. Hilda was one of those stoic older school women who rarely cried. "Please, I'm begging you now, think carefully before you do anything. And talk to Jack. He's leaving today. Why don't you go see him after you've taken the children to nursery? Promise me you'll at least do that."

Lucy hadn't any intention of taking the children to nursery. "You won't mention anything to Kitty about all of this, will you? Not until I've sorted out what I'm going to do."

"Of course I won't. She won't be round to see me anyway, she'll have sent me to Coventry for not going to her birthday party."

The monitor alerted Lucy to the boys waking. It sounded like Jordon was shaking Cory and telling him to wake up.

Lucy sighed, "Peace is shattered. I'd better go up."

Hilda picked up their cups. "Jordan was saying that Mrs Graham is leaving today to have her baby and they're having cakes. Cory thinks the baby is coming tomorrow, bless him."

Lucy smiled, loving their innocence. "I'm not letting them go to nursery."

"No?" Hilda widened her eyes, no doubt thinking they should go. But there was no way she could drop them off and leave them. Not now. She surprised herself she was still there when her urge during the night had been to get the boys dressed and leave as soon as she could.

"I tell you what," Hilda said moving to the sink, "why don't we shower and get the boys ready. I'll ring Jack and ask him to come round. I can look after the children while you have a talk with him. Then you can decide the best way forward."

"I don't want you taking them anywhere I can't see them."

"I won't. We'll wrap up and play on the swing and climbing frame. And in the shed, they love to play post offices."

"What about the shop?"

"It won't hurt to stay closed for one day. I'll ask Iris next door to put a note on the door, saying we're closed due to sickness."

Chapter 29

Oban

Lucy's anxiety level was high sitting in the kitchen waiting for Jack. She dreaded seeing him, but there was part of her that dreaded not seeing him, which was bizarre.

He tapped on the front door and came in the house. His eyes scrutinised her face as he came into the kitchen. "Hi."

Her tummy still did the usual leap at the sight of him, which she didn't want to happen. He wasn't quite the enemy, but he was near enough. "Hi." She didn't want to appreciate how the blue shirt he was wearing somehow made his eyes warmer, or the tight jeans that enhanced his long masculine legs. He was too rugged to be a male model but he wore his clothes as if he was one.

"Hilda asked me to come round."

"Yes, I know. Can I get you a drink? I've just made fresh coffee."

"Great, black please."

They sat down together at the kitchen table which had always been the hub of the house. Her and Hilda spent countless hours with the boys doing craft work, colouring and playing games. The silence between them was as awkward as the table separating them.

"You're leaving today?" she asked.

"Supposed to be. I had to see you before I went. I couldn't leave things as they were."

"Why, so you could try and persuade me to come with you?"

"No. I think you need some time to make that decision. I know how big this is for you. And if I'm truly honest, if you don't come, I wouldn't blame you. In your shoes, I might not either. But now someone knows of your existence, it's a whole new ball game. You really aren't safe here."

"I know that, that's why I need to leave."

"Yeah, but my way, with you giving evidence, you'd be safer than you've ever been."

"But what about the boys? The Montgomerys are going to want access to them once they know of their existence." She swallowed, stifling an urge to cry. All night she'd been like it, imagining her precious sweet little boys being entangled with that family. It was horrific. They'd tarnish them. They were evil.

"I understand that fully." And she could tell he did. Jack didn't say anything to pacify. But sympathy aside, he was pragmatic. "But if we get the conviction, Leo will spend time in jail. By the time he gets out, the children will be older. I can't see the courts thrusting two little boys on Avery any time soon. Grandparents don't really have any legal rights, and when Leo gets out, he'd have hell of a game as a convicted murderer getting any visitation rights. The most he could possibly get would

196

be supervised access, and you'll fight that every step of the way."

She took a deep breath in. "Look, you're a good man, Jack, I know that now. And I understand how much you hate the family and want your sister out of there, but you have no idea what you're dealing with. Trust me on that. They're monsters, all of them."

"I don't doubt that for a minute." He reached across and took her hand. The strength of a man was comforting and not something she'd ever had. "But I promise you, I'll take care of you. I won't let anything happen to you or the boys."

"You can't promise that."

"I can. And I'm not saying it's going to be easy. But working together we can bring Leo down. I'm not entirely sure about Avery, but whatever happens, I have a way to keep you safe. Remember what I suggested. You tell me the whole story, everything you know about the family, and I write it down. Not for publication, it'll be your insurance policy. And we let the Montgomerys know we have it. That way, it wouldn't be in their interest for any harm to come to you. Therefore, actually giving evidence would protect you. They wouldn't dare harm you."

"We can't be sure of that, though."

"No, we can't. But it has to be better than what is happening currently. Someone knows you're alive, Lucy. That person sent me that message and I found it. What if that person gets to the Montgomery's? They'll come looking for you then. We both know that."

Her tummy clenched hard. He wasn't saying anything she hadn't already thought of. "That's what I don't get. Who? I've been supposedly dead for five years. There's a headstone with my name on it, for God's sake. How has somebody found out I'm alive?"

"I really don't know," he shook his head, "I haven't got the answers but you must understand it makes you a target. I found you so others can. But I can offer you protection if you'll tell me your story and give evidence in court."

She fought to stop her eyes filling with tears but the situation was horrible and she didn't know what to do. "You have no idea what you're asking me to do."

"I have every idea. And even though I've not known you long, I do know you're a brave woman, and an intelligent one to have pulled off what you did. You shouldn't be living your life in hiding. You're a brilliant designer with two children to bring up. You have to embrace life, not hide from it."

"I'm scared, Jack. I've spent so much time looking over my shoulder, terrified this day would come. And now it has, I don't know what to do."

"I know that. Let me help. We can banish that fear, together. Let me look after you. Every step of the way I'll be with you. I'll protect you, I promise. I want you safe to live your life so you don't have to look over your shoulder all the time. You deserve that, Lucy."

"So, what are you suggesting, I come to London and turn up at the trial? Then what?"

"I don't have all the answers yet. But what I do know is, the barrister leading for the prosecution, Justin Coffey, I went to uni with him. If you agree to meet with him, he'll tell us both what you can do from a legal perspective. He may well say we can't have you turning up in court to give evidence. I don't know."

"Have you spoken to him about me?"

"Of course not," he frowned, "I've not said a word to anyone. Jenna doesn't even have any idea who you are. And believe you me, I've wanted to tell her so many times. If only for the satisfaction she'd get that she isn't legally married to Leo, you are. But I haven't as I didn't want you put in danger."

"It's just a piece of paper. If she's been living as his wife, she'll be his wife. Me turning up won't alter that. Leo won't let go of what he sees as his. And what about when it comes out I'm living here, in Oban, then Leo will know she's been here and met me when she came to visit you. I dread to think what he might do to her."

"He won't find out Jenna has met you. He thinks she went to Cornwall. And by the time he sees you in court, it'll be all over for him. He'll know you can get him banged up for the rest of his life."

"You're that sure."

"As sure as I can be."

"If I came to London to give evidence, I'd want the children with me."

"They'd be better staying here."

"I can't leave them."

"You can. Hilda will take care of them."

"It's not safe. If someone knows who I am they may go after the children."

"They won't. It's you that's going to testify. No harm will come to them. Just give your evidence in court, and I'll be with you every step of the way."

"If only it was that simple."

"I promise I'll not let you down."

"It's not you I'm worried about."

"Then I'll not let them get to you. I'll protect you from them. You just have to trust me."

"Where would I stay in London?" It would have to be a hotel with security. That had to be a consideration.

"With me at my home. I wouldn't let you out of my sight."

"You'd do that?"

"Absolutely."

"Do you know when the trial is?"

"Yes. April 15th.

She sighed, that was only ten days away. Could she do what Jack wanted? He was absolutely right, she couldn't keep hiding. Not now someone knew she was alive. And although she barely knew Jack, she trusted him. She had an innate feeling he'd take care of her. She'd sensed it from the first time she'd seen him that he was one of the good guys.

"Okay." Her voice was barely a whisper, "No more running."

"Good girl," he said, "you'll not regret it, I promise."

"I already am," she said feebly.

"Okay, I need to go get off and then speak to Hilda."

"Are you leaving Oban now?" Her tummy tensed at the thought of him not being around.

"No. I said I'd look after you – I need to ask Hilda if I can move in."

"Move in? You can't be serious."

"Oh, I am. Very serious. I'm not letting you or the boys out of my sight." He grasped her hand, "We're going to do this. You're going back and you're going to bring that family down for what they did to you and Jenna. And once that's over, well who knows . . ." his rich brown eyes warmed with affection.

"Who knows what?" Did he mean the two of them? The flutter she always tried to suppress reared up.

"Anyway," he ignored the question, "we've got a trial to prepare for."

She watched from the patio door as he made his way into the garden. The boys ran excitedly up to him and he gave them both a swing round. They squealed excitedly.

Jack was talking to Hilda. What a man he was, preparing to help her. She'd never had anything like that in her life, it had always been just her. It was only with his help she was prepared to go back. Jack was pragmatic and would sort everything out. But there was one thing he couldn't. He didn't know any more than she did who had found her in Oban. And the burning question was – if it wasn't the Montgomerys, then who?"

Chapter 30

London

Bridget returned from town to Oak Ridge and entered her small office near the utility area at the back of the house. She switched on the laptop which she had sole access to for co-ordinating domestic issues such as ordering supplies for the kitchen, washing and ironing of the family linen, which she outsourced and online food shopping for the chef.

The office was her domain and used only for family business, therefore she couldn't use it for the information she wanted hence the trip to town first thing to use an internet café. Her research into medication and its side effects was best done where it couldn't be traced and in town she'd got exactly what she'd wanted.

She heard voices approaching. If she didn't know who was coming, she felt him. That was the affinity she had with Avery. She could sense him from a distance. Her office door was slightly ajar, the way she liked it. She wanted the cleaning staff that worked in the mornings to realise she was watching at all times.

Avery appeared at the door accompanied by a man of similar height to him but much heftier.

"I thought I'd find you here, Bridget. Let me introduce you to Steve Cooper. Steve, this is our housekeeper, Bridget, the Montgomery special asset. What the family would do without her, I don't know."

She blushed and shook Steve's hand, "Pleased to meet you," and gave Avery her secret smile, "you're too kind."

Avery shook his head, "Not kind at all, it's the truth. Anyway, Steve's going to be around for a while from next week. He's going to be our live-in security, what with the court case coming up."

"I see. Welcome," she greeted.

Steve nodded.

"Steve's going to be spending time around the house, so can we find him a bedroom, and if there's somewhere he can eat privately, that would be good."

"I have just the place for you. Would you like to see it now?"

"It'll be fine, wherever it is," Steve said looking very much like the type of man wherever he laid his hat, was his home.

"It's only for a few days," Avery said, "it's to make sure that Susan and Jenna are protected from any press attempting to stick cameras in their faces going to and from the house. Mainly on the days we have to attend court."

"That sounds sensible," Bridget said, puzzled about it all. She'd never known them to have personal security around the house. At work in the nightclubs she was pretty sure they had something. It would be foolish not to the business they kept."

"I'll just take Steve out the back so he can get a feel for the place before he gets off."

"Will it be Monday you're starting?" her eyes flicked from Steve's to Avery's.

"Yeah, I'll be here on Monday morning."

"I'll make sure everything is ready for you."

"Great," he nodded, "thank you."

Avery held the door letting Steve walk in front of him. Before following him out, he turned his head, "I'll be back shortly, Bridget, if you stay put," he winked, "I need to just go over a couple of accounts with you, I think there may be an error with one of them."

"Fine, I'll wait here then," she nodded and watched them go. Her day just got so much better. Sickly Susan was out playing bridge, and Avery was coming back for her. She'd find out then exactly what Steve was there for – she wasn't buying this house security crap, not one bit. She opened the top drawer in her desk and took out her powder compact. Staring at herself in the small mirror she refreshed her face to dampen down the heat that had caused her skin to flush. A quick spray of her Vera Wang perfume and she was ready for him.

Chapter 31

Oban

Jack, true to his word, hadn't left Lucy's side. Hilda had fussed around like a mother hen, sorted him out with the sofa bed in the dining room, and spent time cooking and preparing meals which Jack heartily tucked into each evening.

Lucy was amazed how practical he was. He encouraged her to allow the children to go back to nursery, telling her what she already knew that it was important for the children's stability and development. He'd accompanied her to speak to the staff and the story they'd come up with was the children's estranged father returning to the area and the possibility he may turn up at the nursery. Lucy was reassured by their promise to be extra vigilant and would call in the first instance should they be worried. Internet access to the nursery gave her added reassurance as she was able to check on them throughout the day.

The days were long and she was on constant alert but Jack being there helped enormously. She'd never had anyone to lean on before. They'd decided that she wouldn't go to the shop, and only left the house each day to take and pick up the boys from nursery. Hilda still went to the shop and, during the time she was away from the house, her and Jack went over her life with Leo. If he was shocked, he never showed it. He just listened with the recorder on and comforted her when she got upset. Jack's tactile caresses she found soothing – but the elephant in the room wasn't ever discussed. The time wasn't appropriate but she knew he felt the attraction between them as much as she did.

It was Thursday afternoon when Kitty called at the house. It was half day closing so it was usual for her to call in after her lunchtime shift at the pub finished. Lucy had dreaded her turning up. Seeing her meant more lies with Jack now residing in Hilda's house.

"Hello, hello, hello," Kitty smiled as she came into the garden where her and Jack were sitting at the garden table. Jack quickly reached for his iPhone that was recording and switched it off. To anyone's eyes, it would appear they were a couple having a coffee together, but Kitty wouldn't accept that. She'd be busting to know why Jack was even there with her.

"Hi, Kitty, how are you doing?" Lucy smiled a bright welcome as did Jack, "Do you want a coffee?"

"I'm okay, what are you two up to? Where's Hilda?"

"Inside. She was having a nap last time I poked my head in."

"Ah right." Kitty was staring at the two of them suspiciously. She'd have to offer her some explanation.

Jack beat her to it. "Hilda's putting me up, I've had a leak at the cottage. The agency's onto it but it's going to take a few of days to sort out."

"You're stopping here?" Kitty scowled, "Where are you sleeping?"

"In the dining room. Hilda's let me crash on the sofa bed."

"Bloody hell, that's uncomfortable for a bloke. You can you come and stay at mine if you like. I've got a spare room with a double bed you can use. I don't know why Hilda didn't suggest it."

Lucy stared, wondering how Jack was going to get out of that.

"That's really kind of you," he smiled at Kitty gratefully, "thanks for the offer. I'd best not though, people might get the wrong idea, you know, a male and a female in the same house together."

"Who cares? I'm not bothered what anyone thinks. It's far too cramped staying here. Tell him, Luce, he'll be much better at mine."

"Erm . . ."

"No," Jack said firmly, "I'll leave things as they are. I'm going back to . . . Birmingham anyway at the end of the week."

"But what about your writing? I'm not being funny, but it's a bit busy in this house with the boys. Wouldn't you rather be at mine where you'll have peace and quiet?"

"To be honest, I've put the book on hold with the problems at the cottage. And as I say, it's only for a few more nights then I'm going anyway. But I really appreciate the offer."

"Suit yourself," she shrugged, "the offer's there if you want it. I'll just nip and see Hilda." She walked towards the house swaying her bottom, which was well on display with the tight-fitting jeans that clung to every sinew.

Once Lucy was satisfied Kitty was out of earshot, she grinned at Jack, "Phew. You got out of that really well."

He rolled his eyes playfully, "I did, didn't I?" She had to stifle the urge to reach out and touch him. It wouldn't be appropriate for any physical contact between them. Jack being with her wasn't about the two of them and she guessed that was why he never talked about himself. His whole focus had been on her and the boys, but each day spent with him was a day in which her feelings grew. Not only was she attracted to him, she respected him and his resolve. He wouldn't fail at anything and as each day passed recording their sessions, even though it was hard for her reliving some of the experiences she'd long since buried, it was almost cathartic. The affinity she developed with Jack made her feel they could achieve anything together.

"I'll just nip inside and see them both," Lucy said, "she'll be leaning on Hilda to get her to make you change your mind."

"Go then, quickly," he urged standing up and reaching for his coffee. He headed down the bottom of the garden, "Let me know when the coast's clear."

She grinned, which she seemed to do far more since he'd been around. Before Jack had arrived in Oban, she'd been quite serious, but she had to be. Danger was always lurking, and it still was. But with Jack around she felt less anxious.

As Lucy was about to walk in the back door, she stopped. Kitty was questioning Hilda.

"Well something's going on. Are they together?"

"I don't know what you mean by together."

"Yes you do, Hilda. Sleeping together, is that why he's here?"

"No, they aren't *sleeping together,* but even if they were it's none of our business."

"It seems odd to me that he won't come and stay at mine. And when did this leak he's on about actually happen?"

Good old Hilda picking up on the story. "The other day, Tuesday I think. What does it matter? He's leaving soon anyway, it's only for a few days."

"Yeah, but it's odd that he'd choose here rather than mine when I've got much more room."

"Well, in fairness, he hardly knows you, so he may not want to put on you. That's all it'll be."

"He hardly knows you but he's staying here. I bet you something is going on between them. I've never seen Lucy as much as talk to a bloke while she's lived here, yet I come today and she's having coffee in the garden with the most eligible bloke around here for miles."

"You read into it what you like. I'm just offering the man a bed. What he and Lucy do is entirely up to them, I'm not interested."

"Liar. You'll be encouraging it. You'll want Lucy to be with him."

"Kitty, I haven't got time for this right now so can we please shut up about them if you're staying."

"Oh, don't worry, I'm not. I'll leave you all to play happy families together. It's just typical though. I really like Jack and Lucy told me she wasn't interested, but now she seems to have the hots for him. It's Lucy Smyth's world alright, don't you think?"

Lucy came away from the door and walked down the garden to Jack. She didn't want Kitty to know she'd heard her. The reference to Lucy Smyth's world hurt. There was no point in going in the kitchen though and refuting the allegations about liking Jack. Because it was close to the truth, she did like Jack – much more than she cared to admit.

Chapter 32

Oban

It was the day Lucy came face-to-face with Justin Coffey, the barrister prosecuting Leo, which made the whole thing she'd agreed to, real. Jack had left earlier in the day and headed to Glasgow airport to collect him and the detective assigned to the case and driven the eighty miles or so to bring them to Oban. Lucy couldn't go to London until the trial. Surprise was going to be the driving force to the whole case. The question Jack wanted to know as much as she did was, would she be allowed to give evidence at the trial?

Accompanying the barrister was Mike Frampton from the police witness protection programme, a mature man with a cautious manner, but nevertheless confident. He appeared to be mid-fifties and Lucy would bet he'd be a thorough cop. Although he wasn't involved five years earlier with the witness protection programme, he'd explained he knew the background as to why she previously wouldn't give evidence even though the police had gone to enormous lengths to facilitate her escape from Oak Ridge.

Justin Coffey, the barrister, was not much older than her. Jack knew him personally as they'd gone to university together and was confident if anyone could bring Leo down, it was him. She could tell from the introductions that he was something special. He had an attentiveness about him – a sharpness that was hard to quantify, but she just knew he'd be a force to be reckoned with in a courtroom. Jack said he was exceptionally bright and one of those that sailed through university with a first.

They were all sitting around the dining table in Hilda's cosy home, topped up with refreshments courtesy of Hilda. Jack and Justin talked about their friendship and uni days. Lucy knew Jack had been corresponding with him regularly by phone so there was no real need for such a catch-up. But it did put her at ease, which she felt had been their intention.

"Shall we get down to business, then?" Justin asked her.

"Yes, ready when you are," she was relieved to have Jack sitting close to her.

"I need to be frank with you both. To have you appear in court without informing the defence you are a witness is not doable. The law states that both the prosecuting and defence barristers have to be made aware of each witness that will be appearing well in advance, so they can prepare for cross-examination. It's prohibitive to introduce random witnesses whatever relevant information they might be able to provide."

"Yeah," Jack agreed, "but surely there must be exceptions. You can't possibly divulge Lucy being alive when the shock impact is what we are going for. If we inform the defence, then Leo Montgomery will know she's alive. And maybe they'll argue who could believe a word she says. She'll be branded a liar by the very nature of the deception that has taken place to get her away from Oak Ridge. We need the surprise element to scare the shit out of Leo," he glanced at her, "Sorry."

"It's fine," she shrugged.

"Yes, we could introduce a new witness at the proceedings, but as soon as she walks into court the case will be adjourned. Leo would be shocked to see the wife he thought was dead is actually alive and well. The adjournment could compromise the case. It might even prove to be gold dust for the defence. They could use Leo's distress to say he is unwell and unfit to stand trial. It could go on for endless months, if not years with a clever legal team."

Justin Coffey was right. It was exactly what Leo would do.

"Isn't there any way they'll hear her evidence?" Jack asked.

"No, I'm afraid not. Not without us giving legal notice."

"So I've dragged you over here for nothing?"

"Not quite. Hear me out. Leo is going to be pretty shaken to find out Lucy is alive and will use that to his advantage. He's a hard case, we know that, but nevertheless, even he's going to be shocked that the wife he thought he'd buried is still alive. I'm certain his defence will press for Lucy not to be able to give evidence." He paused to take a drink of his water before continuing. "That said, we can still bring Lucy into court for the element of surprise even though that's all we'd get on that particular day. The judge will adjourn and see the defence and I in his chambers and then I'd have to disclose what Lucy is going to testify. Which brings me onto," he looked directly at her, "I've read your original statement you gave to the police that confirms categorically Leo killed Isaac Davey. And your intention would be to testify to that under oath?"

"Yes, of course." She wasn't sure what he was getting at. Wasn't that why he was there?

"Then we have one thing in our favour, an airtight case on paper. Sadly though, that won't be enough."

"So you can't get a conviction even with me?" she asked, not knowing if it was elation she felt at not having to testify, or deflation that she couldn't. Jack would be so disappointed. He thought he was going to be able to help Jenna. Now it sounded like he wouldn't.

Justin shifted in his seat. "I don't think you'll even get to testify, which is the whole reason why I'm here. I wanted to discuss a scenario which I think is a gamble that may work. Conversely, it might not. We all have to be prepared for that to be the case."

"Go on," Jack urged.

"If we went ahead with me calling you into court as a witness, we'd get the shock, horror, the judge summoning me to his chambers. And then there'd be a delay of a few days while the judge decides on arguments the defence and prosecution put forward as to whether you can testify. I'm nearly one hundred percent sure you won't be able to as I've already said. But . . . and it is a big but, the reason I have come today is to find out if you know more about Leo breaking the law than killing his chauffeur, as heinous as a crime that is, of course." He didn't wait for her to answer. "If you do have more on the family, and Leo knows that, it may be that we might be able to get him to change his plea to guilty to the lesser charge of manslaughter. That's the gamble he'll have to take. His thought process will be that you are going to disclose his illegal activities, in which case, is it better to admit to a manslaughter charge and you not giving any evidence?"

"What's the difference in sentencing?" she asked.

"Much less for manslaughter, but he would serve a period of incarceration."

"I see."

Mike Frampton chipped in. "Jail is still a good outcome and one we'd be satisfied with. It'd be a start. There's so much more, we know that. But the elusiveness of any evidence regarding the Montgomerys makes it difficult for anything to stick. They cover their tracks well. And of course they don't carry out these misdemeanours themselves – they use others."

Justin continued, "So, yes, it will always be somewhat of a gamble and the only thing that is absolutely essential for us to even consider any of this working is," he stared directly at her, "that you know more than him killing the chauffeur."

Six questioning eyes were on her. Waiting. It could be the difference between going to court or fleeing. But it wouldn't be fair to turn back now. She'd come this far with Jack's support, and she was warming towards getting Jenna released from a life so similar to her own past.

She cleared her throat. "I know enough to put Leo Montgomery behind bars until the day he dies."

Chapter 33

London

Jenna was sitting in the lounge. She was perfectly dressed, with perfectly matched accessories. Even her hair was perfectly styled, as was expected for Leo Montgomery's perfect wife. Leo had told her they were going out for lunch in the city with his parents and she was waiting for him to return from golf. Her phone pinged – it was a text message from Jack.

Sorry I missed you. I'm fine, just busy. You okay? X

She'd been expecting him back in London days ago but he was still in Oban. The last twice she'd called him, he hadn't answered, which she didn't understand. Surely, if he was writing this so-called book, his phone would be close by? They were days away from the trial and she so desperately wanted to see him before it. She barely got through each day in her Oak Ridge prison, and seeing Jack always made it bearable. But for some reason, he didn't appear to be in any rush to return to London and it upset her not seeing him, especially after their time together in Oban. Leo hadn't bothered asking about her trip, which was an enormous relief. It wasn't that he couldn't know she'd been in Oban, her fear was how furious he'd be that she lied through omission.

She redialled to try again to speak to Jack but had to cut it when she heard Leo's voice. He was talking with someone and they were approaching their suite. As he came through the lounge door with a man she hadn't seen before, she stood up. He was stocky, late thirties and not someone who looked Leo's type at all. Any male associates of his were invariably dressed as immaculately as he always was. This particular man was dressed only in casual attire.

She smiled a greeting.

"This is my wife, Jenna," Leo said as if he was a normal husband, "this is Steve Cooper, Jen. He's going to be our security for the next couple of days until we get this trial over and done with."

She shook Steve's hand.

"Pleased to meet you, Mrs Montgomery."

"No need for any formality," Leo said, "it's Jenna." He spoke to her, "Steve's going to be living in for the days he's here. Bridget's set him up with a room."

"I see," she nodded, puzzled as they'd never had in-house security before.

"You'll hardly notice I'm here, I can assure you," Steve said. "I asked if I could meet you to say hello, so you weren't startled when you see me around the house. But I've met everyone now, so there won't be any surprises."

"Well I'm glad you did," she smiled, "it's reassuring to know you'll be around."

"I hope so," he nodded, "nice to meet you." He followed Leo towards the door.

"You've never hired live-in security before," she said when Leo returned.

"I know I haven't. It's with the court case coming up. Dad thought it wise to have someone accompanying us to and from court."

"I get that, but why is he staying in the house? That's the bit I don't understand."

"You don't need to understand. Steve's around now and that's the way it is." His eyes were drawn to her abdomen. "Why aren't you wearing that belly thing?"

"I don't want to, Leo, please don't make me."

"I am making you," he said. "This lunch with my parents is so we can show everyone you are damn pregnant." He made his way towards the door, "I'm going to get changed. Make sure you're wearing it when I come back."

She sniffed back the tears as she made her way to the bedroom. If she cried she'd only have to reapply her make-up and Leo would be even angrier having to wait.

The pristine new belly was on the bed where he'd left it, glaring at her like a beacon all newly wrapped. The label read, *'Carefully crafted ultra-realistic fake baby bump used to perfectly recreate the natural shape and stages of pregnancy, used extensively for stage and screen performance, advertising and medical training'.*

As if. There was nowhere that said anything about it being used as a tool to hood-wink people.

She took the flesh-coloured bump out of the packaging and removed her suit. Even though the bump

219

was sized small, suitable for three to four months of pregnancy, the zip on the skirt she'd been wearing wouldn't fasten with it on. She felt sick. How she was going to eat lunch she had no idea. She reluctantly placed the bump across her abdomen and fastened the shoulder straps to ensure it stayed securely in place.

Inside her dressing room, she selected a dress which was loose fitting and would accommodate the bump. It was difficult to avoid seeing herself with the wall-to-wall mirrors, and the first thing that sprung into her mind was she looked like some sort of pantomime joke act. It was utterly abhorrent having to wear it and the hate she felt for Leo was magnified more than ever. When she watched murder dramas on TV, she fantasised about thrusting a knife into him, just to be free of his relentless abuse. His parents were equally as evil, making her go through with the charade. What sort of people were they? She was mortified at the thought of enduring lunch wearing the stupid bump and, if that wasn't bad enough, the sex-on-demand afterwards when Leo had been drinking was what she dreaded equally as much.

Chapter 34

London

Lucy arrived in London the day before the trial. Jack had wanted the boys and Hilda to remain in Oban but she couldn't have left them. They still didn't know who the person was that knew she was alive. Even though the brakes failing and the push at the crossing could have been legitimate accidents, there was no getting away from the fact someone had sent Jack the email and text telling him she was alive and where she was living.

They'd all flown together across country, Hilda and the boys, her and Jack. The boys had been so excited; they'd never experienced the joy of flying. Jack had won their little hearts by taking them into the airport shop and buying them aircraft models and a teddy each dressed in a pilot uniform.

Once they'd arrived at Heathrow and headed for the car park, they were met by Anita who Jack introduced as one of the secretaries at work. She'd been tasked with purchasing bumper seats for the boys so they could travel safely in the car. They loaded up and Jack drove them to his home which he'd described as a town house in Belgravia. Even though she knew the district was an affluent area of London, she hadn't expected Jack's house to be quite so grand.

"Oh my goodness me," Hilda gasped, taking the words out of Lucy's mouth as they gazed around the impressive hallway, "I can't believe you've been sleeping on a sofa bed in my dining room when this is how you live. I'm so embarrassed."

"Hey, don't be," Jack put an arm around her, "I loved staying at your house with you looking after me. You're the best cook in the world."

"Go on with you," she pushed him playfully.

Jack laughed. "I'll show you all to your rooms. I've asked Freda my capable girl Friday, or maybe I should say Lady Friday to sort things for me. I've had two single beds put in one of the bedrooms for the boys, and I've put you right next to them, Lucy. There's actually a door separating the two rooms, which you can leave open and it'll give you peace of mind."

"Come on," Jack said to the boys. I'll race you to the top of the stairs."

The boys ran ahead up the huge staircase squealing with delight.

"I wonder who takes care of all this," Hilda said to her, "I can't see Jack keeping it as pristine as this."

"I can hear you," he said from the top of the stairs. He put on a playful posh voice, "I have staff, of course."

They learned over dinner Jack did of course have staff. It was quite a surprise to Lucy exactly how Jack was living. She knew he wasn't poor by the style and cut of his clothes, his educated accent, and his truck was a top of the range model. But she hadn't anticipated he was as wealthy as he appeared to be.

"This meal is lovely, Jack," Lucy said, "whose idea was it to have pizza for the boys?" she asked as the boys devoured a slice each.

"My chef Kouri, he's fabulous. You'll meet him while you're here. He's a great guy, there's nothing that man doesn't know about food. When I told him the ages of the boys, he set to making them pizza. But I tell you now, they aren't you average pizzas. Kouri's all about nutrition."

"Yes, I noticed the spinach heavily disguised with the tomato sauce."

"Yep, that's Kouri for you."

"Well, this chicken is to die for," said Hilda, "and he went to all this trouble for us."

"He would do. His whole life is devoted to food. He loves it. He comes in every second or third day and leaves me food to warm up. I'll get him to come more frequently while you're here." He turned to Hilda, "Do you think you can manage not cooking for a few days?" he asked, clearly wanting to pay her back for taking care of him."

"Go on then, if I have to," she winked, taking a sip of her wine.

"Can we go outside?" Jordan asked.

"It's getting dark out there," Jack said firmly, "maybe tomorrow. But what you can do is play at exploring in all the rooms upstairs. And, if you look carefully in the wardrobe in your bedroom, you might find some new toys to play with."

"Can we go now?" Cory asked.

"I'll come too," Hilda got up from the table, "it'll give you both a chance to talk about," she hesitated, "you know what."

"Thanks Hilda," Jack said, "we'll get rid of all this mess, and then when the boys are in bed, we can all have a drink and a chat together."

Eventually, Hilda and Lucy had got the boys settled and to sleep. It was all strange for them sleeping in new beds and having a different bedroom. They'd been so excited with their new toys, too. Jack certainly was a thoughtful man.

The early part of the evening was spent in the beautiful room at the back of the house which overlooked a stunning terrace. Between them they talked about the forthcoming court case. Jack wanted to go over everything precisely so that she and Hilda understood.

Finally, Hilda gave a great display of fake yawning and took herself off to bed. Lucy knew she'd be comfortable in her bedroom with a wide screen TV, and an ensuite bathroom to die for. The bath alone was huge with a Jacuzzi feature so she didn't feel bad Hilda excusing herself. And she had an overwhelming desire to be alone with Jack. Yet, despite craving for some intimacy with him, she wasn't entirely sure that Jack felt the same way. She was sat next to him on the sofa as near as she was able without it being too intimate, but his focus seemed to be resolutely on the court case.

"I've texted Jenna to say I'm back in London."

"She'll be pleased to hear from you."

"Yeah, I'm purposely avoiding ringing though."

"Why?"

"I think the less communication between her and I right now the better. Once you've appeared in court and it's all out in the open who you are, she can come here and see you."

"That'll be nice. I'd like to see her again."

"Yeah, me too. We normally meet each week for lunch which I always look forward to. I do miss the old Jenna, though. Those Montgomerys have wrecked her life. She's a shadow of her former self."

"I hardly dare ask because I reckon I know the answer, but how did she get with Leo in the first place?"

"It's a long story." His jaw tensed and his brows drew together, "And there's a certain irony, telling you it all."

"It's okay," she squeezed his hand, "I've spent days telling you all about my life, I know how hard it is."

He took a breath in. "Jenna worked in the financial district when she met Leo. I didn't have any idea it was Leo Montgomery she was seeing, she never told me, I just knew she was seeing someone. She implied it was casual, but I could see changes in her. I knew it was more than that. She was glowing. I was going through a particularly stressful time at the newspaper so didn't see her as often as normal but I knew she was fine as she had this new bloke. So I wasn't worried she was lonely or anything. She had a good social life anyway. We still texted and spoke occasionally." He paused to take a drink of his wine.

"I was sort of expecting her to say to me any day, let's go for dinner so I could meet this guy and then they would probably do the engagement marriage thing. But it never happened. I did of course ask how things were going, but she was vague, so I concluded maybe it was him, and that he didn't want to be tied down. She said he was a widower so I assumed he was taking it slow.

"I now know, according to Jenna's description, that he *wooed her with his wealth and an abundance of enthusiasm.* She later described it to me as a romance she thought only happened in women's fiction. But that was much later when she'd began to despise him.

"He whisked her away to Antigua in the West Indies, which at the time I thought was nice. I'd liked to have met him but I was busy, and at the end of the day, she was an adult. I couldn't be playing the big brother when she was clearly in love.

"It was during that holiday, he asked her to marry him. But he wanted to do it there. She told me a year or so into the marriage that Leo Montgomery's persona in the early days had been nothing short of persuasive. She'd asked if I could fly out as she desperately wanted me to give her away, but there wasn't the time. Leo reassured her they would have a ceremony in the UK at some stage. Excited and in love, she believed him, but she'd been naive because that never materialised. She'd returned home from the West Indies to find her flat had been emptied and everything moved into Oak Ridge. That had been a big enough surprise, but there was more to come. Leo persuaded her to give up her job, *to*

226

concentrate on us, and she foolishly did. Overnight, she became precisely what Leo wanted her to be. From an independent girl around town, she became Leo's beck-and-call wife.

"You don't need me to tell you about Oak Ridge. As you know it isn't a pleasant place to live despite its opulence. It became almost her prison. And the thing Jenna hated most of all was the regulatory evening meal with Avery and Susan. And still to this day she loathes it."

Memories flooded back to Lucy's mind. Jenna's life was exactly the one she'd managed to escape from. She felt Jack's pain for his sister. She'd been where Jenna was and her heart went out to her. When Jack brought Jenna to Oban to visit, she'd known something wasn't right about her.

She squeezed Jack's arm. "If I had any doubts at all about giving evidence before, now I know categorically it's the right things to do. We'll get her out of there, Jack, just like I did. If we do nothing else, we'll free her from those monsters."

He used the back of his fingers to stroke her face. "You are one hell of a woman, do you know that?"

"And you are one hell of a man. Jenna is lucky to have you."

Their eyes locked. Was it a glint of desire she saw? Warmth surged though her, overwhelmed by his masculinity. She couldn't help but appreciate his attractiveness; she willed him to reach forward and kiss her. The mood between them was perfect. They could go upstairs and comfort each other. She so desperately wanted that, but Jack clearly didn't. He tapped her leg, "Right, come on, let's make a move. We've a busy day tomorrow. I want to show you a small kindergarten round the corner I've found for the boys."

She stood up. "I'm not sure about that, Jack," he was striding ahead and she rushed to keep up. "I don't want them leaving the house."

"It won't hurt to take a look though. We'll all go tomorrow together and see what we think."

Did he ever stop organising? Jenna was so lucky to have him as her brother. If anyone could free her from the Montgomery chains, then he would.

She'd bet her savings he never failed at anything.

Chapter 35

London

Finally the day of Leo's trial had arrived. Jenna checked herself in the full-length mirror satisfied she looked every bit the glamorous wife in her pale blue dress and jacket and cream shoes and handbag. She'd had to buy the dress a size larger to accommodate the fake belly.

Jack had called to say he was back in London but couldn't meet with her. He'd explained he'd got flu type symptoms so it was best they skipped lunch. Apologising, he'd said he didn't want to pass it on to her with her being pregnant and she hated herself for not telling him there wasn't a baby. It was probably a blessing in disguise though. Jack would have never tolerated her being humiliated with a phoney pregnancy. It was unlikely now she'd see him until after the trial. It seemed a long time since their weekend in Oban together. She still got twitchy thinking about it. If it came out that she'd not been in Cornwall, she was fearful what Leo might do for deceiving him.

Leo came into the bedroom looking strikingly slick – as far removed from a murderer as only he could be. His Prada suit would have cost hundreds as well as his highly polished Berluti shoes. He'd had his hands manicured and if she wasn't mistaken, he'd had his eyebrows groomed alongside his fashionable haircut, gelled to perfection.

"All set?" he asked.

"Yes, I'm ready."

The public following the trial would see them as a glamorous rich couple – they wouldn't know that every night she prayed her husband would be found guilty and go to jail. He was the opposite of everything she believed in. There was no good in him so to be free would be such a relief even though she'd still have Avery to contend with. As far as she was concerned, if Leo had murdered someone, which she was quite sure he was capable of, then he deserved to be punished.

"It's going to get a bit more intense as from today," Leo said picking up his wallet and phone from the dresser, "the prosecution are likely to say some awful stuff about me. None of it will be true, though, they'll just be painting a picture to try and get a conviction."

Yeah, right.

"So you must keep your expressions impassive, look to Dad to lead you. The jury will be watching you, wondering if you believe what you are hearing, so remember, don't give anything away. I need you to do this to perfection, Jen. Don't let me down." His tone was laced with threats.

"I won't."

"And when this is all over, we'll go away somewhere nice together. How about that?"

She felt the urge to vomit. As if she wanted to go anywhere with him.

"That'll be nice," she said. "Let's hope it's over and done with quickly, your mother doesn't look well with it all."

"Yeah, I spoke to Bridget about it. She's keeping a watchful eye on her."

She wanted to bite back, God help Susan if Bridget was keeping a watchful eye – she wouldn't let her look after a pet hamster.

He carried on. "Dad says that as soon as it's over, he's going to get her some medical help. He's worried about her too. Hopefully, the trial won't be long though, they don't have any evidence, it's all circumstantial. Curtis reckons by the end of today, or tomorrow at the latest, the case will be thrown out."

"Let's hope so," she said, wanting to cross her fingers behind her back like she did as a child when she told lies.

She reached for her designer handbag from the bed, carefully chosen to match her Louboutin shoes. She had to get away from him before he suffocated her.

Avery and Susan were waiting in the hall in all their designer finery which was to portray how rich they were. Avery had a mantra that clothes maketh the man, which he certainly lived by. He was always well turned out and today was no exception.

Steve, their new security man, was stood with them and Bridget was hovering as usual with her supportive guise which camouflaged her wanting-to-know-it-all-face, fussing round Susan who looked like death warmed up.

"You've got everything," Bridget reassured Susan, "I've checked. Glasses, tissues, and gloves in your bag. And I've put in some paracetamol in case you get one of your bad heads."

"I've got one now," Susan said with a face so pale it was bordering on translucent, "but thank you, Bridget."

Avery took on his I'm head of the family, persona. "Okay then, let's get this done. Remember ladies what Curtis said. We have to display a united front and give Leo our total support. And do bear in mind that the cameras will be on us the whole time."

They made their way to the waiting cars. A vision of Jack sprung into her mind. However sick he genuinely had been the last few days, she knew today he'd be in court. She recalled an earlier conversation she'd had with him before he went to Oban when they'd met for lunch. He'd said things would kick off when he came back. Yet things had gone deathly quiet. But she knew from old, when Jack was quiet – he was invariably up to something.

Unease surged through her as McNeil held the car door open.

Chapter 36

London

"All ready?" Jack asked Lucy as he stood at the front door looking devilishly handsome in his grey suit and tie. It was the day of Leo's trial.

"As ready as I'm ever going to be," she sighed. The night had been terribly long. She'd yearned to knock on his bedroom door and go inside, curl up next to him in his bed and sleep with his strong arms reassuring her. But he hadn't indicated anything like that would be welcome so she'd tossed and turned all night and was still awake when dawn peeped through the curtains.

"Mike will be here shortly," he told her, "stay close to him. I've told him even if you want to pee, he's to stand outside the toilet door. And he's not to relinquish you to anyone but me."

"I wish I could go with you."

"Me too. But as a witness you can't. And I've got to go into court so I can see you when you come in. Mike's got a room for you both so you're not visible until they call for you." He lifted her chin with his hand, "When you step into the courtroom, I'll be watching you, and I won't take my eyes off you for a second. So when you walk towards the witness box, I'm walking alongside of you, willing you on. Don't forget that."

She nodded, loving him for his reassurance. She hated the thought that in less than an hour she'd be face to face with the family she'd escaped from. The thought of seeing Leo and Avery was responsible for the huge knot in her tummy, which was getting tighter by the minute. The urge to open the front door and run was overwhelming.

Jack reached for her hands and grasped them tightly.

"You can do this. Remember, you aren't going to be able to speak today. It's just the formality of you being announced and walking in. No doubt there'll be hell on after that, but we'll be out of there. Trust me, we'll be home within an hour, I promise."

"I know," she sighed, "it's the thought of seeing Leo and Avery again. I wish I could be behind a screen or something. That life seems so long ago, I was a different person then. I feel like I'm morphing into Grace Montgomery again. You'll probably not recognise me when I walk in that courtroom and have to face them with a totally different persona."

"I'd recognise you in a pitch-black coal mine," he said and his lips found hers in the gentlest kiss. A kiss that made her want to rake her fingers through his hair and drag him upstairs. But it was over before it had even begun. She saw tenderness and kindness in his eyes and wasn't sure how to respond.

"That's for good luck, and to say," his strong arms wrapped around her, "you've got this." She fitted perfectly against him with her head barely touching his jaw. The hug between them was a first, along with the kiss. It felt warm and comforting, and it gave her strength. She wouldn't let them down. Jack and Jenna, although Jenna didn't know it yet, were depending on her. Her desire to help Jenna was becoming stronger the closer she became to Jack. They were decent people and deserved a life without the Montgomerys dominating it.

Hilda came rushing through to the hall with the boys.

"Aren't you taking us?" Cory asked looking cute in his Peppa Pig sweatshirt ready for nursery. Jack had found them a small kindergarten close to his house, and while Cory seemed fine attending once he was there, he was still unsure each morning about going. Jordan was wearing his Paw Patrol jumper, looking forward to whatever the day brought to his childhood life. The kindergarten situation was far from ideal, she'd have preferred them to stay in the house but she knew two boisterous boys couldn't be locked inside with Hilda all day. And Jack had spoken to the staff and explained that the children must be supervised at all times. He'd used the story again about her estranged husband looking for the boys and was confident due to the small group of children attending, the boys wouldn't be found. And as he'd said reassuringly, the Montgomerys had the trial occupying them. They'd need an outcome from that before their focus turned to anything else.

She smiled lovingly at her precious boys and squatted down to their level. "No, we aren't taking you today, Hilda is. She wants to see your new nursery."

"Where are you going?" Jordan asked.

"We're going to see someone about our flights to go back home."

"I want to stay here," Jordan said jumping up and down, while Cory, clutching his teddy, asked, "Can I come with you?"

"No, sweetie, you have to go and have fun at nursery and we'll see you later. Come on, let's have a great big hug, all of us, like we do at home. She wrapped her arms around both boys and Hilda did too, just as they did in Oban when they were leaving for nursery.

Cory reached out for Jack, "You as well." And Lucy's heart melted as Jack walked forward and joined in the hug.

It was a day of reassurance for each of them.

Chapter 37

London

As predicted, as they arrived at the court, the cameras were on Jenna and Leo as they exited the car. Steve did his best to get them through the crowds but the police had to step in to help form an inroad to the court entrance. It was a relief when they got inside and the door closed behind them. Leo's barrister, Curtis Grantham, was waiting in the foyer for them. He was dressed up in his gown and wig looking exactly like you would expect a barrister to look – all academic and persuasive. Leo said that once you got to know Curtis, he had a compelling manner which had you believing everything that came out of his mouth was gospel.

"Good morning," Curtis greeted them with his moustache perfectly groomed and curled. Leo had been confident that while his appearance was eccentric to say the least, he was the best and if anyone could get the case dismissed, then it was him. Seemingly he had a great track record with scores of cases. That's why they'd chosen him and paid the hefty fee he charged. And they hadn't stopped paying yet. There was more to come at the end of the trial, however it went.

Jenna smiled at Curtis, "Good morning."

Avery and Susan shook his hand. Avery looked slick and confident, and while Susan was clad in her designer dress and coat, she looked pale and frail. Jenna felt sorry for her. She wasn't her favourite person, particularly for the way she pandered to Avery and Leo, but nevertheless, she loved Leo and would be anxious for him.

As if to appear like a loving husband, Leo leant forward and kissed her cheek. "Try not to worry. I've got to go with Curtis. I'll see you shortly."

He kissed his mother's cheek and nodded at Avery, "Dad."

"Good luck, son. We're rooting for you."

An encouraging nod was all she could manage. Leo, still trying to portray himself as husband of the year, said, "Dad'll look after you."

As if Avery Montgomery *looking after her,* would give her reassurance. She couldn't think of anything worse. As far as she was concerned, he should be on trial as well as her husband. They were joined at the hip, so whatever Leo had done, his father would be involved. He'd just slipped through the net. But that wasn't a surprise, he was brighter than Leo and had been around longer. And she knew there were occasions that Avery had to sort out mess Leo created.

The insufferable Avery, standing a few steps away, reached to take her arm and she was forced to accompany him and Susan who looked increasingly like she was going to collapse any minute. Her carefully applied make-up was much heavier than usual – if the intent was that way to disguise her ill health, it wasn't working.

They had to stand and wait until the doors opened to allow them inside the courtroom. Avery held Susan's arm and she followed with the ridiculous false belly on show. She took her seat next to Avery. He was doing his best to be upbeat, smiling and nodding to people he knew, while overtly holding his wife's hand. Oh, how they all looked the part, the Montgomery family supporting Leo. She wanted to stand up and scream to those that had already taken their seats, what a hateful man she was married to, and as far as she was concerned, he most likely had killed Isaac Davey and there'd most probably be others too. Maybe it hadn't been Leo directly carrying out the heinous crimes himself, but she was sure he'd have orchestrated them. And Avery would be involved – she wouldn't put anything past him. He controlled Leo's strings. Yet the evil bastard was sitting next to her playing the big I am. How could he be so relaxed about seeing his son standing trial for murder? What a horrible man he was, and Susan too. She might look crap right now, but what sort of a woman had she been all these years – content to be married to a thug, and rearing one too. It disgusted her.

She scanned the gallery and spotted the only decent thing in her life. Her dear brother, Jack seated at the end of the row. He was sitting next to a couple of men who looked like detectives. Jack's warm loving eyes met hers. It was a relief that he looked fine, not that she was totally convinced he'd been ill. She daren't smile at him. Avery would be watching her closely, but she gave him a look which she hoped conveyed how much she wished she could have sat next to him.

As she continued to study Jack, the expression on his face was one she recognised. She'd seen similar on him when he was a small boy and had done something good. Unease crept through her veins. Leo would go ballistic if Jack had interfered in any way. But she knew her brother. He'd said he'd bring Leo down, and in that instant she feared this was going to be his moment. It was as if something pinged in her brain. Like driving through thick fog which suddenly clears and you could see the way forward. He had been avoiding her. And she now was fairly sure she knew the reason why.

He'd wanted to protect her from whatever was about to happen.

Chapter 38

London

Jenna watched Leo as he was brought into court accompanied by a security officer and taken to the area reserved for the defendant on trial. If he was nervous, it didn't show. Curtis Grantham had tutored him well. After a few minutes, the court usher asked them all to stand and the judge walked. He was an elderly man, tall and distinguished. They waited until he took his seat and they all took theirs.

The jury then filed in, one after the other. She counted eleven of them, six male and five female and prayed they'd be strong enough not to fall for Leo's charm. The judge addressed the barristers for opening statements.

Justin Coffey for the prosecution stood and faced the jury first. He appeared to be young. She always imagined barristers to be over fifty, rather like Curtis Grantham who must be pushing sixty. This particular barrister was only mid-thirties by the looks of him. And good looking too – not that looks should sway the jury. She hoped desperately he'd present a compelling case and it wouldn't be thrown straight out, as Leo and Avery were expecting.

"Ladies and gentlemen of the jury, may I respectfully remind you all, you are sitting here today in pursuit of justice. Isaac Davey, a married man, a family man with children, and a law-abiding citizen, who sadly has had his life taken away prematurely." He paused, Jenna imagined that was about impact, and was done to give the jury time to assimilate what was being said.

The prosecuting barrister continued, "But one autumn evening, he didn't return home. His wife and daughters are here in court today," he made an elaborate indication with his head as to where they were sitting in the courtroom, "and they are desperately seeking justice and closure, so they can try and move on with their lives. The police believe that when Isaac Davey went missing over five years ago, he was killed shortly afterwards. We all know that a man cannot simply disappear. Not a family man who liked nothing better than spending time when not working, with his wife and two daughters. The prosecution believe one man knows exactly what happened to Isaac Davey, and that man is on trial today.

"The defence will no doubt argue that all the prosecution have is circumstantial evidence, and indeed, before we even begin, I agree. We don't have a body and we don't have forensic evidence. But what we do have is a man that left his home one evening to go to work for the Montgomery family and never returned. We ask that you listen carefully to all the information presented today, and I'm confident you will come to the only conclusion . . . that Isaac Davey was murdered. And, if you conclude that is indeed the case, then you'll need to consider Mr Leo Montgomery, who is on trial today. And as difficult the concept of murder is, we urge you not to lose sight of Mr Isaac Davey, a man that worked hard and did his best to provide for his family. We owe it to him, indeed it is our duty, to ensure justice is carried out in this courtroom. The accused's defence will be that he has no knowledge of what happened to Mr Davey. I put it to you, Leo Montgomery knows exactly what happened and we are going to prove to you that he was responsible for Mr Davey's death."

Curtis Grantham stood to address the jury. He had a confidence about him which made Jenna feel uneasy. If the Montgomerys believed he could get the case thrown out, she believed it too. And that was the last thing she wanted.

He kept his voice low. "Leo Montgomery has not killed anyone. In court today, we have a happily married man, with extensive business interests. He is law abiding with not even a parking ticket against his name. The prosecution has no body, no forensic evidence, nor any conclusive evidence whatsoever, only a theory, that Mr Davey has been killed. Mr Montgomery has fully co-operated with the police every step of the way, and, from the lack of any evidence, we can only conclude that he is innocent of any crime. He stands trial today with the belief and absolute faith in the legal system that the jury will come to that conclusion too. I ask that you listen

243

carefully to the information presented; I use the word information purposely as it won't be fact or evidence, it will be supposition. It is therefore my intention today to press for the absolute acquittal of an innocent man."

He took his seat. That appeared to be it. She'd expected more, but his delivery had been believable and convincing.

The judge invited the prosecution to call their first witness. Justin Coffey stood up. "Your Honour, I would like to call my first witness, Grace Montgomery."

Grace Montgomery? Jenna must have misheard.

"What the hell . . ." Avery muttered. She could feel the tension in him, sitting by her side. The silent courtroom waited while a door opened in the distance.

Grace Montgomery was the name of Leo's first wife . . . but she'd died. Jenna remembered when she first met Leo, going with him to put flowers on her grave one Christmas. It must have been to impress her in the early days as he'd never been since, not with her anyway, and she doubted he'd go on his own. He never mentioned the woman.

Footsteps were coming closer to the courtroom. Jenna glanced across at Jack. His face was impassive but he was staring intensely at the courtroom door. She switched her focus onto Leo who was wearing an expression she'd never seen before. The high colour she'd noticed earlier on him, which she'd put down to anxiousness, had completely disappeared, and ashen replaced it. He looked like he might be about to faint.

She didn't get it. Grace Montgomery was dead. Leo was a widower. How else could he have married her?

The courtroom door opened and a woman was led inside.

"Jesus Christ," Avery muttered and Jenna could easily have said the same. She couldn't quite believe what she was seeing. The woman held herself tall, her walk measured and steady as she made her way into the witness box, and there was no doubt about it, it was Lucy Smyth who lived with Hilda that she'd had afternoon tea with in Oban. But why was she walking towards the witness box? Why would she be at Leo's trial? And why had they called her Grace Montgomery, Leo's late wife's name?

Lucy had certainly undergone a transformation. Gone were the jeans and tee shirt she'd seen her in. Stunning didn't come close to the vision walking towards the witness box in a smart suit and with a full face of make-up. And the thick-rimmed glasses had gone. She could see it was Lucy, but it didn't seem like her. Her persona was totally different.

Curtis Grantham appeared confused and turned to her husband who hadn't taken his eyes off Lucy. He was staring at her, as if in a trance. And then, rather like a light-bulb moment, in that second she got it. This wasn't Lucy Smyth coming into the courtroom to give evidence – this was Leo's first wife, Grace Montgomery. The woman he thought all these years to be dead, was clearly very much alive. And Jenna knew categorically it was down to Jack. That's what the writing retreat was all about, the rubbish about Cornwall, not returning when he said he would, and not seeing her before the trial. He'd planned all of it.

If this woman was indeed Leo's first wife, she must have faked her death. And that could only mean she'd outfoxed the family. And nobody ever outfoxed them.

"Objection Your Honour," Curtis shouted as he stood up, "I'd like to call for an immediate recess. Grace Montgomery, if this is indeed her, is officially dead. This is obviously an enormous shock to my client and his family. This woman is supposedly deceased," he repeated, glaring at Lucy Smyth in the witness box.

The judge addressed Justin Coffey. "This is highly irregular, Mr Coffey as you well know."

"Yes, Your Honour. If you will allow me, I'll give an explanation to the court. Grace Montgomery has vital evidence that formulates the prosecution case. For that reason, she has been placed in witness protection but has willingly co-operated with the police and my legal team and wishes to bring her evidence to court."

The judge only took a moment to consider before raising his head toward Leo. "Mr Montgomery, in light of any possible further evidence, your bail is relinquished and you will remain in custody until further notice."

Jenna nervously bit the inside of her lip as she witnessed the discomfort pass across Leo's face. He'd be mortified at being incarcerated. Furious wouldn't come close. And, glancing at Avery – she guessed they'd both have murder on their minds right now.

The judge addressed the court, "The court will adjourn temporarily." He directed his icy glare at Justin Coffey. "I'll see you in my chambers, Mr Coffey," and less fiercely addressed the defending barrister, "and you, Mr Grantham." He banged his gavel against the sound block. They all stood while the judge exited the courtroom.

Jenna's eyes were drawn to Leo. He stared furiously at Avery as he was led away by the security man at the side of him. Not a glance her way, just a fixed glare at his father. She knew exactly what would be going through his mind. Some sort of deal. He thrived on them. His plan now would be to make one with his first wife. But would she? She'd risked her entire life coming to the court – her dear brother's efforts had paid off. But there'd be a price to pay. And even though she'd known nothing about it, it felt like a ghost had walked over her grave, and each step she took alongside Avery, was edged with tension. After today, she had a gut feeling she might end up somehow being the one to pay.

Chapter 39

London

Jenna had no choice than to accompany Avery and Susan out of the courtroom, Avery's grip on her elbow was firm. She could feel the rage in him. The foyer was filling up as they filed out. She glanced around to find Jack, but she couldn't see her brother anywhere.

Avery's grip on her elbow tightened and she was marched alongside him out of the court towards the waiting car.

There were shouts from the reporters. 'Did you know the first Mrs Montgomery was still alive?' 'How much did your husband know, Mrs Montgomery?' 'Are you still supporting your husband?' – the questions went on, one after the other. But the one that had slammed her the most was, 'How do you feel, Mrs Montgomery, now you aren't legally married?'

They fought their way to the welcome privacy of the Rolls Royce and the doors were firmly closed behind them. Cameras were at most of the windows but started to disperse as the driver slowly managed to move through the crowds.

Susan broke the silence. "I don't understand . . . where has she been all these years? Leo saw her in the chapel of rest. How can she be alive?"

"I have no damn idea," Avery snapped. He turned his furious face to Jenna, "Do you know anything about this?"

"Of course not," sweat began trickling down her back, "how would I know anything?"

"Through that bastard brother of yours, he'll have something to do with this."

"He's been away," she said trying to keep the nervousness out of her voice, "I haven't seen him."

"You have!" his eyes blazed murderously, "You went to Cornwall to see him."

"Avery," Susan put her hand on his, "please . . . can we just leave this until we get home."

"No, we can't, Susan. Our son is likely to be going to prison now depending upon what Grace bloody Montgomery has to say for herself. And we need to find out who's damn responsible and just how much she knows!"

Susan wouldn't give up and Jenna was grateful. It gave her time to think.

"Jenna's had a shock too, remember. The man she thought she was married to, it's clear now she isn't. We all need to time to adjust to Grace returning, not just you."

"Time!? We need answers!"

Avery's expression was thunderous as he turned to her. "Where did you stay in Cornwall?"

"Why do you want to know that?" she replied, trying not to show how much she was shaking.

"Just bloody tell me, woman!"

"St Ives."

"Where in St Ives? A hotel? What's the name of it?"

"It wasn't a hotel. Jack had rented a house. I stayed there with him. But why are you asking all this? What has this got to do with Leo's first wife being alive?"

He didn't answer. He didn't need to. She knew how his mind was working. There was no way she was going to divulge anything that might implicate Jack.

"What's the address?" he barked.

Susan came to her rescue again. "Avery, this is getting us nowhere. All it's doing is sending my blood pressure up. Can we leave off the interrogation for now? We'll be home soon, we can try and work it all out then."

Fury raged in his eyes and she spotted he'd involuntary clenched his fists. His anger was misdirected at her. The outrage was for Lucy Smyth aka Grace Montgomery. She'd beaten the family and nobody did that.

"I want the damn address," he glared at her.

Jenna took a deep breath. Thank goodness she'd holidayed at St Ives with her parents. She knew where they'd stayed as a child and this particular street shared the same name as her grandmother.

"Dorothy Avenue."

"What number?"

"I can't remember," she scowled convincingly, "I don't even think it had a number on the door."

The silence was thick between them. Susan started to sob, "Poor Leo. I can't bear to think of him in a cell. We have to get him out, Avery."

250

"I will," he growled, "just back off and give me time to think."

Jenna stayed silent and continued to stare out of the window. Her normally slow and stilted heart seemed to have gained an extra beat, she wasn't legally married to Leo Montgomery and might never have known if it hadn't been for Jack. Her job now was to protect him at all costs. She was telling Avery nothing other than what she already had.

The Rolls pulled into Oak Ridge and was slowly driven along the imposing drive way to the main door of the house. Bridget was standing at the door waiting for them. Jenna had come to the conclusion the housekeeper never had a day off. She couldn't remember a time when Bridget wasn't visible at the house.

Steve Cooper got out of the accompanying Audi and moved towards the Rolls and opened the door. He reached forward to help a fragile looking Susan out.

"Thank you, Steve," Susan mumbled. Her weakness was evident as even holding onto him, she stumbled.

He caught her with his other arm "Are you alright, Mrs Montgomery?" It was evident she wasn't. She could barely stand. Avery rushed to help.

Susan's voice petered out, "I don't feel . . ."

"Let's get her inside," Avery grabbed onto her as well as Steve. "Bridget," he instructed, "call a bloody ambulance.

Chapter 40

London

Jenna laid in the bath trying to relax after the traumatic day. Every muscle ached and her head throbbed with the tension. Even though she now had a break from Leo while he was in custody, he wouldn't be there for long. Avery would have him out of there in no time, she was sure of it. She'd tried to call Jack but it went straight to his answer phone which was frustrating her. She wanted to find out how he'd discovered Lucy Smyth was Leo's first wife and how she'd faked her own death. It was unbelievable she managed to pull that off and fool the Montgomerys.

She rubbed the luxurious lather into her aching arms and shoulders, trying to fathom why Jack wasn't answering his phone. There was no reason for him to ignore her calls now it was out in the open. Surely he could speak now? Where was Lucy staying – was she at his house with him? Was there something going on between them?

She dressed again after her bath intending to go and see if Avery was back from the hospital; Susan had looked pretty grim and out of it when the ambulance came. But the thought of seeing him again caused her chest to tighten with anxiety. He'd be furious about Leo being in custody and she feared he might continue with his interrogation of her, as if she had something to do with it. Thankfully there was no way he could link her to anything, nevertheless there was no Susan to protect her right now.

As she walked into the lounge to call Jack again, her phone wasn't where she'd left it on the coffee table. She stood for a few seconds, puzzled. A phone just couldn't disappear. The thought crossed her mind that Bridget may have been in snooping but she wouldn't take her phone with her . . . would she? She'd have to go and find her. Opening the door to the landing, she was surprised to see Steve the security man sitting on a chair with a small table in front of him playing on an iPad.

"Hi, Steve, what are you doing sitting out here?"

He shrugged. "Avery's instructions."

"I don't understand."

As much as she dreaded it, she'd have to go and confront Avery. She made a move to pass Steve but he stood up. "You're to stay in your room, Mrs Montgomery."

"Stay in my room? What are you talking about? Will you get out of my way, please?"

Steve didn't move.

"Have you been in my suite and taken my phone?" she glared.

"No. That was Bridget."

Unease slid through her. "Why? Why has Bridget taken my phone?" she moved again to pass him, but he put his arms out to stop her.

"I don't know what's going on here, but you're frightening me. And I'm warning you now, you can't keep me in my room. I need to see Avery and Bridget."

"They'll come to you. I'll call them."

"Steve," she gave him what she hoped was a persuasive stare, "whatever you've been told to do, this isn't right. If I were you, I'd go now before you get too involved with this twisted family."

As if she might have been listening, Bridget appeared from nowhere and made her way towards them. Jenna's heartrate accelerated. She'd always hated Bridget but had never been frightened of her. Now she wondered if she should have been.

"What the hell is going on, Bridget? I want my phone back now. You had no business taking it."

Bridget didn't answer. Her persona seemed to have shifted. The way she was glaring, as if she was assessing and deciding on her next move. Anxiety was creeping down Jenna's spine. Being alone in the house with Avery was frightening enough, but now it appeared he might have an evil sidekick.

Avery came into view from the top of the stairs and walked towards them. It was a ridiculous situation, all of them stood on the corridor.

"What's going on?" Jenna challenged, "Steve won't let me past."

"No, he won't," Avery said with a warning glare, "it's best you rest in your room tonight."

"What do you mean rest? You can't keep me locked in my room. Why? I understand you're upset about the trial . . . we all are," she added, "but that doesn't give you the right to hold me prisoner. And why has Bridget taken my phone?"

"It's just for a short while. You'll get it back."

"I want it now. I need to speak to my brother. He's expecting me to ring him. He'll be worried if I don't, so please, get me my phone."

"Not yet, maybe tomorrow. It's been a hard day for everyone, Jenna. It's best you take it easy tonight. It's obvious you're not yourself," he added patronisingly. "That's what shock can do to you, it's perfectly understandable."

The tears that were threatening started to roll down her cheeks. "I'm not being locked up like a prisoner. Jack will be here for me and you'll be sorry," she turned her glare to Steve, "and you. What sort of a person are you that you take this instruction from him? It's breaking the law holding someone against their will."

Steve's face was impassive.

"Just do as you're told, Jenna." Avery reached forward to touch her arm.

She pulled away from him. "Get your hands off me."

His tone changed, as if it was a normal family chat. "Susan sends her love by the way. They're keeping her in for a few days but she'll be back in no time, I'm sure. Then all this nasty business will be over. Oh, and when Steve goes off later tonight, another chap is coming. That's Greg, he's a quiet chap so won't bother you. Bridget will make sure they have food so don't be worrying about that."

Had Avery gone mad? And Bridget, why was she getting involved in his agenda? Surely she wasn't party to all of this? Resigned she was going nowhere, she glared at Avery with as much hate as she could muster, and turned back to her lounge. Closing the door behind her, she headed straight for the windows. Although she was on the upper floor, she'd take her chance of somehow getting out. But they were all locked. Could she throw a chair through one of them? They were double glazed so it was unlikely they'd break. Her hands were starting to shake as she made her way to the fire exit in the spare bedroom which had steps leading to the garden. It was locked as well.

She wandered frantically from room to room trying to figure out a way to escape. Her body was shaking with rage.

How long could they keep her locked up for?

Chapter 41

London

Lucy couldn't sleep following the trial, her emotions in turmoil. She was desperate to go back to court, give her evidence and then she could return to Oban. It didn't matter now if someone knew who she was. The more she thought about it, the conclusion she came to was the incidents were genuine accidents and not the more sinister idea that they were attempts on her life.

The night dragged on endlessly. As much as she tried to block the Montgomerys out, Leo's face haunted her, fearful of what he and Avery would do for revenge. Stunned didn't come close to describing Leo's face when she walked into the court room.

Sleep was intermittent. It felt like she spent more time awake than asleep. And she longed for Jack's arms to comfort her, which was made worse by him being just along the landing.

After endless tossing and turning, the morning light was beginning to creep through the blinds. She checked the clock and saw it was five minutes before five. There was no point in lying there; she wouldn't go back to sleep and the boys were only about an hour from waking up. She put on her robe and headed downstairs for some coffee. Jack's state of the art kitchen was a delight, as was the rest of the house. But knowing him now as she did, she wouldn't expect any less. He'd make a success of anything in his life and his house reflected his achievements.

Lucy carried a mug of coffee upstairs to Jack's room and she tapped on his bedroom door. There was no answer. Assuming he was in the ensuite, she went inside and left the drink on his bedside table. The bed was a surprise as it looked as if it hadn't been slept in, which was puzzling. He had a woman that came in each morning, but it was too early for her.

Lucy moved towards the ensuite door and listened for the shower. But there was only silence. She tapped on the door. "I've left you a coffee, Jack." Nothing. She tried again before gently opening the door. The bathroom was empty. Despite telling herself not to panic, she made her way downstairs with fear pulsing through her veins. As she passed the front door, she willed for him to come in, sweating in running gear or something.

"Jack," she called as she quickly checked around the downstairs rooms. He didn't answer and there wasn't a text message from him, either. She tapped on Hilda's bedroom door and went in. "What is it?" Hilda sat up.

"Jack's not in the house and his bed hasn't been slept in." Lucy eased herself down on Hilda's bed.

"When did you last see him?"

"Last night when I came to bed. He was on his computer, about eleven I think."

"Maybe he's gone out early for something?"

258

"I don't think he has. Something's wrong. Jack has barely left my side since Oban. I'm starting to get a feeling that something's happened."

Hilda wrapped her arms around her. "It's alright, love, nothing will have happened to him. Let me put some clothes on and come downstairs. If he's not back by then, we'll have to speak to Mike Frampton."

"Mummy," a voice called from the bedroom next door.

Hilda threw the bedclothes back. "You see to the boys and we'll get them some breakfast before we do anything."

Both of them tried to keep busy with the children's breakfast. While Lucy made them eggs and soldiers, she kept an eye constantly on the door, willing Jack to walk through it. Her worst fears were coming to fruition, which she daren't say out loud. What if he'd been taken?

"I don't like Edward," Cory said, "he hurt me."

Lucy didn't like to see the anxious look on Cory's normally cheerful face. "Edward at nursery?"

Cory nodded. "He pushed me," he said, pulling a woe-is-me face, sure to gain sympathy.

"Well, that's not nice. Did you tell Mrs Henry?"

"No."

"You must if he does it again. That's naughty."

"I don't like nursery," Jordan chipped in, "I want to go home."

"We are going to, just a few more days. We have the aeroplane tickets so we'll be going soon and then you'll be back with Mrs Leam."

"Do you want them to go to nursery today?" Hilda asked munching on a slice of toast. Lucy's tummy was tied in too many knots to think about letting the children go anywhere.

"Not until Jack's back."

Jordan heard Jack's name. "Where's Jack?"

"Work, sweetie, he had to leave early."

"I think you'd better ring Mike now," Hilda said. "Go in Jack's office and I'll get the boys washed and dressed."

"I think I will."

Lucy closed the door behind her in Jack's office and called Mike Frampton. As she waited for him to answer she gazed around his office at the walls with photographs of Jack's life. There were plenty of him with Jenna, and ones with what appeared to be his parents, university photographs, all pictures which demonstrated Jack's vibrant life.

"Mike," she said as he picked up, "Jack seems to have disappeared."

"Disappeared?"

"Yes. He wasn't in the house when I got up this morning."

"When did you last see him?"

"Around eleven last night. I went to bed and he was in his office."

"And he's not nipped out, you don't think?"

260

"I don't, no. I was up at five and his bed hasn't been slept in."

"Has his car gone?"

"No, the keys are here."

"What about his phone?"

"It's not here. Not that I can see."

"Okay, I want you to stay indoors, we're coming over. Don't answer the door until you know it's me."

"Okay."

She cut the call feeling better having made it. If Jack turned up, it didn't matter. The main thing was doing something. The scenario of something happening to him was too frightening to contemplate. Her feelings for him were growing daily and even though she wasn't sure what his were towards her, she hoped when all the court business was over, there'd be an opportunity to explore how they both felt.

She needed to speak to Jenna and cursed herself for not having a number for her. But it was probably better not to worry her. A thought had crossed her mind that Jack could be with her, but it was unlikely so early in the morning. And he'd said he was keeping his distance so as not to implicate her in anything until after the case. He thought it was safer that way until she left Oak Ridge, which was the next part of his plan.

Lucy was sat with Hilda on the settee, Mike Frampton and another man from the police was with him. Hilda had done her usual sterling job of entertaining the boys and making tea for everyone.

Mike took a sip of his drink. "We're checking CCTV around the area to see when he left."

"How long will that take?" Lucy asked anxiously.

"Not long, I hope."

"Jack won't have just left," Hilda said, "something isn't right."

Mike nodded. He knew as well as they did Jack wouldn't just disappear. The likeliest explanation was he'd been taken. And nothing was going to be achieved by them all sitting and skirting around the issue which they all suspected had happened. She'd known it from the moment she saw Jack's bed hadn't been slept in. A wave of acid welled up from her belly. If she wanted to help him, there was one way she could try. But it would mean confronting Avery.

"I've got to go to Oak Ridge," she said firmly, "it's the only way to help Jack."

"Absolutely not," Mike said. "You wouldn't be safe, not when Avery knows you're going to testify against his son."

"I can't sit here and do nothing."

"We don't know if Jack's even there."

"Oh, he won't be there," she said, "You know this family don't dirty their own hands. Someone will be holding him. It's their leverage to stop me testifying."

"If that is the case, then there's nothing to be gained by you going there. If Avery's got Jack, he's not going to let him go because you've turned up. On the contrary it'll incense him."

"I don't care, I'm going. I have to at least try. And when he hears what I have to say, I think he'll let him go. We can't just do nothing."

"What is it you're going to say?" Mike asked. "You need to tell me before I consider anything."

"We don't have time for this. I'm telling you now, they'll have him. And they're going to hang on to him to stop me giving evidence."

"So why go and see Avery if that's the case?"

"Because I have to. These people are evil. I have something on Avery that will terrify him. I think he'll let Jack go when he hears it."

"And what if I allow you to do this and something happens to you?"

"That's unlikely right now, you know that as well as I do. Avery won't do anything to me, that isn't the way he operates. They're holding Jack purely to frighten me."

Hilda's face was pale, "I'm with Mike, love. These are evil people. He could do anything to you."

"Look," Mike said with a degree of sympathy in his voice, "it's admirable what you are trying to do, but if anyone is going to visit Avery Montgomery, it's the police, not you."

"And what do you expect him to say. Yes, we've got Jack and we won't let him go until you stop me from giving evidence. Come on, you know he's not going to admit anything to you. This is all to get at me. This is their style. It's to show me they win every time."

"Then you need to tell me what you've got that makes you think he'll relent."

263

"I can't. You have to trust me."

Mike's face was tight and grim. It was unlikely he was going to budge.

"Do you think I want to go back there?" An edge of impatience crept into her voice. "I don't, but I have to. I can get them to release Jack. You have to at least let me try. By all means wait outside the house so he knows you're there, but I have to go in alone."

His eyes narrowed, "It's what you're going to bargain with that worries me. What are you going to say, that you'll not give evidence if he lets Jack go?"

"No, I'm not going to say that. Avery knows I have a lot of evidence on that family. The death of Isaac Davey is chicken feed. She glared at Mike and Hilda with determination in her eyes. "I'm the only hope right now. I need to go to Oak Ridge."

Mike stared at her as if weighing up the options, while Hilda's eyes filled up and she tried to stem the threatening tears with a tissue.

"We have to try," Hilda said, "but please go with her, Mike. He wouldn't dare harm her with the police there. I know Lucy, if she thinks she can do it, then at least let her try. This girl doesn't make rash decisions. She knows the family better than anyone and if she thinks she has a chance to help Jack, then we should let her. I'm terrified we're too late and something has already happed to him."

Lucy took Hilda's hand. "I know how worried you are, but you're right, I know this family. They won't have harmed him, I'm sure of it. There's too much hanging over them at the moment to risk anything. I think there is a way I can get him released, but that involves me seeing Avery on my own."

"But what is it you're not telling us?" Hilda asked, fear replacing the normal vibrancy of her eyes. "Why can't you tell us what you're going to say to Avery? At least let us know that."

"I can't. It's best you don't know. But I promise you both, I've got an ace card and I'm going to use it."

"Okay," Mike said. "We'll do it. But we'll be right behind you."

Adrenaline spurred her on. She grabbed her bag and jacket, desperately wanting to slip out of the house quickly, but Jordan spotted her wearing her coat.

"Where are you going?" he asked.

"I'm popping out to the bank to get some money for our trip home. You stay with Hilda and I'll be back soon. If you're good, I might even treat you to some Maltesers."

Cory's eyes lit up. "Promise."

"I promise. Come and give me a big hug, both of you."

She fought back the tears as she wrapped her arms round them in turn and hugged them both tightly. A little bit of normality before heading for the lion's den.

"Mummy loves you to the moon and back," she kissed their heads.

"Are you crying?" Cory asked.

"No, sweetheart. I think I've got a bit of a cold coming on. I might have to call at the shops and get some medicine. So if I'm a little while, don't worry, Hilda's here with you."

It almost felt like slow motion as she took Jack's car keys out of the kitchen drawer. She didn't want to go in a police car. They could follow if they wanted, but no way was she having them go inside Oak Ridge with her. What she had was for Avery's ears only. And once he'd heard it, she was as sure as she could be he'd let Jack go.

Her biggest fear though was – she might be too late.

Chapter 42

London

Lucy drove Jack's Range Rover along the leafy London suburbs towards Hampstead Heath. A journey she'd made so many times when she lived at Oak Ridge, with the chauffeur, Isaac driving her. The innocent man that was only guilty of being a friend to her and for that he'd paid with his life. Leo believed they'd been having an affair when all they'd done was stop off for a couple of bar meals. But Leo didn't believe that. He was insanely jealous. And poor Isaac had paid the greatest price.

Every emotion possible ran through her, anxiety and nausea being the most prominent. She wasn't going to be physically sick, but she felt an overwhelming need to the closer she came to the house. But adrenaline spurred her on. She could do this. She had to for Jack who'd done so much for her. They'd grown close and she was starting to imagine a life with him in it permanently. He was a decent man and had done his best for his sister and for her. She owed it to him, even though the next few hours were going to crucify her.

While she was driving to Oak Ridge, memories that she'd managed to bury came rushing back. The unpleasant years she was married to Leo who desperately tried to control her, and her insufferable in-laws, Avery

267

and Susan living in the same house. She used to beg Leo to move to a home of their own, hoping that in some way, she could make their marriage work if she got him away from the influence of his father. Avery was poison. But Leo was like a lapdog with him. If Avery told him to jump, he'd ask how high.

As she turned right into the tree-lined road that led her towards Oak Ridge her tummy plummeted as the police car that was following her flashed its lights and pulled over. Mike had been as good as his word. He would sit there and wait.

She continued on her own, clouds growing darker ahead. A bad omen, she thought. Memories returned of how unhappy she'd been living there. Never had she imagined she'd ever have to return once she got away. The endless years she'd thought up plots to leave until eventually she found one. It had been five years since she'd spoken to Avery. And that wasn't nearly long enough. But right now she needed to get Jack back – that was her focus. She couldn't afford to think he might become another of the Montgomerys victims.

Chapter 43

London

Wrought iron gates barred Lucy from driving up to the front door of the house. An electronic speaker was attached to the adjacent wall which she had to get out of the car to access. She pressed the speak button. Her heart raced as she waited for someone to answer.

"Good morning, how may I help you?" Even after five years, she recognised Bridget's voice. She didn't let on though. No need to acknowledge the housekeeper who was almost like an additional Montgomery, such was her loyalty to them.

"I'm here to see Avery."

"Is he expecting you?" She'd know damn well he wasn't.

"Tell him it's Grace Montgomery."

It started to rain as she waited. She wouldn't put it past Bridget to leave her standing there longer than necessary just to spite her. But she was confident Avery would see her – she'd gamble her life on it.

Bridget's voice returned on the intercom, "If you'd like to make your way to the front door."

Lucy got back in the car as the gates slowly opened. She made her way up the winding drive towards the mansion. As she exited the car, she knew Avery would be watching her on CCTV. Nobody got anywhere near the entrance without an invitation.

The solid oak front door was in front of her. Imposing – like a demon guarding the gateway to hell. To her, even the handle had teeth, and each grain of wood induced fear. It was going to take a huge heap of courage to pass through it.

The door creaked open and Bridget the witch was eyeing her up and down. A few more wrinkles and the odd grey hair, but she was exactly as Lucy remembered her. Elevated, as if she owned Oak Ridge and didn't just work for the family. There was no greeting of acknowledgement between them.

"Come in. Mr Montgomery is in the sitting room. Would you like me to take your coat?"

"No. I won't be here that long."

The evil Bridget was too well trained to question. But she'd no doubt be eavesdropping at the doorway. Lucy needed to circumvent that. What she had to say was for Avery's ears only, she couldn't afford the information to get into the wrong hands. There wasn't a soul that knew what she was about to tell him. And she hoped that would always be the case.

"If you'd like to follow me."

She walked along behind Bridget. There was a certain irony in being shown to the sitting room – it wasn't as if she didn't know the way. The hall was similar to how she remembered it. It had been decorated, but it was still the same old-fashioned hallway.

Bridget opened the sitting room door and gestured with her hand to go in. The evil bastard was standing by the fireplace, facing her as if it was an ordinary day and he stood like that all the time. He'd aged well. There might be a few more lines on his face and his hair slightly thinner, but the wickedness in his eyes was still there. That was innate in him.

"Can I get you anything?" Bridget asked Avery, as if she was there for a social visit. He didn't even bother to ask if she wanted anything. "No, we're fine, if you'd close the door behind you, please."

Adrenaline rushed through her as she heard the door close. He'd terrified her all the years she was married to his son, and he still did even now. He was a bully and a murderer. But the one thing she had learned with Jack's support was, bullies needed standing up to. That's why she was there. She couldn't allow him to win. Not with this. It was too important. And if things weren't as serious, she'd have enjoyed today. Nobody ever got one over on him. Leo being on trial would have seriously inflicted pain. That's why he'd taken Jack. It was his leverage. What he didn't know was, she had leverage of her own.

He raised his eyebrows. "I can't imagine why you've come here. You and I have nothing to say to each other."

She boldly stared into the darkness of his eyes. "Why have you agreed to see me then? You could have said no."

He shrugged. "I was curious as to why a scheming bitch that faked her own death, would want to see me. You're bold, I'll give you that."

"I'm not bold, Avery, I'm here because I want something. And you're going to give it to me."

"I wouldn't give you a damn cold," he spat, "you know that. And I can't imagine what I could possibly have that you want. And whatever it is, I can assure you, you're not going to get it. So, this *visit* is a complete waste of time."

"We'll have to see about that. But before I say anything to you, get rid of Bridget from outside of the door. You won't want her hearing what I'm about to say."

Pure hatred flashed in his eyes. But he'd be scared of what she might say. He too was hiding things that only the two of them knew. She watched him stride towards the door. He was still an attractive bloke, if thugs were your bag. He had a presence about him that she could see people would be drawn to. He opened the door, and just as she suspected, Bridget was hovering in the hallway.

"We would like some coffee after all Bridget if you'd be kind enough to fetch us some, and maybe some pastries. No rush." If she didn't understand that was code for clear off, then she'd be pretty thick. And cunning Bridget was far from that.

"Of course," she heard Bridget answer, "I'll do that right away."

272

He closed the door and moved back towards the place he'd left. He must have thought he looked more imposing stood by the fireplace. He never offered her a seat, but she wouldn't have taken it anyway.

Lucy forced herself to be assertive. "You've taken Jack Carr. And if he isn't still alive, then I'll make sure you'll spend the rest of your life wishing he was."

"I have no idea what you're talking about," he snarled.

"I know you're holding him somewhere," she challenged, "and you think that by doing so, I won't reveal in court what I know about your precious son."

"Do you think I care what you think?" he spat, "I have no idea what you're talking about. And if that's all you've come here to say, then I suggest you leave. I've more important things to do with my time than listen to your ludicrous allegations."

"Yeah, me too. I'd rather not spend a minute longer here than I have to. But before I go, you better listen carefully. If Jack doesn't come home today, I'll be spilling my guts, big time. You got off lightly with me leaving like I did, but you need to understand that if anything happens to Jack, then you'll be going down for a long time. It'll be my mission to make sure of it. And because I know exactly how your twisted mind works, I have written everything down I know about you and your thuggish family. So if anything happens to me, it's going straight to the newspapers. And believe you me, I know lots. You and I both know Isaac Davey's murder is small change."

The ridges of his neck became dangerously pronounced. "Do you really think you can pull off what the entire police force has tried to pin on this family for years?" His face flushed with rage, "Do me a favour and piss off. I'm not interested in what you think of this family. I have lawyers that'll eat you up and spit you out you stupid little bitch."

"You're sure of that, are you?" she raised an eyebrow. "I tell you what, if you're that confident, then I will leave. But before I do, is Susan around? Maybe she'd be interested in hearing how you raped me five years ago. What do you think the penalty would be for that?"

Her eyes clashed with his . . . remembering. The high puce colour of his face drained.

"Oh, I see, not so confident now, are you?"

"Any police or court would just see this as revenge," he spat, "made up lies by the whore you are. As if anyone would believe you. Get out of here, you pathetic slut, and take your ridiculous accusations with you."

"They aren't ridiculous and you know it. And very soon the whole world will know it. Unless you stop it. Let Jack go and I'll keep quiet."

"Keep quiet? Have you heard yourself? Do you really think anyone is going to believe you over me . . . a woman who faked her own death? Who's now back with a preposterous allegation from five years ago that her father-in-law raped her. Do me a favour. Even you can see nobody would believe you. You have no proof, it's your word against mine."

She reached in her bag for her phone and brought the screen up with her boys on. She turned it to towards Avery.

"There's my proof."

Momentarily, he looked confused, until the penny dropped. His expression was one of shock more than surprise.

"As you can see, I have all the proof I need of what you did to me, you sick bastard. Look closely, Avery, at your twin boys and remember, as much as it saddens me, they have your DNA. And do you know what? If this comes out, you'll face the wrath of your wife, the newspapers, and the law. But you and I know there's a greater force to be reckoned with here . . . Leo. He'd never forgive you, ever. So let's not have any more talk of lawyers eating me up and spitting me out."

The anger on his face was contemptuous. He'd know absolutely she was right. Leo would never forgive him.

"So . . . release Jack today unharmed. If he isn't, then you need to understand what I'll do."

The silence was palpable as they glared at each other.

His venomous eyes blazed murderously. "And if Jack did miraculously turn up . . . what then?"

"Get your son to change his plea to manslaughter and he'll get what he deserved for killing Isaac Davey. He did it as he believed Isaac and I were having an affair, which never happened – it was all in Leo's head."

"Leo will never go for it. He's going to be walking out of there by the end of the week a free man."

"Not when I give evidence he isn't."

She could see the cogs turning in Avery's brain. He wasn't stupid. She had the upper hand and he knew it. Her only hope was she wasn't too late.

She played her ace card. "Let Jack go and get Leo to plead guilty to manslaughter. I'll go back to where I came from and divorce him. You need never hear from me again." With clenched teeth and utter contempt, she continued, "But if anything happens to me, or any of my family, then believe you me," her eyes narrowed as she warned, "I've left the evidence to expose the lot of you."

She couldn't stay a minute longer. She'd done what she set out to do. On the surface, she was confident as she made her way towards the door – inside she was an angst-ridden wreck. As she walked into the hall, approaching with a tray of refreshments, was the evil housekeeper.

"I think maybe Avery could do with something a lot stronger than coffee right now, Bridget."

Chapter 44

London

Jenna jumped in fright as the lounge door swung open and Bridget sauntered in without knocking, something she'd never done. She was carrying a tray of sandwiches and fruit and a pot of tea. She placed the tray on the coffee table. There was an air about her. As if she was now in charge.

"You won't get away with this, I'm warning you," Jenna glared at her, "you'll end up in prison for what you're doing. My brother will see to that."

Bridget's eyebrows rose "And what exactly am I doing? We're trying to look after you. You're not yourself with the stress of the court case, anyone can see that."

"What do you mean, *I'm not myself*," Jenna snapped as she stood, "I'm perfectly fine. I need to leave this house and try and sort my own life out. I have solicitors to see. I'm sure you know by now, I'm not even legally married to Leo. I have no reason to stay here. We need to stop this nonsense now so I can leave."

"When Avery has spoken to the lawyers and Leo is released, you can talk then, when he's home, and sort everything out with him."

"When did you get so bloody grand, eh? You're forgetting your place. I don't know whether you've got grandiose ideas in your head that you're part of this family, but trust me, you're not. You're nothing but a servant. And if you think by assisting Avery you are going to somehow be in his favour, think again. When Susan comes home and hears about this, you'll be long gone from this house. I'll make sure of it."

The housekeeper moved swiftly towards the door, but hesitated before leaving. The new elevated Bridget clearly had more to say. Her mouth formed into an unpleasant twist, "You've always looked down on me, as if you're someone special. But you're not. You can't even hang onto a baby. All you had to do was sit back for nine months and produce an heir. But you couldn't do that, could you? You're just a useless piece of eye-candy. This family will be well rid of you."

The woman had gone mad speaking to her that way.

"Get lost, Bridget and take your stupid tray of food with you. Run along and do the washing up and whatever other skivvy tasks you're paid to do. And don't set foot in my room again."

Bridget's eyes filled with venom as she left the room and slammed the door shut behind her.

Jenna picked up a stool in a rage, intent on hurling it at the window, but one glance outside stopped her. Steve was out there on the lawn, smoking, looking up at her with a smirk on his face. Dammit! She tried to think of a way out. During the night she'd opened the door to the landing but there was an even bigger gorilla than Steve

278

baring her way. The windows and the fire escape were locked. If there was a fire, there was no way out for her. Bridget must have removed the key that was always in the door to the fire escape. The wrought iron ladder that would assist her escape was so near, yet so far.

As she kicked a chair in frustration, her dressing room sprang to mind. There was a small door behind her shoe rack that led somewhere, maybe to the loft. She'd never even looked inside before but it might be a way out. She quickly made her way there and moved the heavy shoe rack to one side and opened the small door. It was pitch black inside. If only she had a torch, or her phone with the light, she'd be able to tell then whether it was an escape route. She daren't just climb into it. She wasn't even sure if, further along, there was even a floor.

She slouched back on the dressing room carpet frustrated, and hunger gnawed at her stomach. She couldn't eat any of the food Bridget brought for her. God knows what might be in that. Tears stung the back of her eyes, which she tried not to give in to. Crying wasn't going to save her. Where was Jack? She was expecting him every day to turn up, beating down the front door. Surely he'd be worried about her and questioning why she hadn't been in touch. Why wasn't he?

And then the awful realisation dawned on her. Bridget would be texting him from her phone, pretending to be her. The tears flowed then, running down her cheeks. And before long she was sobbing like a baby.

There didn't appear to be any way out.

279

Chapter 45

Bridget had Jenna's iPad and phone. The pass code was easy – Jenna's birthday. Silly bitch. There was a message from her brother, sent just after the court case.

How you doing? Won't call until the dust has settled. Bet it's a relief to have a reprieve from Leo? Let me know you're okay X

Bridget checked Jenna's text history and carefully examined how she texted her brother. She couldn't find anything to indicate Jack was behind Grace Montgomery's appearance from the dead, although Avery thought it had to be something to do with him. She sent a non-committal text back in the style she thought Jenna would use.

All good. Be better when I see you. Enjoying the peace! Catch up soon X

She put the phone in her pocket and made her way to the sitting room. As she opened the door, it crushed her to see Avery slumped in a chair clutching a glass of whisky. The ridges of his neck were dangerously pronounced and his skin was a motley purple colour. She feared for his blood pressure and wanted to console him. Sitting next to him on the sofa was a first, but there was no need to worry about anyone catching them together.

Jenna was locked in her suite, ably guarded by Steve, so she wasn't going anywhere, and Susan was in the hospital.

She stroked his arm, "The nerve of Grace coming to the house, how dare she after all this time. You've got more than enough on with Susan being admitted to the hospital, and the trial."

"Yeah, she was always trouble that one. We underestimated her." He took a swig of his drink, "I still can't believe she managed to dupe us."

"Yes, but she'll have had help, remember that. Anyway, you said yesterday it was unlikely she'd be able to give evidence in court. Is that still the case?"

"I'm not entirely sure anymore. She knows plenty about this family, she could do us a lot of damage. She's sharp that one, much brighter than Jenna."

"But won't she be seen for exactly what she is, throwing allegations around and out for revenge?"

"Maybe," he shrugged, "who knows? I'm going to have to go and speak to Leo's barrister, Curtis Grantham. It's one stinking mess, that's for sure. Leo's going to have to change his plea now to manslaughter."

Her voice went up slightly, "Change his plea? Why would he have to do that? Surely nobody will believe Grace?"

"I don't honestly know." He shook his head wearily, "What I do know is, it's going to be too much for Susan. She's ill enough without all of this. I can't have any more stress put on her; she needs to concentrate on getting well."

Bridget's tummy contracted hearing him talking kindly about his wife. Who cared about her? She'd got rid of her, hadn't she? By the sound of things, the paracetamol in particular had caused damage to her liver – there'd even been talk of a possible transplant in the future.

"How is Susan? Any update?"

"Nothing more than we already know. The overdose of tablets has caused extensive damage." His voice was edged with tension, "I blame myself, I could tell she wasn't right. She was getting muddled. When I saw her yesterday she said as much. She'd been taking too much medication to help ease the pain." His forehead creased, "I should have been around more to help."

"You mustn't blame yourself. You've been trying to support Leo with the trial. It's been massive for you both. If anyone should feel bad it's me. I've been giving her pain medication each time she asked. I should have been more careful."

He rested his hand on hers, "You're a good woman Bridget, don't be hard on yourself. If Susan asked for her tablets, it's not for you or anyone to question it."

Her heart ached for him. She wanted to offer him some comfort and relief; he only had to say the word. But that didn't appear to be on his mind. He stood up. "I've got to make some calls and then go and see Leo's barrister. I'm hoping he can pull some strings so I can at least get to talk to Leo directly. It's no good on the phone. Can you call McNeil to come and get me, I've had too many to drive."

"I'll do that now." She stood up and reached for his arm to give it a gentle squeeze, "Whatever you do, it'll be the right thing for Leo, I know it will. What about Susan, are you visiting her today?"

"Of course. I'll go there, too. They might have some more news today. The main thing we have to do now is somehow hope we can get her home."

Home? He'd been having too many whiskies. Why would he want her home? She'd worked bloody hard to get rid of her so they could be together. The last thing she needed was Susan coming home. Not now the coast was clear for the two of them.

Chapter 46

London

The waiting was endless. Since Lucy had returned from Oak Ridge and threatening Avery, her and Hilda had drunk endless cups of tea and coffee, waiting. All they could do was entertain the boys until their bedtime. Mike Frampton was at the house trying to co-ordinate the search for Jack but Lucy knew they wouldn't find him. The Montgomerys were too clever for the police. They'd have used every method at their disposal to take him without being caught. She knew many of their old haunts, particularly the one where Leo had forced her to watch while gorillas beat the hell out of Isaac Davey until the poor bloke couldn't take any more and had passed away. She remembered clearly where they'd done that, in an old barn they owned miles from the city. But they'd since knocked the place down and built houses on it, which would destroy any forensic evidence of that crime, and the many more she was sure they'd committed there.

Once she'd settled the boys to sleep, Lucy came back down stairs and Hilda had poured them a large brandy. Lucy could tell she'd been crying.

"I'm getting scared now, I have to admit," Hilda said wearily.

"Me too. But Avery isn't a fool. He'll let him go, there's no longer any need to hold him."

"But what if they've harmed him?" Hilda's eyes welled up, "From what you've said, they do that to people. I'm terrified."

"He'll be okay. Trust me, they'll let him go," Lucy said with a conviction she didn't truly feel. But she knew it would be foolish of Avery to do anything bad to Jack, not when the police were on high alert and the trial of Leo. But he was holding him, she was certain of that. She could feel it.

A bang on the front door made them all jump and stand up. "Wait," Mike held his hand up.

Lucy's heart was pounding as she gripped Hilda's hand, praying it was Jack. They followed Mike towards the front door.

"Who is it?" Mike asked.

The voice that came back was the familiar one, which had been with Lucy since the day he'd found her. "It's me."

Mike unlocked the door and Jack walked in. The man she now knew she loved, was alive. She rushed forward and hugged him as if she'd never let him go. Tears streamed down her face.

"It's okay," he reassured, "I'm alright."

Relief flooded through her, she clung on to him desperately. He was alive. She didn't want to let him go, but she had to. Hilda was hovering. She too flung her arms around him and hugged him tightly, "Thank God you're safe, Jack. You had us scared there for a while."

They sat together in the lounge. Lucy had a desperate urge to take Jack into a room so they could be alone. She wanted to feel his arms around her again. But for now, she had to be content with just having him there.

"I can't tell you anything," Jack rubbed the back of his neck, "I wish I could. I went out onto the terrace for a cigarette, the next thing I knew I was grabbed and a rag was pressed to my face. Chloroform I guess. I don't remember anything after that. I woke up wherever, handcuffed to a bed. I had one of those sleep flight masks over my eyes and a gag in my mouth. Someone was with me in the room the whole time."

"How many of them?" Mike asked.

"No idea. I sensed just one. If there was another, they didn't communicate with each other."

"Did they speak at all?"

"Only to say not to try removing the sleep mask. I guessed it was someone working for the Montgomerys and the idea was to stop Lucy giving evidence?"

"Yeah, we think that's pretty much it."

"Then how come they let me go?" The line of his mouth tightened, "What was the point?"

"You'll have to ask Lucy that. She went to see Avery."

A spasm of anger crossed Jack's face. He glared at her, "Please tell me you didn't?" Her silence spoke volumes. He reeled back at Mike, "Why the hell did you let her do that? He could have harmed her."

286

"I think that was unlikely, given the current situation. And she did a good job of persuading us it was the only way to get you released. As it turns out, she was right. You're back."

Jack gave her a look that told her there was more to discuss later. He carried on, "About an hour ago, they bungled me into a car, still wearing the blindfold and dumped me a mile down the road. I have no bloody idea where I've been."

"That's good," Mike said. "If you'd seen anything and you were able to expose them, you might have not been released so easily. How far away do you reckon you've been?"

"Maybe about fifty minutes, it's hard to tell." He turned to her, "Have you told Jenna? I need to speak to her, she'll be frantic."

Lucy shook her head, "I haven't got her number so I couldn't let her know anything. I daren't ask when I went to Oak Ridge where she was as I didn't want anyone to know I'd met her. The last thing I wanted was to compromise her."

"You didn't see her?"

"No. Just Avery and Bridget the housekeeper."

Jack reached for his phone. "They threw this at me the same time they threw me out of the car. I can't believe it didn't break." He glanced at his messages, "There is one message from her saying she's okay, but I'm not so sure I believe it."

"Why wouldn't you believe it?"

Jack sighed, "I've tried ringing her but she won't answer."

"I'm sure it's nothing," Hilda said. "She could just be resting. She'll be out of there soon with a bit of luck."

"Yeah. They don't have anything on her, thank God. We agreed driving back after Oban we wouldn't speak about the trip, and as far as I know the Montgomerys thought she'd been with me in Cornwall. I'll try ringing again in a bit.

Later that evening, after Mike had left and Hilda had discreetly gone to her room, Jack topped their wine glasses up, before trying Jenna's number again.

"Still no answer," he said, and stared intensely at her. "I've sent messages and they've delivered, but no reply."

"You don't think they'd harm Jenna do you?" Lucy asked, knowing that she wouldn't put it past the evil bastards.

Jack sighed.

"I really don't know what to think. Tell me what it was you said to Avery? Truthfully. How did you get him to release me?"

"I just told him I was all set to give my evidence regardless of whether you were released or not. I said I could say only what I knew about Isaac Davey's death, or a whole lot more. It was entirely up to him. But if he let you go, I'd only give evidence about the chauffer."

"And he bought that?" he was scrutinising her face. He didn't look convinced.

"I guess he must have done. They released you."

288

"Yeah, thanks to you. It was a brave thing to do." He took her hand, "You must have been terrified going back to Oak Ridge."

"I was," she said, "but the thought they might do something to you, terrified me more."

"Me too. But I kept thinking why would they? The police would be all over them if I hadn't been released. They wouldn't want that. But I did think they'd hang onto me a bit longer. It doesn't make sense they let me go on your threats."

She shrugged but couldn't look him in the face.

"That's not all, is it?" he pressed, "tell me. I don't want secrets between us. I only want to move forward with honesty. You want that too, don't you?"

"Course I do."

"We've got a lot of evidence collated that you've told me already. But I have a feeling you're holding back on me. Avery wouldn't let me go on your threats. Why would he? He held me for a reason. So you must have said something and it had to be good for him to release me."

Much as she loathed to, she had to tell him. Jack wouldn't let the matter drop. "Okay," she swallowed, "I'll tell you what leverage I used. It's not very pleasant though."

"I'm listening."

His hand grasped hers tightly while she began to explain the horrendous night Avery had come to their suite of rooms. It had always been a mystery as to why. It was most unusual for him to do that.

"I was keeping my head down purposely as the escape was only two days away. I'd avoided going to dinner with Avery and Susan. Because I was supposedly ill, I could get away with that, which was a relief. Anything was preferable to sitting with those two.

"That particular night, Leo was out, doing the rounds at the nightclubs, and I was flicking through TV, sitting in just a nightdress when Avery tapped on the door on some pretence of an issue concerning Leo. I was uncomfortable as I was half dressed and I could see he'd been drinking. As soon as he saw me, he had an odd look on his face. I asked him politely to leave, making an attempt at a joke that I wasn't dressed for visitors, but he came and sat on the sofa. Before I knew it, he attempted to kiss me. I pushed him away, which only incensed him. He ripped my nightdress off and forced himself on me, in my own lounge, on our sofa. I have no idea what made him do it. As horrible a man as he is, it seemed totally out of character, even for him."

She wiped her wet cheeks with her hand. It was painful reliving something she'd never said out loud to anyone.

"It was terrible, Jack," she sniffed, "I wanted to go to the police, but the plan for me to get away from Oak Ridge was only days away, so I wasn't in a position to get any retribution." She reached for a tissue to blow her nose. "I probably wouldn't have dared go anyway. What was the point when your own husband would believe his father rather over you?"

290

Jack pulled her to him and wrapped his arms around her. "You are the bravest woman I know. And do you know what? I love you for your strength. You amaze me."

His words thrilled her and instantly made her mood go from darkness to light. She reeled back. "What did you say?"

"That you're a brave woman . . ."

"No, Jack. The other bit."

"That I love you?"

She couldn't take her eyes off his. "You do?"

"Yep, I do." He took a huge breath in. "Those aren't words I've used a lot in my life. And never with a woman I've only ever shared a chaste kiss with. But right now, I feel like a schoolboy anxiously waiting to see if you feel the same."

"Oh, Jack, she said, her heart swelling, "I think I've loved you from the day you first walked into the shop."

His huge hands clasped her face and he brought his mouth unhurriedly down on hers. This kiss was gentle at first, and as her lips opened to invite him inside, he deliberately deepened it. She became lost in the magic of his masculinity and found herself matching him as his mouth demanded more. Sensations ran through her, the like of which she thought she'd never experience again . . . but he abruptly stopped and pulled away. A bereft feeling flooded through her as he steadied his breathing. "I think we need to get the next few days over with and then we'll concentrate on us, shall we?"

He was right. Now wasn't the time. Her heart gave a leap at the thought of future intimacy with him, but that would have to wait. Soon they'd have as much time as they needed to explore their feelings for each other. He was back and that was all that was all that mattered.

As she lay in her luxurious bed with the boys sleeping peacefully near-by, she couldn't sleep for excitement. Jack felt the same way as she did. She said a little prayer, thanking God he was safely back with her. It had been the longest day of her life. Returning to Oak Ridge after five years had been traumatic, but it had been the right thing to do. The pallor on Avery's face when she'd shown him the boys' picture made her confident he'd release Jack, which he'd had to do. He needed to understand for every action there were consequences. Avery prided himself on being sharp. This time though, he wasn't as clever as he thought he was. She'd outsmarted the family once before and she was certain she'd done it again – a lie had many variations. The question now was, on the strength of what she'd told him, would he, to save his own skin, get his son to plead guilty to manslaughter?

She'd put her life on it that he would.

Chapter 47

London

Lucy exited the car outside the court accompanied by Jack. The judge was going to allow her to give evidence which must have meant that Leo wasn't intending to plead guilty. Nerves were making every hair on her body stand on end. She'd prayed so hard she wouldn't have to.

Jack held her hand tightly as he escorted her towards the court door with the help of the police making a pathway through. The crowd numbers had increased tenfold since her first appearance when nobody knew about her. She couldn't ignore the taunts. 'Where've you been hiding, Mrs Montgomery?' 'Are you here to put the final nail in your husband's coffin?' It was a relief when they made it inside the foyer and the doors closed behind them.

Justin Coffey was there to meet them and ushered them both into a side room. "Leo's changed his plea – guilty to manslaughter."

"No?" Jack shook his head, "I can't believe it. Thank Christ."

"We've got exactly what we wanted. I've met with his brief, they're going for guilty on the grounds of diminished responsibility. They'll put forward Leo was under stress at the time and have medical assessments, which he'll milk for all its worth to get himself a lesser sentence." Justin shrugged, "Murder would have been better but it was always a challenge getting a conviction. He could have walked if the jury found him not guilty."

Jack scowled. "I'd have preferred life."

"Yeah, but it's still a good result." Justin looked directly as her, "You did it, Lucy. He'll be behind bars and have plenty of time to think. You'll always be out there and can expose him at any time. And another cause for celebration is, now you're free, you can live a life where you aren't hiding anymore."

"Yes, maybe so," she pulled a face, "but there's part of me that thinks I'm never going to be able to breathe easy."

"That'll pass, I'm sure. Get a few months under your belt and you'll be fine. Five years is a long time to have spent looking over your shoulder."

"Do you know if Leo's here?" Jack asked, "I'm wondering if Jenna's around?"

"No, he's not here. I saw his father briefly first thing, not sure why he came though if his son wasn't appearing in court."

"Maybe to see the barrister?"

Justin shrugged, "Maybe. Who knows?"

They made their way to the court exit and stopped to their goodbyes. Justin playfully thumped Jack's shoulder, "And as for you, my dear friend, you set out to free your sister, and you've done exactly that. Jenna's not even legally married to Leo so, it'll be easy to extract herself from the family now."

"Yeah, you're absolutely right. I can't thank you enough." Jack shook his pal's hand, "Give us a couple more weeks and we'll get together for dinner. Jenna as well. How does that sound?"

"Sounds good to me."

"I'll be in touch then."

He gave Lucy a friendly hug and smiled kindly at her. "Sentencing will be next week sometime, I would think."

"Good." She wouldn't be there but she was certain Jack would be, to see Leo go down.

A movement caused Lucy to look to her left while Jack continued to speak to Justin. "Lucy's keen to get back to Oban, so I'll see if I can get her a flight for tomorrow. I'm going to be here for sentencing though."

Avery was obscured from Jack and Justin as he leant against a pillar staring directly at her. She caught his piercing narrowed eyes, still glowing with fire. She'd won – and he'd hate that. She'd beaten him. And by taking him on, she'd taken on the family and finally escaped their evil clutches. Now, thankfully, so would Jenna. But the best bit as far as she was concerned was, she had a hold over them. For as long as Avery was alive, he wouldn't want exposing. He couldn't cope with his son knowing what he'd done to her. That's why he persuaded Leo to change his plea, to save his own skin. They couldn't afford for her to give evidence. Avery had so much to lose if she spoke out. He could deny it all he wanted that he hadn't raped her, but she had the evidence that he had – or so he believed.

Jack touched her arm. "Are you ready?"

"Yes," she said, "let's get out of here."

Chapter 48

London

Jack had taken Lucy to a favourite bistro of his in Chelsea where they welcomed him like an old friend and gave them an intimate table away from the main hub. Hilda was looking after the twins and had urged Lucy to go out and enjoy herself before they returned to Oban the next day.

For the first time in years, she didn't have worry of constantly looking over her shoulder. He hadn't discussed their future or anything, there hadn't been any time for that, but they'd become so close, she was certain it wasn't the end for them.

Jack ordered food for them both telling her she wouldn't be disappointed with his choice. She happily let him. It was a delight to see the charming and charismatic Jack in action chatting to the waiter.

He raised his glass of wine. "Here's to the bravest woman I know."

She raised her glass, "And here's to Jack Carr, my hero who literally saved my life," she gazed intently into his eyes, "who I'm going to miss so much."

"Me too," his warm eyes mirrored hers with affection, "and I'm going to miss the boys. I don't want to think of going back to my house without them there."

"What, no cartoons on the TV, yoghurt stains on the kitchen table, and no more being woken up at five thirty each morning?"

"Ah, there is that, I suppose," he grinned. "Anyway, have you thought about what you're going to call yourself now? Are you going back to Grace?"

"Definitely not Grace Montgomery."

"What about your Christian name then, and sticking with Smyth. You could be Grace Smyth?"

She shook her head, "I'm happy with Lucy Smyth. I think I'll keep that. It's the business name and I've been much happier as Lucy than I ever was as Grace."

The waiter appeared and they began to eat their scallops and chorizo starters.

"What do you think?" Jack asked in between bites, "I told you this food was amazing."

"It certainly is. Thank you for bringing me. It's so nice to be out and feel normal without a constant knot in my stomach."

"Yeah, I bet. It would have been great if Jenna could have joined us, but we'll do that next time." His brown eyes twinkled, "I wanted you to myself tonight."

"I'm glad you did. But I am looking forward to getting to know her properly."

"Yeah, me too. You'll love her. I know I'm biased, but she is special. Sadly, she lost her mojo the day she married Leo, but it'll come back. Once I get her out of Oak Ridge, which I can do now, then the old Jenna will return. She's been through a lot, I probably don't know

298

the half of it. She puts on a brave face when I'm with her."

"I think you've been the best brother ever. You came and found me. Everything you've done is for her, she's lucky to have you."

He took her hand. "I wish someone had been there for you. I hate that you had to do it all on your own."

"Yeah, but let's not talk about that now. It's a night for celebrating."

"You're right. Oh, and by the way, I heard from Jenna. She replied to my texts. Seems Hilda was right, she was resting up with a migraine. I'll ring her tomorrow after I've taken you all to the airport and make sure she's okay. She'll be waiting to see how many years Leo gets banged up for. After that, I'll go to Oak Ridge and get her. I want to see that battleaxe of a housekeeper. It sounds like she wants hitting with a shovel."

Lucy laughed. "You are funny. That's exactly what she deserves."

"Thankfully, Jenna doesn't have to stay there now; and she's not even married to Leo, which in itself is worth celebrating."

"No," she sighed, "unfortunately though, I still am."

"Yeah, well, we'll soon get you out of that."

"Good." She took a mouthful of wine, "I'm not being awful, but it's such a shame about Jenna being pregnant, isn't it? It ties her to the family."

"Yeah, it does, but we'll bring him or her up as a Carr. It doesn't matter who genetically fathers a baby. Look at Jordan and Cory and how they've turned out."

Her stomach tightened. She quickly changed the subject. "You'll be a fantastic uncle to Jenna's baby, you're great with kids."

"I do my best. Anyway, I want to talk about us." He took her hand again, "I don't know about you, but I'm not sure about a long-distance relationship. I want you with me all the time," his eyes glistened causing her heart to flutter, "but I'll give it a go for a week or two."

"A week or two? That's not long."

"Okay then," he grinned, "four."

She rolled her eyes, "So after I leave tomorrow, when do I see you again?"

"How about next Friday?" It'll give me time to get Jenna moved into my house. And then I need to get back to the newspaper."

"Friday sounds good to me. I'll ask Hilda to get the sofa bed ready, shall I?"

"You must be joking," he scowled playfully, "they were the worst nights of my life. My feet were freezing sticking out the bottom all night. And it sent me mad knowing you were only up the stairs. I can't tell you how many nights I laid there frustrated as hell wanting to creep up to your room."

She smiled, loving him for his honestly. He paused while the waiter removed their plates. "I've still got a few months lease on the cottage."

"I thought you only had it for a month?"

"I did, but once I met you, I knew I'd need longer so I extended it. Maybe we can stay there together, with the boys, and then we can get to know each other properly? Although I must say," his eyes reflected warmth and honesty, "I feel I've known you forever."

"Yeah, me too," she said, wondering exactly what she'd done to be so happy. But before he went any further, she needed to share with him one concern.

"You're okay that I come with children?"

"Yeah, of course. I love kids. I want at least five of them."

"Five!" she squealed, "you can't be serious."

"I am. Deadly."

"Right, quickly moving on," she laughed, loving his enthusiasm for life. "I am looking forward to having a week in the shop to get sorted, and then Friday, you'll be coming. You'll fly up from now on, won't you?"

"Definitely. I only ever travelled by car so there were no flight records. I didn't want the Montgomerys knowing where you were once I found you."

"It's such a relief I can go back now and relax. Although we never did find out who tipped you off about me, did we?"

"No, and I don't suppose we will. But it doesn't matter now."

"No, it doesn't, thank goodness. I spent so long worrying that someone had discovered me with the car brake incident and being pushed into the road. But I think now, looking back, they were just accidents."

"Yeah, I'm sure you're right."

They returned to Jack's house after dinner. It was all quiet as they stepped into the darkened hallway. Jack carefully closed the door and locked it.

Without turning on any lights, he took her by the hand and led her through to the kitchen.

"A celebration," he said, keeping his voice low as he took a bottle of champagne from the fridge.

Lucy didn't need to ask what they were celebrating. They'd waited long enough. Tonight was their night.

"To us," Jack said as they clinked glasses.

"To us."

"Tasty stuff," Jack said and Lucy found herself burning up as he took her glass and placed both glasses on the counter.

"Oh, Jack," she said as he cupped her face in his hands.

She melted into his kiss as his mouth met hers and kissed him back, hands in his hair, their breaths soon becoming frantic.

No words were needed as Jack broke away, tugging her towards the stairs by the hand.

They made their way upstairs and she peeked at the boys before joining Jack in his room. He closed the door behind her and pushed her against it, bringing his mouth down on hers. Their lips moved effortlessly together. It was hardness meeting softness. His muscular body was liked steel against hers.

Not once did he pause. His mouth relentlessly devoured her, and she matched his ferocity. She couldn't breathe, but didn't want to. His huge arms enveloped her, and hers wrapped themselves around his neck as if she possibly could get any closer.

She met him kiss for kiss, nipping, sucking and biting. Desire swept over her. He felt as amazing as she always knew he would. She was eager to ride the tidal wave of lust that was making her insides shudder.

"I want you so much," he groaned as they effortlessly sank onto the bed, tearing at each other's clothes, his eyes consuming her naked body. "God, you're so beautiful," he sighed and the longing in his eyes thrilled her. She moaned with pleasure as he began the exquisite exploration of every inch of her.

She welcomed the weight of him as he moved his body onto hers. His lips were consuming her mouth again. The taste of herself on him excited her and she weaved her fingers through his hair as she met his need with a newfound desire of her own. Long, slow, mind-blowing kisses, each one seducing her beyond reason. His mouth was compelling.

"I need to be inside you," he breathed, reaching down and easing himself into her, sealing his body fully with hers.

Their joining went deeper than physical pleasure. His lips grazed everywhere; along her jaw, over her throat and then back to her lips.

"You're incredible," he breathed against her mouth, "I knew you would be."

She breathed his name over and over as the pressure mounted.

"You're so beautiful," he said.

And for the first time in years, as she crested the wave of heady emotions, Lucy felt alive again.

Chapter 49

London

Bridget gazed lovingly at the man asleep by her side. Her and Avery had made love during the night and now she was ready for him again. She snuggled into his nakedness, dropped a kiss on his shoulder, and he grunted awake.

It didn't take much coaxing before he was on top of her. God, how she loved him. It gave her a thrill they were actually in Susan's bed. She'd come to him during the night, stripped naked, and eased herself into bed with him. It felt right. She was where she should be. He was half asleep anyway and by the time he came round properly, he couldn't object to her being in Susan's bed as he was already deep inside her.

The coast was clear for them now. Jenna was still locked in her suite of rooms with security guarding her, and Susan was banged up in the hospital. It wasn't looking good for her, even though Avery was in denial and talking about her coming home. Bridget smiled with a sideways grin. Not quite the outcome she'd hoped for, but near enough.

"Are you going to the hospital this morning?" she asked as he flopped back on the bed.

"Yes. I've got to meet with the doctors today. They want to discuss the treatment options available. After that, I'm going to see Leo. They'll be transferring him next week."

"Well, I hope it isn't too far away. He'll be relying on you to visit regularly. And Susan of course," Bridget added, praying she wouldn't be around much longer.

"Yeah, me too." He got up from the bed. She loved to see him naked. For a man his age, he still looked fit. And she liked he wasn't embarrassed about his body.

"I'll have something ready for you tonight when you come back," Bridget said, "we can eat together." She was finally going to sit at the table where for years she'd served the whole family.

Avery was distracted, leaning on the dresser and checking his phone. She sidled up to him from behind and wrapped her arms around his chest. "Did you hear what I said?"

"Yeah, sorry," he pulled away from her, "I've got a lot on my mind. I'm going to have to tell Susan today about Leo changing his plea and that he's going to be permanently in jail. She's going to be devastated."

"She doesn't know yet?"

"No, of course she doesn't. She's too ill. I don't want to tell her but I can't avoid her questioning any longer. I've had to keep saying the case is still adjourned. Worrying about him isn't helping her recovery."

Bridget injected as much sympathy into her voice as she could. "I guess you can't keep it from her for ever, she needs to know."

"Yeah, no point in pretending any longer," he said as he made his way towards the ensuite.

"I'll make myself useful while you're gone. I've given Frank and the cleaners a couple of days off. I thought it best while this Jenna business is ongoing."

"Good idea. There's no need for you to do any food for me, though. I don't feel like eating much and I'll be late getting back. Get the security guys a tray though would you? And Jenna, she'll want something."

No way was she bothering with Jenna. The stupid girl wasn't eating any of the food she'd left her anyway. Each tray was untouched. She could starve herself to death for all she cared.

"It's no trouble, honestly," she said as he closed the door to the ensuite. Bless Avery, he was such a good man thinking of her well being. Her mind drifted to the main dining table the family used. Tonight they could have an intimate dinner together. Like a normal couple. It would be nice to cook something for him herself. She rarely got the chance to show off her culinary skills.

Bridget pottered around the main kitchen in the house. It was Frank the chef's domain normally, but she knew her way around. She oversaw everything in the house, that's why she was so good at her job.

She found some smoked salmon in the fridge, boiled some eggs and made a light mayonnaise. Not quite up to Frank's standards, but it looked appetising enough. The main course was easy. Beef stroganoff was a particular favourite of Avery's which was simple enough to do. She made a balsamic vinegar sauce and left the beef marinating so it'd be tender when she cooked it. She'd have everything ready in the warming trolley so she could dish up for her and Avery in the dining room and only have to leave to fetch their desserts.

Her next task was the dining room table. Susan had always insisted on formal dining each evening so she wanted to do the same for Avery. She took the fine china out of the cupboard the family used for entertaining. She set places for her and Avery opposite each other. It was going to be their first dinner together, the first of many, she hoped. She took the silver candelabra from the sitting room and placed it on the centre of the table. She always associated candlelight with romance. All that was missing was the wine. Again she selected one of Avery's favourite deep red clarets. She opened it and left it on the table to breathe. She stood back admiring her efforts. Everything was perfect. All that was missing was the man himself.

Avery returned to the house much later than she'd anticipated. She heard him go upstairs and talk to Greg and waited in the hallway until he came back downstairs.

"Hi," she smiled, loving the feeling of him coming home to her. "I've got dinner all ready in the dining room."

He scowled, "I said I didn't want any food when I came back."

"Yes, I know you did. But I thought that was just for my benefit with Frank being off. Anyway, it's been no
308

trouble, it's done now. You might as well have something. Can I get you a drink?"

He looked tired. It would have been a long day for him. She wanted to help relieve some of the pressure.

He sighed, "A large whisky and ice, then."

Bridget felt it was best he ate something and then he could rest. Sleep was important so she'd encourage him to go to bed – with her, hopefully. She longed to hold him and cradle him to sleep. Like the previous night. She'd hardly slept at all. In the darkness of the master suite, she'd gazed around the room she knew so well, where each morning she'd take tea to sickly Susan. Finally, she'd earned her place next to her love.

"I'll get that for you right now. You go take a seat in the dining room, and I'll be there shortly."

She almost did a hop, skip and a jump from the sitting room with his drink. The table was set beautifully, the food was warming, and she was wearing her new deep red cashmere sweater which she felt sexy in. When did life get so good? But as she opened the dining room door, Avery wasn't sitting down at the table as she expected. He was standing with his back to it, staring out of the bay window. Quite why, she had no idea. It was pitch black outside so he couldn't see a thing.

"Here you are," she handed him his drink. Three fingers of whisky with two ice cubes, just how he liked it.

"What's going on, Bridget?" he indicated with his head towards the table, "who've you set the other place for?"

"Me, of course. I thought it might be nice for us to have dinner together for a change."

His pained expression troubled her. He didn't look overjoyed to be dining with her. Maybe he had some bad news at the hospital? Her heart accelerated hoping it was the case.

"Is everything alright?" she asked. "Have you been given some news at the hospital? Come and sit down and you can tell me."

"I don't want to sit down," he snapped, "and I don't want dinner either."

"But I've made your favourite, beef stroganoff, and I've got the bottle of claret breathing."

"What don't you get?" his expression was tight with strain, "I'm not sitting down to an intimate dinner with you while my wife's in hospital."

"But you're happy to fuck me in your wife's bed, that's alright, is it?"

"Look, Bridget," his mouth formed an unpleasant twist, "it's been a tense few days. My wife's fighting for her life, and right now I've got my daughter-in-law under house arrest. I really don't want any more grief."

"I'm sorry, I can see you're tense. If I've added to your stress, that wasn't my intention. Do you want me to clear up the food and make my way home?"

He pulled out a chair at the end of the table, not one of the ones she'd set intimately for their dinner, "Sit down for a minute would you."

She took the offered seat and he took the adjacent one.

"We've had a great time you since we became intimate . . . what is it, a year or so?"

"Three."

"Three? Well, I've appreciated all your years' service and everything you've done for this family, and our relationship. Right now, I can't do anything about Leo, we just have to wait until he gets out. But I can look after Susan, she needs to be my whole focus. So, in light of everything that's gone on, particularly with regard to you and I, maybe it's time you started looking for a similar job, somewhere else."

"Another job?" her voice went up an octave, "what on earth do you mean? This family's my life. And you, Avery," she reached for his hand, "I can't leave Oak Ridge. Why would you even suggest it? I've nowhere to go, this is my home."

"I'm not talking about tomorrow," he said, "I'm just saying, now might be the time to begin the process of looking. I'll make sure you get severance pay for all your years' service. You'll not be out of pocket, I'll see you right, I promise."

"What are you saying – you want to us to finish?"

He moistened his lips, almost as if he was nervous. "I think its run its course and now might be the time to move on. I know we'll never get another housekeeper like you, you're unique and have served the family well. We'll always have fond memories of you."

Her muscles stiffened as she watched him reach for the open bottle of wine that was meant for the two of them.

"I promise we'll look after you," he said wearily. "Now, if you'll excuse me, I'm going to take this with me and get some rest. It's been a long day."

He paused in at the doorway. "I'm sorry, Bridget. I have to concentrate on Susan and her coming home. There won't be time for anything else. And now that Leo's best option is to pleading guilty to manslaughter, we'll let Jenna go in the morning. Her and that brother of hers can't do anything to hurt us now."

"Are you sure? What if she goes to the police and says we held her against her will?

"We'll just deny it. She's highly strung, nobody in their right mind would believe her. I'll sort it tomorrow. Goodnight."

Goodnight? He'd thrown in a huge grenade and all he could say was goodnight? Her insides burned with pain as she watched him leave. He wanted rid of her and he wanted to replace her at Oak Ridge. Over her dead body. She was their housekeeper. There wasn't anybody else that could do her job.

She moved towards the heated trolley and piled the uneaten starters on top ready to take to the kitchen. She began to clear the table, making sure she left the dining room in perfect order before she went home, just as she always did. That was her job and exactly what was expected of her. And she never did a bad job . . . ever.

Bridget paced the room in her own house, ready to burst. She was going crazy since Avery's rejection. After all her service and hard work, making sure Oak Ridge ran absolutely perfectly, and keeping Avery satisfied sexually. Yet he was discarding her as if she was a bloody domestic on a temporary contract. He wanted her to leave the only home she'd ever had. Well, he wasn't going to get away with it. Over the years she'd learnt from the family. Revenge was their motto. It wasn't wise to cross them. Now, it was her time to step up.

As far as she was concerned, after all her years' service and loyalty, she was a Montgomery.

Chapter 50

London

It was pitch black outside when Bridget made her way through the garden to the outbuildings and found the storeroom where the petrol was safely kept that the gardener used for the lawnmowers. There was always a good supply, that was her job, ensuring staff had the appropriate tools to work with. She located a wheelbarrow and swiftly moved the four canisters to the house via the back door, and quietly unloaded them into the sitting room.

Next, with purpose, she climbed the spiral staircase to Jenna's rooms. Steve had left earlier, something about his son being unwell. Greg, the other security chap was sitting on a chair on the landing desperately trying to stay awake.

He nodded a greeting to her as she approached.

"You can get off now, Greg," she whispered.

He stood up, no doubt eager to be going home to his own bed. "You're sure? I can stay until morning."

"I'm quite sure. Avery asked me to let you know. It's late I know, but you'll be paid fully, don't worry about that. If you follow me, I'll show you out."

The house was in darkness as they moved towards the staircase and made their way to the back entrance of the house. She'd disarmed the alarms and opened the door to let him out.

"Cheers. Let me know if I'm needed again?"

She nodded. "Mr Montgomery will be in touch."

She closed the door behind him and leant against it. Why had Avery tossed her aside as if she just worked for him? Especially when she'd freed him from ball-and-chain sickly Susan, who was unlikely to make a recovery and, if so, she was quite prepared to smother the sickly bitch her with a pillow anyway.

And how dare that stupid dimwit wife of Leo imply she was a servant, after all the love she'd bestowed on the family. Jenna was going to wish she'd never said that by the time she'd finished with her. Bridget South was much more than a servant and there wasn't anyone but her that could take care of Oak Ridge. It was her domain.

With speed, she made her way towards the sitting room to retrieve the petrol containers lined up where she'd left them. Taking three canisters with her, she placed a fourth on the bottom step of the stairs. She started to hum to herself as she liberally dowsed petrol in the main sitting room the family used, next she moved onto the dining room. She gazed at the immaculate table with the linen run perfectly in place, just how it should be. There was no evidence of the intimate dinner she'd planned earlier with Avery. With a steely determination, she drenched the table with petrol and the surplus on the floor, and left the normally closed door, wide open.

She walked back into the entrance hall and continued to pour petrol everywhere, resting the empty canisters at the bottom of the stairs. With a rush of adrenaline she picked up the canister she'd saved. As she climbed each step of the huge spiral staircase, she poured the petrol behind her. It was almost cathartic that the house was going to go up in smoke. Avery had dared to suggest the family would get another housekeeper – well they wouldn't now. She'd see to that.

Hadn't Avery always said the family couldn't do it without her?

Chapter 51

The petrol fumes were stinging Bridget's eyes and catching in the back of her throat as she placed the last canister on the top step of the stairs. That part of her plan was almost done. All she needed was one match. She touched her pocket to check the box was there; she'd removed it only minutes earlier from the kitchen drawer.

She glided along the landing as only she could do, silently. Another thing she'd perfected over the years, quietness. She didn't want to wake Avery. It was unlikely as he'd been drinking most of the day and when he'd returned from seeing Susan he was throwing it back. He'd even taken the bottle of wine to bed that she'd selected for their intimate dinner.

As she approached his room, she paused outside the door. Her love didn't want her anymore. He said it so must have meant it. And he said they would get another housekeeper. How dare he? They'd never find anyone as good as she was. She knew that, and Avery did. And what was going on in his head with all this Susan business. Since when had he been devoted to her?

She slowly turned the door knob and stood quietly inside the room bathed in darkness. Avery was fast

317

asleep on his back in the huge King bed. He looked peaceful. He belonged to her. The thought of sickly Susan being back in the bed beside him made her more determined it wasn't going to happen. That was her place now. She deserved it. She'd been loyal to him. They were going to be together on that tropical island and he would fish all day and she would tend house. That was still the plan – but now it would be in a different life.

Light through the drapes was shining on the small console table that always held a fascination for her. It beckoned like a beacon. The gun inside was the attraction. Growing up on a farm, she'd been taught how to use to them. Her father had shown her how to shoot and even though she hadn't handled a gun for years, she knew her way around one.

Quietly and slowly, she opened the drawer. The gun was still there as it always was. She reached for it and removed it from its pouch. It was heavier than she'd thought as she opened the chamber to make certain it was loaded. She counted six bullets – she needed three.

As she made her way towards the bed, she stared at her love sleeping soundly. Now was their time. They would be together. Her and Avery. Always.

She leaned forward and grasped the pillow at the side of him. It was an irony that it was Susan's pillow she was holding as she walked around to the side Avery was sleeping. She looked closely at the man who'd been her world. Even before they'd become intimate, she'd loved him from afar. She couldn't remember a time since she came to the house to work, that she hadn't.

"I love you so much, my darling," she whispered, as she placed the pillow level with his chest. She pushed the barrel of the gun against it and squeezed the trigger, blasting him through his heart.

Chapter 52

London

A loud bang woke Jenna. She sat up in bed. Had she been dreaming? Her digital clock on the bedside table showed ten minutes past two. She made her way to the bedroom window which overlooked the back of the house and the extensive gardens. Leo's office was visible but it was in darkness and she couldn't see any security lights on.

She swayed and had to grab the windowsill. Not eating was beginning to take its toll; she felt light-headed and queasy. The bang reverberated in her ears. What was it? She filled herself a tumbler of water from the bathroom tap and glugged it down.

It was the second night of being held prisoner. Each time she tried to go out onto the landing, there was a gorilla barring her way. She'd tried to engage with Steve but he didn't answer any questions nor rise to the bait when she goaded him, saying that as soon as she got out, she was going to the police.

Thoughts about Jack caused her the most distress. He'd have her out of there in no time if he knew what was going on. But he'd be getting texts from her phone via Bridget so wouldn't have any idea of what she was going through.

She quietly opened the door to the landing and peeped out. Neither Steve nor the other man was there. Had they gone to investigate the bang? It didn't matter. It was an opportunity to escape, even though she was in her nightdress. There was no time to go back and change, she had to make a run for it. She left the door open, not wanting the click to alert anyone, and tiptoed along the landing as swiftly as she could, terrified that Steve might return at any minute. There was a dreadful smell of petrol, causing her eyes to smart. The possibility of an explosion made her move with greater urgency. She almost reached the staircase when the door to Avery and Susan's bedroom opened.

Her heart rate stumbled over its own rhythm as Bridget stepped out. Jenna stopped. She was trapped. The spasm of anger on Bridget's face made her look predatory – like a mad woman. And her eyes, glowing with savage fire were terrifying, but it was her hand clutching a gun that caused sheer horror to rush through her at the thought she might be about to lose her life. She raised her hands defensively.

"What are you doing, Bridget?"

The first bullet hit her hard in the abdomen. Burning hot pain seared through her. She tried to grasp herself . . . a second bullet hit her . . .

And then darkness.

*

Bridget stood over Jenna where she'd fallen. Her dead eyes were wide open. Blood seeped from her torso,

321

pooling on the floor. The bitch looked scared, even in death.

"I'm much more than just a servant," Bridget snarled.

She turned towards the banister, opened the box of matches and selected one. A solitary little match, that's all she needed to destroy Oak Ridge, her home. She struck the match across the sandpaper, and watched the tiny flame begin to burn down the stick, before tossing it over the banister and down to the hallway. She heard rather than saw the hallway erupt in flames. By that time, she was walking away and back towards Avery.

Still carrying the gun, she opened the door to the master bedroom and climbed onto the bed next to her dead lover. It was her place, not Susan's. It was where she should be, next to her love. She lay on her back and lifted his cold hand to her mouth, kissing it gently before resting it back down, keeping hers linked to it.

"See you on the other side, my darling."

She lifted the gun to her heart and pulled the trigger.

Chapter 53

Oban

Lucy was driving Hilda to the shop. Both were eager to get back but the early morning traffic was heavy, making their progress slow. The children had been excited the previous day when they'd arrived home, racing around the house and garden full of energy. That morning they'd been eager to return to their nursery that was familiar to them.

"So, what do you think long term for you and Jack?" Hilda asked, "Oban or London?"

"God knows, it's been a complete whirl, hasn't it? We honestly haven't had a chance to discuss anything about our future. He's not keen on a long-distance relationship, that's for sure. He's kept the lease on at the rental for a couple more months, so that's good. It'll give us time to really get to know each other. I must say, I'm missing him already and I only saw him yesterday."

Hilda grinned, "That's love for you. I just knew you two were meant to be together."

Lucy smiled, "I'm glad you did, there was a time when I was ready to uproot and leave Oban."

"Yes, you were, but Jack was never going to let that happen. He's quite a man, isn't he?"

"He is. And while I don't want to live in London, that's where Jack's life is. He has the newspaper and Jenna there. So we'll have to see."

"What's Jenna going to do now? I guess she'll leave that prison you both lived in now?"

"I would think so. Jack said he's going to Oak Ridge today. She'll move in with him initially I would think. There's nothing to keep her there now she's not married to Leo." Lucy pulled a face, "That's the next thing for me, I've got to formally divorce him now."

"Good. The sooner you do that, the better."

"Definitely." She pulled up outside the back of the shop. "I'm looking forward to getting back to normal after all this time, aren't you?" she smiled at her dear friend. All they'd achieved had been with her help.

"I am, yes. It's certainly been a rocky few weeks."

"It has and you've been a brick. I couldn't have got through it without you. I can never repay you for being there for me, and Jack. You've been like a mother to him as well as me."

"Go on with you . . ." Hilda dismissed, turning to get out of the car.

As Hilda unlocked the front door and switched off the security alarm, they grinned like children at each other.

"I can't believe we're back," Hilda said opening the till.

"Me neither. Such a lot has happened since Jack first walked in, hasn't it?"

"You bet, but it all worked out in the end."

324

"It has, yes. Right, I'll check the workshop."

"I hope you find it in better order than the till and cash box," Hilda frowned, "I'm telling you now, if this is it and Kitty's not banked the takings, there will be trouble. I'm just going to give her a quick ring."

"Oh dear, I'll put the kettle on," Lucy said and made a hasty retreat.

Lucy checked the workshop stock. Several pieces were missing. The most expensive stones were locked away, but those she'd been working with and kept to hand in a drawer, were gone. She wasn't sure what to do. It would be hard to tackle Kitty, she wasn't a thief. A thought came into her mind which she had to quickly brush away. Had Tricky been in there? She wouldn't put it past him to steal from them.

Hilda came into the workshop.

"Here," Lucy nodded to the mug, "I've made you tea."

"Thanks, love. I've spoken to Kitty, apparently she has been to the bank. I'll check online later. It doesn't sound like we've taken that much though." She shook her head. "Why am I not surprised? You know what her sales technique will be like, take it or leave it. Anyway, you're never going to believe it," she widened her eyes, "she's asked if she can come round tonight and bring Tricky. Apparently they've got some news."

"What sort of news?"

"Lord knows. Whatever it is, it'll be a ten-day wonder."

"Do you think she might be pregnant?"

"I doubt that very much. Kitty can barely look after herself let alone a baby."

Lucy was relieved she hadn't mentioned the missing stock. She was going to subtly find out if Tricky had been in her workshop. But not right away. It was best to settle back in first and concentrate on Jack arriving on Friday.

"I'll pop out after lunch and get us a couple of pies from the butchers," Hilda said, "Kitty likes those and I guess Tricky Dicky will eat them. I can hardly see him as the vegetarian type can you?"

"No, I can't." Lucy pulled a face, "I wish he wasn't coming. He makes my skin crawl. You don't think they're getting married or anything do you?"

"Let's hope not. I don't want him in our lives at all. She's an air-brain for even entertaining him."

The shop doorbell chimed. Hilda stood up, "Someone's early. I hope this isn't those Jehovah Witnesses. I took a brochure from them a few weeks ago and when I got out the van this morning, I saw them in a pack down the road, loitering."

Lucy smiled, "Oh heck, that'll be why they're back then. Rumour has it they put a chalk mark on the wall of anyone gullible they can entice into their flock."

Hilda rolled her eyes, "I wouldn't put that past them."

Lucy took a sip of her tea. It was a huge relief to be back in Oban. Whatever happened in the future, she really didn't want to leave the place. A warm happy feeling

326

gripped her, thinking of Jack, but there was still a touch of unease. The question that still lingered in her mind about who'd tipped him off that she was in Oban. They never did find out.

Her ear became attuned to the shop. Was she imagining it? Hilda was talking to a man and her heart leapt at the familiarity of the voice. She rushed through.

"Jack," she ran towards him and threw her arms around him. It seemed completely natural. He hugged her tightly – too tightly. Something was wrong. He shouldn't be there until Friday. She pulled away, "What is it?"

His face was crestfallen. He swallowed, "Jenna's dead."

Had she heard him correctly? "Dead . . . Jenna?"

"Oh, my Lord," Hilda said, "Come in the back and sit down."

Lucy couldn't take her eyes off his tortured face as he took the stool Hilda pulled out for him.

"Tell us," she urged, "what's happened?"

A chill ran through her as in barely a whisper he said, "The housekeeper shot her and Avery, then turned the gun on herself."

All three of them sat stunned. It was eerily quiet.

She took his hand, "Bridget? She did that? I don't understand. Why?"

"I don't know. She set fire to the house as well, so it's all a bloody mess. Jenna was found on the landing, Bridget and Avery were on the bed."

"Bridget and Avery?" Lucy scowled. It was one of those moments that you just couldn't quite believe. Bridget and Avery, together?

Hilda got up, "I'll go and make some tea," and left them together. Lucy stood up and wrapped her arms around him as he sat. His head rested on her abdomen. "I'm so sorry, Jack, truly I am. What a terrible tragedy. Poor Jenna."

She held him tightly, trying to give him strength.

He took a deep breath in, "I just wanted to be with you, so got a flight and drove straight here. I couldn't stay in London."

"You did right. Stay here with us. It's a terrible shock, you need a few days to come to terms with it."

"Yeah," he nodded. "I've brought some stuff with me. Thank God I've still got the lease on the cottage. I'll crash here for a few days and then go back to make the funeral arrangements."

"Here we are," Hilda came in carrying fresh mugs of tea. "I've managed to find some brandy, so I've put a little tot in . . . for the shock," she said putting one in front of each of them. "I'm going to ring Kitty and cancel tonight. Whatever she has to say can wait a day or two."

"Don't cancel anything because of me," Jack said wearily.

"It's fine," Hilda said, "it's not as if we were looking forward to it. It'll keep."

Lucy watched Hilda fussing round them both. What a remarkable woman. She'd dropped everything to come to London with her to help with the boys. Every step of the way she'd been there for them. She truly was the dearest friend anyone could have. Lucy gave her an affectionate glance while still clutching Jack's hand, "Thank you."

Chapter 54

London

Lucy looked around the church at those attending Jenna's funeral. There were plenty of people dressed up in their finery. She recognised their type, she should do, she'd lived as part of the clique for so long. Jack couldn't stop the Montgomerys' friends and associates attending. The service was simple enough. Jack had written the eulogy and discussed it with the vicar.

Lucy couldn't help but cry for dear Jenna who had been cruelly taken. She hardly knew her, having only met her briefly, but through Jack she felt she did. And Jack's pain was her pain. He blamed himself for not going to Oak Ridge sooner but as she'd tried to reassure, nobody could possibly know what Bridget was capable of. Such heinous crimes were unimaginable.

The undertakers came in after the service had finished and wheeled Jenna's coffin outside the church. Jack had requested the internment was private, and the order of service booklets had instructed those attending who wished to attend the wake, to make their way to a local hostelry he'd organised.

Her and Jack stood at the graveside clutching each other's hands. They'd come through so much together, all down to Jack's tenacity, yet the one person he'd been

330

trying so desperately to save, wasn't going to be there with them for the promising future that beckoned.

They stood hand in hand at the graveside while the vicar said the usual words before the coffin was lowered into the ground.

"Bye, Jen," Jack threw a rose onto the coffin, followed by a handful of soil.

"Come on," she whispered after a reasonable amount of time, "let's go." As they walked back towards the church, Lucy's eyes were drawn to a woman in a wheelchair wrapped up in a blanket. As they got closer she realised who it was. She'd aged considerably, appearing almost like an elderly woman when she couldn't be more than sixty at the most.

"It's Susan Montgomery," she told Jack, not sure if he had met her before.

He stiffened.

"She looks ill, be careful," Lucy warned.

Susan was clearly waiting for them. Her tiny eyes were haunted with inner anxiety and her complexion seemed jaundiced.

"Could I have a word? I've not come to cause any trouble."

Lucy wasn't sure what Jack would do. He was glaring and possibly not sure what to say.

"Please, Grace," Susan asked in a suffocated whisper. It felt strange after all the years that had passed to be called Grace – the name she associated with so much sorrow.

"What do you want?" Jack asked.

She turned to the woman stood with her, "Could you give me a minute, Sonia please?" The accompanying woman moved away.

Susan looked ghastly and painfully thin. Lucy doubted she had long to live.

Her mouth was tight and grim. "I want to offer my deepest condolences, I'm terribly sorry for what happened. I liked Jenna and wished her no harm. I came today as I wanted you to have some closure. I don't know entirely what happened that night but I have an idea, if you'll hear me out."

"Go on," Jack said.

"My brain isn't what it once was, so it's taken me a while to work things out. I believe now that Bridget was slowly poisoning me. I'd been unwell and got muddled up with my tablets, but I think she was giving me extra disguised in drinks, on top of my legitimate medication."

"I don't understand," Lucy said, "why would she do that?"

"I think she wanted Avery. And the only way she could get him was by getting rid of me."

"Bridget and Avery?" Lucy scowled, "You think they were having an affair?"

Susan looked knowingly at her. "Avery, and sadly Leo, were not adverse to a pretty woman. So yes, I think probably Avery may have been having sex with the girl. And the fact she was found on my bed with Avery confirms it really."

"So what has this all got to do with my sister?" Jack asked.

"Only that I think she was in the wrong place at the wrong time. The night of the fire, Avery visited me in hospital. The doctors spoke to both of us and suggested I had high levels of paracetamol and opiates in my system, almost too high to have accidentally overdosed myself. They said the blood levels indicated it wasn't recent, it had happened over a period of time."

Susan slowly closed her eyes. Lucy saw the anguish as she opened them and carried on.

"I was terribly confused and the trial hanging over us had taken its toll. Before Avery left me that night, I mentioned that Bridget had been helping me with my medication and maybe she'd been accidentally giving me too many. It was just an off the cuff statement and that was it. But I think now maybe he tackled her, I don't know. But clearly something happened for her to have gone on the rampage like she did. Maybe your sister confronted her too, we'll never know. That's all I came here to say. I'm sure it won't help your loss, but I think it offers an explanation for what happened. I daresay the coroner will come to a similar conclusion."

Lucy nodded. It was sad to see Susan Montgomery's demise. She'd never been fond of her, and it was now apparent that she'd become a victim too.

"And the baby?" Jack asked. "The coroner said Jenna hadn't been pregnant."

"I'm afraid she had a miscarriage."

They'd guessed that. The sadness was Jenna hadn't told Jack, but Lucy reassured him that she probably wanted to tell him in person rather than by text.

A flicker of light appeared in Susan's weary eyes. "I understand you have twin boys?"

"Yes."

"Would it be too much for me to see a photograph of them? I always wanted grandchildren. We both did," a wave of sadness passed across her face.

Lucy reluctantly reached into her bag for her phone and brought up the screen save she'd shown Avery when she'd tried to get Jack back. She handed it to Susan.

"Oh my, oh my. What beautiful little boys." She peered more closely, "I can see they're Leo's. They already have the Montgomery genes, you can tell by their proud little noses."

Lucy's muscles tensed. There were no Montgomery genes – there couldn't be when they weren't genetically related. But she'd vowed to take that secret to the grave.

Susan waved for the carer and handed the phone back. "Please, if you would be so kind, give the boys a kiss from me. I would have loved them so much. I'm truly sorry, Grace for the way in which you had to leave Oak Ridge." She took a deep breath in, "I've been doing a lot of thinking recently; I guess that's normal as you sit in God's waiting room." She looked at Jack who'd remained silent the whole time. "I have to take some responsibility for everything that has happened, and I wanted to come here today and say how sorry I am about Jenna. Nobody deserved that."

The carer appeared and grasped the wheelchair.

Susan raised a hand to stall her and continued speaking to Jack.

"You have a life ahead of you, live it for Jenna. Don't blame yourself, she wouldn't want that."

With tears in her eyes, Susan nodded to them both as she was wheeled away. There was no more to be said. A dying woman had made her peace.

Jack was silent as they walked to the car. It was going to take time for him to come to terms with losing his dear sister. Nobody could have predicted Bridget, but he still blamed himself. The murders were so heinous, particularly when Jenna was so close to getting away from the Montgomerys and Oak Ridge.

There were no words.

Chapter 55

Oban

Gradually Lucy was slowly getting used to being involved with a man having spent so much time on her own, so from her perspective, the long-distance relationship with Jack was good. But it wasn't for him. He'd started looking at houses in Oban and was even exploring setting up a newspaper.

Each weekend he flew to Oban and stayed in the cottage and Lucy spent her time with him there. The way Jack was moving along, it wouldn't be long until they were together in their own home. Jack always included Jordan and Cory in their plans, it was as if he'd always been part of their lives, which she loved him for. He was still mourning Jenna, he found it hard to forgive himself for not going to Oak Ridge and helping her leave. But as she constantly reassured him, he couldn't have predicted Bridget's actions. Nobody could.

That evening, they were getting ready for Kitty coming for supper. Hilda had been putting it off since they'd found out the news Kitty had wanted to share about Tricky moving in which Hilda wasn't happy about. But now, because they'd become a couple, she'd felt obliged to include him in the late night suppers she loved hosting.

"It all looks lovely," Lucy said folding the napkins and placing them in the wine glasses. A twinge of unease clenched her tummy. Even though Jack would be there and she had nothing to fear anymore, she didn't like the thought of sitting down to eat with Tricky. There was something about him which had always unsettled her.

Hilda placed the bread basket on the table, "Of all the decent men in the world, and she hooks up with him."

"I know. He's the biggest slime ball if you ask me. I don't get why he even wants to eat with us."

"He probably doesn't. It'll be Kitty's doing."

The front door opening interrupted them, "Ah, here's someone now," Hilda said. Lucy knew who it was before he even announced himself. She could feel Jack when he was around her. She rushed to greet him, and as always when he'd been away from her, he wrapped her up in his huge arms, which made her feel soft and feminine. But more important than that, he made her feel safe.

"Can't we just slip away?" she whispered to him in the hallway, "I'm dreading sitting down with Tricky."

Jack shook his head, "It'll be fine, don't worry. After today, I think it'll be unlikely he'll be sitting down for any more meals with us."

"Why? I don't understand?"

"You will by the time we've finished eating. Come on," he raised the bottle of wine in his hand, "let's grab a drink, shall we? I've a feeling we're going to need it."

337

Hilda came into the lounge where they were sitting prior to dinner.

"Another half an hour and we'll be about ready, the meat needs a little longer."

Tricky was sitting with Kitty on the settee looking awkward, as if Hilda's house was the last place he wanted to be. Lucy had to keep her eyes averted, grateful he didn't appear to be one for polite conversation.

Jack handed Hilda a glass of wine. "There you go, you'll have earned this, I bet you've been at it all day, cooking for us."

Hilda smiled taking the glass from him, "It's no trouble, I love cooking."

"Well, lucky for us you do," Jack said and held up his glass. "Cheers everyone."

He turned to Tricky who was clutching a can of beer. "Do you want another, mate?" he asked, "we've got plenty. Kitty said you weren't a lover of wine."

"No," he grunted, "I'm not."

"I'll fetch one," Lucy stood up, pleased for an excuse to leave the room. When she returned and handed Tricky a can of beer, Jack was talking to him.

"What sort of work it is you do . . . it's Richard, isn't it?"

"Yeah, but I prefer Tricky. Labouring, stuff like that."

"What, on a building site?"

"And sometimes some farm work."

"Tricky has just been laid off," Kitty interjected, "that's the trouble with labouring, it's not guaranteed work."

"No, I guess not," Jack said.

"That's why we've decided on a bit of an adventure," she said gulping down her glass of wine.

Nobody said anything.

"Er . . ." Kitty glanced at each of them in turn, "do you want to know what it is, then?"

Lucy did her best to look enthusiastic, "Yes, go on."

"Since Tricky's moved in," Kitty looked sideways, as if trying to include him, "we've been thinking. We don't want to spend the rest of our lives stuck here in Oban. So, we're going to Spain. Tricky has got a mate out there and we're going to work in his bar for a while and see how it goes."

The silence was obvious. Nobody thought it was a great idea. Lucy felt uncomfortable, knowing Hilda would have something to say.

"What about your job?" Lucy asked.

"What about it? It's hardly a career working in a pub. Now we're together it seems a good idea to try something different."

Lucy didn't bother pointing out that she'd be doing the same job, just in a different country.

Jack nor Hilda spoke. They must have been thinking the same as she was. Who'd go anywhere with Tricky and what sort of mate did he have that owned a bar.

"Aren't you going to say anything?" Kitty asked glaring at Hilda, "it's unlike you to be quiet."

"It sounds like you've decided, so there isn't much point. I hope it works out for you," Hilda said, her voice devoid of any interest.

Jack took a mouthful of his wine and raised his glass, "Good luck, then."

The conversation had stalled. Jack topped up Kitty's wine glass, which she didn't acknowledge. Her face was full of fury.

"Thanks very much all of you for your enthusiasm," she said sarcastically, "it means such a lot to us."

"Anyone else?" Jack asked, clutching the bottle of wine.

The atmosphere was tense. Tricky was either oblivious, or just didn't want to get involved. He appeared to be completely disinterested in the conversation. She wasn't sure if it was deliberate or if it was ignorance.

Kitty's mouth formed an unpleasant twist. "I know, why don't we talk about your new house with Jack, Luce. I'm sure that'll create more excitement."

Lucy recognised the sarcasm and tried to deflect from it. "Not much to say really. We haven't made a final decision yet, we're going to have another look on Thursday at our favourite to make sure. We do like it though," she smiled at Jack, still excited to think she was going to be building her life with such an incredible man, "don't we?"

Jack met her eyes lovingly, "We do. It's got everything we need, plenty of space and a big garden for the boys."

"I'm surprised you aren't living in London," Kitty said, the negative tone in her voice obvious, "that's where your work is, wouldn't you be better living there?"

"I'm most probably selling the paper," Jack replied. "Lucy wants to stay round here and be close to the shop. And who'd want to leave Hilda anyway?" he winked at Hilda who he'd joked was his surrogate mother, which she absolutely loved. "She's the glue between us all, so we want her to be part of our life still, which she'll be if we settle in Oban."

Hilda's little face was a picture. She was all fluffed up.

Jack carried on. "So . . ." he stared intensely at Kitty and Tricky, "it seems that your efforts to get Lucy to leave Oban have been a complete waste of time."

Lucy turned her head towards him. He'd lost her. She didn't understand what he was saying, but she did notice Tricky shift awkwardly in his chair.

"Sorry?" Kitty frowned.

"Are you?" Jack asked.

"Sorry about what?" Lucy said looking directly at Kitty and Jack.

Jack spoke again. "Haven't you worked it out yet?" he looked at her and Hilda, "these two are the ones responsible for the accidents. Tricky here will have tampered with the brake pipes on the car and he'd be the jogger that pushed you into the road, or one of his mates. Is that right, Tricky?"

"Don't be so ridiculous," Kitty snapped, her face colouring, "why would we do anything like that?"

Jack raised his eyebrows, "You tell me. But you did do it, the pair of you. I know you did."

Hilda appeared equally as stunned as she was. "Tell me this isn't true, Kitty?"

341

Kitty looked mortified. Tricky was fidgeting, as if he was going to make a run for it.

"Why?" Lucy couldn't believe what she was hearing. "Why would you do something like that?"

Kitty's normally pretty face contorted with resentment, "Because I'm sick to death of you being the golden girl," she snapped, "you're not even a blood relative, yet Hilda treats you as if you are one."

Her nostrils flared as she turned on Hilda. "I'm your niece but you haven't a kind word for me. It's all about Lucy and now we all know why." She looked scornfully at Lucy, "You left wealth and privilege behind in London and decided there was equally as rich pickings here. I can see right through you, even if Hilda can't."

Kitty stood up, "Come on," she said to Tricky, "we're going."

"Wait," Jack said firmly, standing up. But Tricky made a run for it. He was out of the door in a second, minus his jacket which Lucy had hung in the closet.

"Leave him, Jack," Hilda said, standing up, "he's not worth it."

Lucy glared furiously at Kitty. "How could you? I was terrified. I thought I'd been found. You had no idea what that family were capable of. What sort of a person are you?"

Kitty started to cry, "I didn't mean for anyone to get hurt. It was just to frighten you. I wanted you to go," she sniffed, "Have you any idea what it's like when I'm pushed out all the time while you're in pole position?"

Jack's voice was calm. "How did you find out Lucy was Grace Montgomery, because it was you that emailed and texted me the information?"

"Does it matter?"

"It does actually," Lucy said, "it matters to me."

Kitty wiped her tears with the sleeve of her jumper. "I was in the doctor's surgery, flicking through a really old magazine and I saw a photograph of Leo Montgomery with his wife, Grace. I was staggered at the similarity to you. I watched you then, and read up on everything I could about the Montgomery family. I found out about his second wife who had a brother that ran a newspaper. So it was easy enough to get his email and message him." The tears continued to flow which was unusual for Kitty. Lucy couldn't remember ever seeing her do that before. Unless they were crocodile tears – she wouldn't know anymore with Kitty.

"I thought we were friends," Lucy said, "I can't believe it, I really I can't."

"I just wanted you to leave Oban and not come back. Before you came along, Hilda looked to me for everything. But you pushed me out. Have you any idea how that feels?"

"I've never pushed you out, not intentionally anyway. Why would you think that?"

"Because it's true. You know as well as I do Hilda thinks more of you than me. All she does is criticise me, but you, oh, you can do no wrong. 'Look at Lucy, how fantastic is the jewellery, how gorgeous are Lucy's boys, Lucy is the best mum', on and on it goes. Whereas everything Kitty does is wrong. And Lucy Smyth gets everything," she sniffed, "Alex at the pub, he wants you, Jack arrives, Lucy gets him. Have you any idea how tiresome the Lucy Smyth appreciation society is? The only bloke not interested in you is Tricky."

Hilda was shaking her head, "Lucy could have been hurt, killed even, thanks to you."

"Well, she wasn't. And she's bagged herself a rich bloke, so no harm's been done."

"What a selfish girl you are. Well you've certainly shown your true colours. You better go and leave us in peace."

"Don't worry, I'm going." Kitty rushed towards the door, "Nobody got hurt, it's no big deal." She walked out and slammed the door behind her.

Jack sat back in his chair and despite the seriousness of the situation, he had a glint in his eye. "Well, all I can say is, every cloud and all that, at least Tricky's not interested in you."

"Jack," Lucy chastised sharply, and turned to Hilda. "I can't believe all this, can you?"

Hilda shook her head, "I could believe most things of that girl, but not this. I could crown her, I really could. I think it's time for something stronger right now. Anyone joining me?"

"Go on then," Jack said, "I'll have a small brandy with you."

Once Hilda had left the room, Lucy tackled Jack. "I'm surprised you're finding this so funny."

"I'm not. It's pathetic really. It did amuse me though the way she said Tricky was the only bloke that wasn't interested in you," he rolled his eyes, "as if that somehow gained him a badge of honour."

She shook her head dismissively. "When did you find out it was them?"

"Around the time of Jenna's funeral. I was thinking about the last time I'd seen her, which was in the car going back to London after she visited me here. I recalled her teasing me about liking you, which I hotly denied by the way." He smiled and his dependable brown eyes crinkled at the edges. "I told her that I wasn't one bit interested in you. Then we talked about the lovely afternoon tea Hilda did for us and Jenna mentioned Kitty and how she felt that she was jealous to death of you." He shrugged, "I hadn't noticed anything, but she clearly had. I guess it's women's intuition and all that. But it got me thinking and I sort of put two and two together. I wanted everything else sorted out before I confronted her. Tricky being here was good. I wanted him to squirm. He looked incredibly shifty when I said about the brakes and pushing you. I've never seen anyone move so fast. He'll be bricking himself now that you might go to the police."

"As if. I've had enough police and legal stuff to last me a lifetime. It does upset me though. I was so scared at the time that Leo and Avery had found me. I almost ran away from Oban and would have done had you not stopped me."

"I know you were scared, but we've put everything to bed now. So there's nothing else, only us moving forward," he reached for her, "no more mysteries and secrets from now on."

She smiled lovingly at him. Hilda came through the door, "I've decided to dish dinner, it won't keep. Let's go and eat that then we need to get our heads together to decide how we move forward with madam after all that."

They followed Hilda into the dining room. Jack had said they'd put everything to bed now. That wasn't quite true. There was one more secret she hadn't shared. However, she'd vowed nobody need ever know about that.

But it still made her uncomfortable that she was keeping it from him.

Chapter 57

Oban

She held Jack's hand as they wandered around the spacious multiple bed-roomed house in Oban with the most stunning views over the bay. Because it was a second viewing and the house was empty, the estate agent had given them a key to look round themselves.

"So, what do you think?" Jack wrapped his arms around her.

"I think it's perfect for us."

He kissed her. "So we should make an offer?"

"Yes, we should, definitely."

"We'll be happy here," Jack said, "I know we will. I can feel it's been a house that's been loved."

"Yeah, you're right, it has a nice feel to it. And it's got everything we need and more."

"Yep, plenty of bedrooms for our brood of kids."

"Steady on with the brood if you don't mind," Lucy said, "I haven't agreed to that yet. But it'll be nice for the boys to have a room of their own when they're older, that's for sure."

"Yeah, definitely."

"I've been thinking also, if we do have more children and we have a girl, we could make sure we include your sister and have Jenna in her name."

His eyes widened with affection, "That's so nice. How did I get this lucky to end up with you?"

"No, I'm the lucky one."

"What about including Grace also in her name. That is actually who you are."

She shook her head. "I don't think so. I wasn't happy as Grace, that's why I ended up marrying Leo, I think. I'd lost my mother, was lonely and he swept me off my feet."

"The same as Jenna. We'd lost our mum and dad and Leo honed in on her when she was vulnerable. I hate that bloody family."

"Me too."

"Will you tell the boys about Avery being their dad when they're old enough?"

She nervously moistened her lips. It was the only blot on her horizon. She had to tell him. Their future was together, they needed honesty between them. He was gazing out onto the lawn, no doubt planning in his mind how it could look in the future.

"There's something I need to tell you."

He turned his head towards her and his eyes narrowed. "Why have I got the feeling I'm not going to like this?"

"Shall we sit down for a minute?"

They sat on the window seat overlooking the garden. Jack had asked that they were always honest with each other and she hadn't been totally honest with him . . . not about everything. It was a secret she was hoping to take to her grave as it was nobody else's business, but she didn't want to keep it from him. It was important he knew.

"You know that night we went out in London together for dinner when Leo agreed to plead guilty?"

"Yeah, the first time we slept together."

She rolled her eyes, "Only a man would remember that bit."

He laughed, "It was a good night. Go on, I'm listening."

"You said to me you wanted total honesty from me, and I explained to you I'd got Avery to let you go by telling him the boys were his and if he didn't let you go, I'd go to the police and have him on a rape charge."

"Yeah, I remember."

She struggled to get the words out. She'd never said them aloud before. And emotionally she'd buried them. It was so horrific.

"So what you saying now," he urged, "it wasn't true?"

"Avery did rape me before I flew to Switzerland to supposedly end my own life, that bit's true, but not the bit about him being the boys' father. I threatened him with that to get him to free you."

Jack blew out a breath. "Well, I can't deny I'm glad he fell for it. But what are you saying, Leo is the twins' father?"

"No, he isn't either."

His handsome face scowled. "I'm finding it hard to keep up here. Who the hell is their father then?"

She was searching for the right words. It meant delving into a place long buried.

"Go on . . . who?"

"You remember I told you to convince Leo I had actually taken my own life in the Swiss clinic, I had to be given a drug which put me in to an unconscious state?"

"Yeah," he nodded, "Midazolam. I looked it up."

"Yes, Midazolam, which rendered me unconscious. It stopped me breathing, which they needed to do. They flooded my system with oxygen so it would continue to circulate, then withdrew it for Leo to see me, which he did from behind a screen. Only my face was visible inside the coffin. They had a diversion tactic if he required longer. I think it was the fire alarm going off. They would have to get oxygen inside me after so long. Seemingly, luck was on their side. Leo had taken one look and was out of there.

"I came round in a chair, like a dentist chair, and the anaesthetist, a fairly old guy, was taking my blood pressure. I was so relieved to have actually woken up and the joy and elation when he called my name and I realised I was alive was immense." Her mind drifted back to the most vulnerable time in her life. "Even now, I can still hear him saying, 'Ah, you're awake, how are you feeling?' and me answering, 'groggy. How did it go?'

"I knew I'd done it. I'd escaped. Finally I was free of the Montgomery family. The doctor reassured me all was well and went to get the police officers who were waiting to move me on. I remember being terribly sleepy and out of it.

"I was taken to a small room to shower in and within no time at all, I was moved away to a safe house. It wasn't until months later I discovered I was pregnant. The only conclusion I could come to was the doctor the police had used had raped me while I was unconscious. I was quite far on into the pregnancy when I found out, but even if I hadn't had been, termination wouldn't have been an option. I decided the baby, I thought it was only one initially, was mine and I'd blot the doctor out. And that's the way it's been ever since. I don't think about a father for them."

She looked up to see Jack's moist eyes.

"It's okay," she caressed the side of his face and looked deep into his eyes. "How unlucky can you get, eh? Not one but two rapes."

He wrapped his arms around her, tightly. "I wish I'd been there to protect you." She loved the warmth of his embrace, she'd never tire of it. Jack was her strength.

He pulled away and his eyes focused on hers. "I'm in awe of what you've been through and I'm going to spend the rest of my life making sure you never have a single sad day in it." He wrapped her in his arms again and for a few minutes they clung silently together.

Relief flooded through her that she'd finally spoken it out loud. It was unusual for her to think about the anaesthetist now, she never did. She'd decided to obliterate him from her thoughts, much as she'd like him prosecuting for what he'd done. But that would have meant at the time exposing she was alive and she couldn't do that. So she remained silent, much as it disgusted her. Now, by telling Jack, it felt like she'd bought herself freedom and a future. She loved him for everything he'd done for her and would spend the rest of her life loving him. And as much as she hated the Montgomerys, the irony was, they had inadvertently brought Jack into her life.

He pulled away from her. "Well, if there are any positives in all of this, this is one. If Leo comes looking when he gets out of prison to see the boys, there'd be no point. Not when they aren't his. Which means you're finally free of that evil family," he kissed her gently. "So, on that heart-warming note, we'd better get a move on." He stood up and reached for her hand.

"What, to the estate agents?"

"No, not there. I'll ring them. We have something more important to do than that," he grinned mischievously as he locked the house door behind them.

"We do?"

She loved him for adding the humour after such a terribly sad conversation. "Tell me," she said as they climbed into the truck, "Where are we going? I've got to pick the boys up from nursery soon."

"We aren't actually going home right now."

"We aren't?" she frowned, "where then?" She reached in her bag for her phone, "I'd better text Hilda to see if she can shut the shop early and pick up the boys."

"No need. She knows. In fact she's meeting us with the boys."

"Meeting us where?"

"I'll tell you when we get there."

"Tell me now."

"You'll have to be patient, Miss Smyth, it's a surprise." He grinned lovingly at her. "Do you know, Smyth has never suited you, Lucy's okay though, you'll always be Lucy to me."

"Never mind about that. Where are we going?"

"Do you like Lucy Carr? I do like the sound of that. It really suits you."

"What are you talking about? If that was some sort of proposal, it was rubbish."

He scowled playfully, "Yeah, I agree, that was nothing like a proposal. And believe you me, when that day comes, there'll be no ambiguity, you'll know exactly what a proposal is."

"Right, can we get back to where exactly we're heading?"

"Okay . . . in the spirit of our open and honesty pact, I can say there might be a Magic Kingdom and a certain Mickey Mouse on the horizon."

"What, Euro Disney?" she widened her eyes. "You don't mean Disney . . . in Florida, do you? You can't be serious. We can't just take off and go. I'd have to get everything ready." She scowled, "And what about the boys?"

"Yeah, I've thought of that."

"So what are you saying?"

"I'm saying, sit back and relax. It's all sorted."

"What's sorted? Jack . . ."

"Well," he said, flashing her a smile, "right now, Hilda and the boys are enjoying a ride in a limo."

"You're joking?"

"Nope, we'll meet them at the airport."

"We're really going to Florida?"

"Yep, one whole month in our own villa."

"I can believe it. You're full of surprises."

"I like to think so," he chuckled.

"But what about packing our cases? Our passports?"

"Hilda has seen to everything, all cases packed. I think she's more excited about seeing Mickey than the boys are."

"Hilda's coming, too?"

"Of course."

She shook her head in disbelief. "Seems like you have got everything sorted."

"I have. All you have to do is sit back and relax."

"You're amazing, do you know that," Lucy smiled lovingly, "I feel so lucky."

"Trust me," Jack winked as the sign for the airport came into view, "I'm the lucky one."

Acknowledgements

As always there are people to thank when producing a book. I come up with the story, but I need to make it desirable to readers. In that respect, I'm fortunate to be surrounded by people who want me to succeed, and for that I am truly grateful.

Firstly, and always top of my list is my excellent editor, John Hudspith. Brilliant insightful editors are a gift to any writer and I thank my lucky stars each day I have John guiding me. I am fortunate to have the fabulously talented Jane Dixon-Smith design the gorgeous cover – and she never disappoints (JD Smith Design). To attract a reader to a book you need a special cover, and Jane delivers every single time.

To my diligent beta readers, Sally and Sue, I'm always appreciative of your input. Your beady eyes are so valuable pointing out all the pesky typos I miss. I'm constantly astounded in how many little idiosyncrasies you find.

Thank you Colin Ward for formatting the manuscript and making it readable, and to my closest and dearest friends (you know who you are), that make me feel I'm the best writer in the world!

I have been fortunate to have had numerous opportunities to give my talk, *'From Bedpan to Pen'* to WI's, book clubs and luncheons. I wish I had words other than thank you to convey how grateful I am to every single person that has purchased my books at these events or downloaded Kindle copies. It is such a delight meeting so many enthusiastic readers who genuinely want me to do well.

Special thanks to the bloggers who enthusiastically share my books when they are released. These wonderful folks are out there industriously helping and directing readers towards my books and for that I want to say a huge thank you. With your help, more people read my stories and that's all I want.

Finally, to all my readers – I couldn't do it without you. Every email, review or message I receive saying you've enjoyed reading one of my books makes all the blood, sweat and edits worth it. Thank you most sincerely.

If you have enjoyed the story, and are able to write a review on Amazon or Goodreads, I would be grateful. Each review gives the book greater exposure which I hope will attract new readers. Any author will tell you, that is primarily why we write. We just want readers to enjoy our stories and I'm no exception. So, thank you in advance if you are able to write a few words about the book. And please do get in touch directly if you so wish, I love hearing from readers.